S0-CAN-302

"Don't stop," Juliette whispered fiercely

Stop? It would have been easier to stop a freight train, Shay thought. Desperation and desire—a volatile combination. It made the ordinary extraordinary. The act of making love took on a whole new dimension.

Greedy, she devoured his mouth. "More. I want more," she demanded.

"Everything I've got...promise," he told her, and then moments later, he was as good as his word as he tightened his hold on her and she on him and their tension built to release.

Slowly, reality returned—bodies cooled, vision cleared, the night once again took on form and dimension. Shay still held her in his arms, not wanting to let her go, positive that if he did, he'd wake up and discover it had all been a dream.

"All right, princess?" he breathed into her ear.

Her answer came, still dreamy with passion as she tightened her legs, reluctant to let him go. "Perfect. But you don't need to call me Princess. I don't use the title."

"What title?"

Her eyes popped open. *Oh, damn!*

Dear Reader,

Haven't you ever wished you could run away from your everyday life and have an adventure? Haven't you ever wished you would be swept off your feet by a bold, handsome man who whisks you away to a life of passion and laughter...with no laundry to do? I sure have.

And this is exactly how Princess Juliette Fortier feels as she sits on a park bench in New Orleans and wishes for a man to sweep her away, temporarily, from the future stretching before her. The only problem is she gets more than she'd bargained for when her adventure begins for real. She gets Detective Shay O'Malley, a hot-blooded cop hot on the trail of a criminal.

I hope you'll love this story as much as I've loved writing about Juliette and Shay. Please let me know. I'd really enjoy hearing from you. You can e-mail me: MEGLACEY@aol.com, visit me at www.eclectics.com or through www.eHarlequin.com or send a letter to: Meg Lacey, P.O. Box 112010, Cincinnati, OH 45211.

Happy reading!

Meg Lacey

Books by Meg Lacey

HARLEQUIN TEMPTATION
734—SEXY AS SIN

Don't miss any of our special offers. Write to us at the following address for information on our newest releases.

Harlequin Reader Service
U.S.: 3010 Walden Ave., P.O. Box 1325, Buffalo, NY 14269
Canadian: P.O. Box 609, Fort Erie, Ont. L2A 5X3

A NOBLE PURSUIT
Meg Lacey

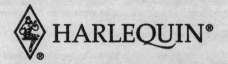

HARLEQUIN®

TORONTO • NEW YORK • LONDON
AMSTERDAM • PARIS • SYDNEY • HAMBURG
STOCKHOLM • ATHENS • TOKYO • MILAN • MADRID
PRAGUE • WARSAW • BUDAPEST • AUCKLAND

If you purchased this book without a cover you should be aware
that this book is stolen property. It was reported as "unsold and
destroyed" to the publisher, and neither the author nor the
publisher has received any payment for this "stripped book."

To dear friend, Robin Graff Reed,
who dropped everything and jumped in when I needed her.

To my terrific editor, Susan Sheppard, who hung in there
and taught me more than I can say. Thank you.

ISBN 0-373-25965-4

A NOBLE PURSUIT

Copyright © 2002 by Lynn Miller.

All rights reserved. Except for use in any review, the reproduction or
utilization of this work in whole or in part in any form by any electronic,
mechanical or other means, now known or hereafter invented, including
xerography, photocopying and recording, or in any information storage
or retrieval system, is forbidden without the written permission of the
publisher, Harlequin Enterprises Limited, 225 Duncan Mill Road,
Don Mills, Ontario, Canada M3B 3K9.

All characters in this book have no existence outside the imagination of
the author and have no relation whatsoever to anyone bearing the same
name or names. They are not even distantly inspired by any individual
known or unknown to the author, and all incidents are pure invention.

This edition published by arrangement with Harlequin Books S.A.

® and TM are trademarks of the publisher. Trademarks indicated with
® are registered in the United States Patent and Trademark Office, the
Canadian Trade Marks Office and in other countries.

Visit us at www.eHarlequin.com

Printed in U.S.A.

1

SHE SAT ON THE PARK BENCH, naked and alone.

Or at least that's the way she looked to Shay O'Malley as his gaze skimmed over her. She was actually dressed in navy-blue silk and dainty heels, but the expression on her face told him she was stripped to the bone emotionally and isolated from the lively activity around her.

Shay sighed. Damn, she looked so young. Or was that because he was studying her with his jaded cop's eyes? He took another look. On second thought, not that young. Early to mid-twenties, at least. He glanced toward the street. In any case, she seemed too innocent and lovely to be sitting by herself on the fringes of the rowdy, wicked Mardi Gras crowd.

He knew immediately that he couldn't walk away. He'd have to make sure she was all right. His damn hero-to-the-rescue complex came out at the most inconvenient times.

Swearing under his breath, Shay shrugged his shoulders, feeling the weight of his old, brown leather bomber jacket as it shrugged with him. Slowly, he walked over to the park bench. "Miss? You look like you got a problem. Can I help?"

The woman gasped, then glanced up at him with an air of surprise that made her seem ill-prepared to face the world. Her ocean-blue eyes were as wide as a child's. Shay wanted to groan as he compared her with the sultry hooker who was flaunting herself by a lamppost near the street.

"You're kind of young to be out here with this type of crowd, aren't you?" Regardless of her actual age, Shay knew firsthand there were too many predators waiting to prey on those who looked like innocents.

Her gaze raced over him from the top of his head to his

toes, but still she said nothing. She only gripped her fingers more tightly together and stared at him, as if he were the devil sent to tempt her to hell.

Shay frowned. "Don't be scared, okay? I won't hurt you. What's your name?"

The tip of her tongue moistened her naked mouth, running slowly over her full bottom lip. Shay felt a jolt that was purely sexual. It singed his gut and quickened his breath. "I said, what's your name?" Uncomfortable at his reaction, he spoke more harshly than he'd intended.

"I..." She blinked, her mouth trembling for a moment, and then she said, "I can't..." She stared up at him, her breath coming a bit faster as her gaze roamed his face, touching on each feature.

He cocked his head, considering her. "You can't tell me your name?"

"I..." Still she stared, then gave a little shrug. "I can't remember."

"You forgot your name."

She looked confused for a moment. "Uh-huh."

"So. Memory's completely gone?" He tried to say it lightly, even though he knew cynicism was sneaking into his tone. His inclination to trust her was at war with his experience as a cop.

She was silent for another moment, then she squared her shoulders. "Exactly."

Shay frowned and tried another approach. "What are you doing out here by yourself? Aren't you with someone— friends, parents...?"

Her head snapped up. "I'm not a child!"

Shay's gaze dropped and he took in the curves beneath the silk of her dress. She was no child, for sure. His gut tightened. Full-grown or not, there was something about her that made him want to shine up his armor and sharpen his lance.

"And I'm not with friends," she continued less vehemently. "I'm alone."

"Okay, you're an adult. Still, isn't there somebody...a boyfriend? Maybe you had a fight or something?" He glanced around the park, then his gaze swept over her again. "It could get rough out here later. If you were my woman you wouldn't be here by yourself."

"Your woman?"

"That's right."

She gave him a hint of a smile. "Do you need a woman?"

He was shocked. He'd have bet his badge she wasn't a hooker. "Are you offering?"

"That depends." Her eyes gleamed with an unexpected excitement.

Shay tilted his head. Now *that* was familiar, that seductive, teasing tone. His eyes narrowed as his gaze came to rest on her mouth. Her lips trembled again, but whether from fear or excitement he didn't know. Maybe he'd misunderstood her tone. From force of habit, he called her bluff. "Depends on what?"

"On if you feel like being a hero."

"You need a hero?"

"Every woman needs a hero."

He gave her a skeptical look. "Not today they don't. Most women would rather be the hero than depend on one."

"I'm not most women."

"I'll say." The words rushed out before he had a chance to think about them. He could feel his neck flush at the sly glance she gave him from under her long dark lashes. "What I meant was, most women wouldn't be sitting here alone on a night like this. Or if so, they wouldn't be alone long." As if to underscore his remark, a group of revelers, dressed to the hilt in colored satin, frothing lace and elaborate headdresses wove past them. Their laughter was accentuated by the rumble that had been growing steadily louder throughout the evening.

She shrugged and touched the wooden slats of the bench. "I came here because I couldn't stay *there* any longer."

"Where's there?"

The woman scowled, avoiding his gaze. "Where I was."

Shay rubbed the spot between his eyebrows where tension was starting to build. Talking to this woman was like being caught in a never-ending loop. "Let's get this straight. You don't know who you are, where you're from or why you're here. That about cover it?"

She shrugged. "That's the story of my life."

"I don't think so, sweetheart. Life has a beginning, a middle and an end. You're still working on the first couple chapters."

"I think my middle and end are already written."

"You're too young to be a cynic. Trust me, I know." Did he ever. No one lost his ideals faster than a cop.

"Aren't cynics merely the flip side of idealists?"

He lifted a brow, studying her in closer detail, now more intrigued than ever by her aristocratic Southern accent and the aura of class she wore. What the hell was she doing out here? "That's pretty heavy thinking for a woman who can't remember her name."

She frowned. "Maybe I read that somewhere."

"Do you remember reading your address?"

She squeezed her eyes shut before saying in a fierce whisper, "No, I don't." She opened her eyes and stared into his, her gaze intense and gleaming with purpose. "Do you believe in fairy tales? In legends coming to life?"

"Fairy tales?" The intoxicating scent of jasmine brought on images of sultry nights under the stars, crushed flowers and soft moans, and Shay shook his head to clear it. They'd warned him in Cincinnati that New Orleans was more seductive than a high-priced whore, but he'd shrugged it off. Now here he was, lurking in a park near the Renard Restaurant on a half-baked tip from an iffy informant and what was he thinking about? "Nah, I don't believe in fairy tales."

"How about fate? Do you believe in fate?"

"I believe in making my own fate."

A self-satisfied smile touched her lips. "I thought you'd say that."

Shay straightened. "What the hell am I going to do with

you?" He shoved a hand through his hair. He had a job to do and he couldn't do it with this type of distraction. He'd already decided that this stakeout was a waste of time and he'd been about to cut bait when he saw her.

"What would you like to do?"

Her voice, soft and provocative, whispered on the breeze as Shay glanced at his watch, then at his companion. Despite the temptation, he made the instinctive decision to protect his undercover status. "I'd better find a cop."

"A cop?" A hint of alarm crept into her question. "Why do you want a cop?"

A gust of wind stirred the branches above them. "Get real. Why do you think? You don't know who the hell you are. I can't leave you here. You'd end up a crime statistic."

"I can't involve the police." Her voice started to rise, which set Shay's warning lights flashing. Why was she so afraid of the police?

"I've got to get you somewhere safe." Shay slapped his forehead with the heel of his hand. "Damn, what kind of...did you hit your head? Is that why you can't remember anything? I didn't even check. Maybe we ought to find a hospital or a clinic." His fingers probed gently in her hair—searching for an injury, he told himself, not because he wanted to touch her. "Let me know if anything hurts."

She slapped his hand away and stood up. "Nothing hurts. Nothing you can see, anyway."

Shay straightened and reached for her arm. "Wait a minute. What do you think you're doing?"

"I have to go now."

"Go where?"

"Anywhere."

Shay grabbed both of her arms and swung her around to face him. "Hold it. You're not—"

"I'll be fine," she said through clenched teeth.

"The hell you will. Look, I'll take you down to the precinct myself."

She tugged her arm away, surprising him with her strength. "No. I can't let you do that."

A jagged flash of lightning split the sky. Shay glanced up, then back at her before grabbing her wrists. "You don't have a choice."

Her eyes abruptly filled with tears and her voice tightened. "No, no, let go. I can't go to the police. I can't have that kind of—please let me go."

He pulled her close, stroking her tense back. "Shh, shh, it's okay, it's okay." What in the hell was this woman mixed up in? he wondered. Should he tell her he was a cop, after all? Not that he had anything but temporary jurisdiction on one specific case, but still—

She struggled, attempting to pull away from him. "I have to go. Please, I'll be okay."

Another crack of lightning split the sky, followed immediately by a roar of thunder. "I'm supposed to let you run away into a storm, without knowing who you are? Forget it, lady. I can't do that. What kind of hero would I be?" The rain started to fall lightly but steadily. All around the area people were running for cover. For a moment, Shay was at a loss. Even if tonight's tip was proving a waste of time, he was still on the job, and he took his duty seriously. But, like every good cop, he knew when to cut his losses. He glanced toward the street and, with no sign of his quarry in the vicinity, decided to bail out. Then Shay pulled his attention back to the woman in his arms. Staring down at her, he cradled her closer. "I have to take you somewhere."

The woman hesitated, then blurted, "Then take me home with you."

"Home with me?"

"Yes. I can stay until the rain stops, and then I'll go anywhere you want me to go."

"That's not the greatest—"

She shivered as the breeze whirled around them. "I'm getting cold."

"Ah, hell." Shay looked down at her, trying not to be distracted by the way the wet silk was clinging to her body, outlining every curve. He stripped off his jacket and threw it over her as the rain started falling harder. "Come on, we'll have to run for it. My car's on the other side of the park."

Shay wrapped his arm around her, tucking her close to his side as they started running. They cut across the grass as the path was now crowded with fleeing people, some laughing, some swearing and some so drunk they were stumbling into each other. A man attempted to grab hold of them to steady himself.

Shay shoved him away. "Go sleep it off, jerk."

"Looks like you'll be doing the same," he slurred with a leering glance at Shay's feminine armful.

Sudden protective instincts leaped to the fore and Shay had to stop himself from punching the guy. "Get out of here before I arrest you." The man moved away and only then did Shay realize what he'd said. He glanced down at the woman next to him, only to see a quick smile cross her lips.

"That was a clever way to get rid of him. I'll have to use that."

Shay chuckled as they continued to cross the wet grass toward the sidewalk. "No one in their right mind would take you for a cop, sweetheart."

"Why not?"

"Because—" Just then the heavens opened, spilling rain in great drenching sheets. Shay grabbed the woman's hand and tugged her along, running down the concrete walk to the side of an old white Porsche that had seen better days. He dug into his pocket for his keys, swearing when his hand stuck in his wet jeans. Meanwhile the rain was plastering his shirt to his chest.

Shay glanced at the woman next to him to see how she was doing under his leather jacket. Marginally better, but not much. He managed to grasp his keys and remove his hand without turning his entire pocket inside out, then leaned down to unlock the door.

Pulling it wide, he began tucking her inside. "In you go, Red."

She stopped halfway into her seat. "What did you call me?"

"Red. I have to call you something."

"Why Red? Why not—"

He ducked his head as a particularly unpleasant gust of rainwater pelted his back. "We'll talk about it when I get in, okay?"

She looked up at him, seeming only then to notice how wet he was. "Oh, of course..."

Shay scarcely heard her "Sorry" as he dashed around the car and slid behind the wheel. He shook his thick hair like a dog coming in from a dunking, and laughed. "Damn, it's kinda wet out there."

The woman stared back at him, looking slightly amazed at his good humor. "Yes, it is."

"I'd offer you a towel, Red, but at the moment I don't have one handy."

"I don't have red hair. So I don't see—"

"I thought you liked fairy tales."

"I do."

"You remind me of Red Riding Hood."

"And you're...?"

"The hero, what else?"

She snorted as she lifted her brow to consider him. "You look more like the Big Bad Wolf."

Shay grinned. "Hey, you're starting to remember already."

She glanced away. "I...suppose so."

"Who knows what you'll come up with by the time the rain stops?" He glanced through his windshield. "If it stops. This looks ready to settle in for the night." He reached for the key and started the car, turning on the wipers and the heat. "We'll have it warm in no time."

True to his word, after a moment the car's heater spat out a blast of warm air that quickly made the small interior feel even more cozy, more intimate. Their shoulders practically touched as they sat in the sports car. They were so close that

Shay was aware of everything about her—the rain-sweet smell of her damp hair, the subtle jasmine perfume she wore, the small, perfect pearl drops that decorated her earlobes, revealed when she tucked her hair behind her shell-like ears. He could hear the soft slide of wet silk as she shifted in her seat, looking for her seat belt, and immediately wondered what it would be like to have that silk shifting against him. He stared at the rain rolling down the window glass, which was fogged by their breathing. They were enclosed in a cocoon of sensuality, and Shay had no idea how to break the spell. He didn't particularly want to, either. To him, the atmosphere seemed thick, laden with unvoiced desires.

She smiled a bit nervously and held her hands, palms out, toward the heater vents on the dashboard. "That feels good. Hot even."

That wasn't the only thing that was hot.

Luckily, he kept his mouth closed, so the thought didn't spill out and make him more uncomfortable than he already was. He was a cop, for God's sake. He wasn't exactly on the job tonight, but even so, he couldn't run around with his zipper at half mast just because he was getting a hard-on the size of California. Not and still call himself a professional. Hell, he couldn't understand it. He'd resisted some of the most gorgeous call girls in the business during his undercover career. It made no sense to jeopardize his integrity with some sexy little waif. Not that this woman was related to his case; she wasn't. Regardless, he'd placed her under his protection whether she knew it or not. Which made this entire situation and his response to it as unethical as hell.

"Whew." Taking his jacket off her shoulders, she folded it on her lap. "It's getting a bit steamy in here."

I'll say. He scowled as he registered her creamy shoulders, which were barely covered by her damp silk wrap. "Keep that on—you're soaked."

"So are you." She indicated her clothing. "I don't want to get your coat any wetter and ruin it."

"You can't hurt that jacket. I've had it practically since I was a kid. Lots of good memories in that jacket."

"What type of memories? Tell me. Maybe they'll help me remember."

Shay laughed, grateful for a chance to get his mind off his groin and back on safer topics. "I doubt it, Red. My favorite memory is wearing that jacket to my first college football game and trying to put the make on Heather Johnson under the bleachers."

"Oh." Then she grinned back at him. "I can sort of relate. Except for the leather jacket, the football game and Heather, of course."

"And you're relating to what?"

"To wearing something that made you feel special."

Shay's gaze sharpened. Pretty astute young woman. It only reinforced his growing unease. Something about this entire situation was off, but he couldn't quite put his finger on it. He didn't know much about amnesia, except it was traumatic for the sufferer. Of course, she had gotten upset when he wanted to call the police, but he wasn't sure that reaction was symptomatic of losing your memory. Or was it? What the hell. He'd spent his entire career adapting the game to meet his rules, so he'd play this situation until it was over, too. It could be worse, he thought, smiling to himself. She could be eighty-eight and weigh three hundred pounds. He checked his mirrors and pulled out into traffic, before glancing over to answer her. "You're right. I did feel special in that jacket."

She smiled, sending him an admiring look. "Still do, I'll bet."

"Now it's like a second skin. I've got it broken in just the way I like it."

Shay saw her absentmindedly stroke the leather on her lap. Desire started gnawing at him again. He set his jaw in a tight line, imposing the control that was supposed to tamp down the fire. As long as he didn't look at her, he figured, he might have a chance of coming out of this with his pants still on.

They drove in silence, each aware of the other. At least

Shay could swear she was as aware of him as he was of her. This feeling couldn't be one-sided. It was too strong and she was too close—way too close. For the first time, he wished he drove a full-size van.

She cleared her throat before asking, "Do you live far?"

He shook his head. "Just uptown a ways, in the Garden District. How about you?"

"I live—" She seemed to swallow her words. "I..." She stared at him, her eyes suddenly huge in her pale face.

"Sorry, just thought I'd give it a try. Take you by surprise and see what happened, you know?"

"Well, it almost worked until I thought about it."

THAT'S THE TRUTH, Juliette thought. She'd almost blurted out her address the minute he asked her, just because she was so conscious of him that he sent her mind reeling. Not once could she ever remember being this aware of a man, being so drawn to someone that she wished he'd absorb her into his bone marrow. It's what she'd have liked to feel about the man her brother wanted her to marry. But she didn't. Of course, her intended fiancé was part of a practical arrangement, one that would unite their family fortunes—a normal occurrence in her social circle, especially since her father was a bit old-fashioned.

Juliette understood the business reasons behind her family's wishes, but she resented—no make that hated—being used as a pawn in some game she didn't want to play. She wanted romance, passion. She wanted a soul mate, a man who could touch her in ways she'd never dreamed of and could make her keep on wanting. What was the matter with a bit of fantasy? Was being swept off your feet by a bold, dashing figure astride a spirited stallion too much to ask? Just then Juliette caught sight of her rescuer's reflection in the glass. A little smile caressed her lips. Or in this case, being swept off by a man wearing a brown leather jacket, beige T-shirt, blue jeans and boots, and driving a beat-up Porsche?

He indicated the window. "What do you think? Anything around here look familiar?"

She carefully avoided looking at the ornate building near the park that had belonged to her family for almost a hundred years and was now headquarters for the family business. "No, nothing."

For a moment Juliette felt guilty for lying to her dark-haired stranger, then she pushed the feeling aside. She hadn't asked for him to come to her rescue, she rationalized, but there he'd been, offering to help her. When a man like this one offered *anything* how could a woman say no? She'd have to be blind, deaf, dumb and 133 years old to resist his appeal. That certainly didn't apply to Juliette, who was 24. Her upbringing might have been grounded in old-fashioned rituals, but her libido was a product of today's world. She stared at his muscular thigh, which looked long and lean through his tight jeans. This man put all of those suave society men she'd always known to shame. Too bad he was temporary. She sighed.

"That was a damn big sigh, Red."

"I know. Everything seems so...complicated...at the moment."

Shay chuckled. "I guess it does if you can't remember anything."

"Yes, that was dumb, wasn't it?" *Of course it was, you idiot! He's not interested in your personal problems. He's only interested in finding a way to deal with the woman he picked up like a stray puppy.* The thought that he might really be attracted to her died a quick death. He was just a Good Samaritan chalking up a virtuous deed for heavenly reward. The thought depressed the hell out of her.

"So, any idea why you were in that park tonight?"

Juliette spoke without thinking. "Escaping."

"Escaping from what?" His voice sharpened and his expression turned to steel.

She shifted on her seat, avoiding his probing glance. "I

don't know." *Liar*, she thought. She was running away from her future.

She'd just bolted from a boring business dinner. For hours, Juliette had sat listening to the discussion, smiling when called upon, uttering polite, meaningless words, knowing that this could be one of the routines of her life from this point on if her brother had his way. She'd have to be perfect on the job, perfect at home, perfect, perfect, perfect! It was enough to make a saint scream! Lately she'd become more and more resentful of her safe, predictable lifestyle. She'd watched her brother and his best friend, the man he'd been pushing as her fiancé in all but name, wheel and deal with business associates until she couldn't stand it another minute. She wanted noise, color, atmosphere, laughter and music instead of a subdued, sophisticated ambiance. She ached for an adventure before she chained herself to marriage. Was that so selfish? Her cousin Carlyne had done it. Carlyne's recent phone call replayed in her mind. *"Juliette, you've got to take a risk, let yourself go. You'd be surprised what might happen."*

So she'd created a bit of a scene, a discreet one, of course, because Juliette couldn't create a major disturbance without someone noticing, and the wrong type of publicity would be very bad for a young woman heading a major charitable fund. She'd pleaded a headache and escaped to the lobby, with her brother right on her heels. After their short, whispered argument, her head really did ache. However, instead of letting the maître d' call a taxi as she'd promised she would, Juliette had escaped into the French Quarter to get some air.

Restless, feeling very much alone and removed from the activity around her, she'd wandered for a while, envying the obvious enjoyment and energy of the people celebrating carnival in New Orleans. In contrast, her own life stretched before her, bleak and devoid of enthusiasm. She'd skirted the Mardi Gras crowds watching the parades and finally wandered into a small park not far from the Renard Restaurant, but secluded enough not to be seen by her brother should he look for her. Taking refuge on a wooden bench, she'd sat down, alternately feeling sorry for herself and wishing she could find a bold warrior who'd rescue her and whisk her off to his bedroom, where they'd live passionately ever after. It was stupid and childish.

Then he had appeared.

As if she'd conjured him up from her fantasy, a man larger than life had strolled into view. Shocked at the real-life warrior who'd suddenly appeared, she had gaped at him as he'd walked toward her. As he'd passed under a streetlight she'd caught the subtle mahogany-red flare of his dark brown hair, which she decided hinted at passion—or was it temper? She had wanted to look away, but his arresting face had captivated her. She had shivered as she took in the broad brow, the slashing dark eyebrows, the piercing green eyes that gleamed like warm jade and had an edge that could cut like a jeweled dagger. He had looked quite fierce as his gaze bored into hers. She'd caught her breath at his aggressively chiseled cheekbones, at the square jaw shadowed by dark stubble. His nose looked as if it had been broken at some point. All she could do was stare at him like a backward child when he'd spoken to her. She had been so stunned that she couldn't say a word, and as she'd stared at him, all she could think was *What if I had no memory of my past? What if I could start my life here and now?*

Why not?

Now, as she sat in the close confines of the car, Juliette slid him a look from under her lashes. Even soaking wet and a bit on edge, the man was impossible to resist, which was good because she didn't want to resist. She'd been yearning for adventure and he'd showed up—the perfect man for a passionate escapade. She studied him surreptitiously. There was danger about him, but still, for some reason she knew she could trust him.

"Well, are you?"

His voice intruded into her thoughts, startling her. "Am I what?"

He adjusted the blower on the heater, then surprised her by sending a penetrating look in her direction, a look that cut into her thoughts and brought her survival instincts to the surface. "Are you warm enough now? I've got it on full blast to dry us off."

"I, oh...yes. Thank you." Juliette glanced away again, suddenly cautious. She had a suspicion that she'd better not underestimate him or push him too far.

A moment later, he said, "You're awfully quiet, Red."

The intimate timbre of his voice sent a current of electricity racing through her veins, leaving behind anticipation and a strange feeling of safety. Juliette stared at his fingers gripping the steering wheel. She wondered how they would feel on her body. Would they be hard and careless or callused and tender, his rough skin igniting flames with each touch? She could picture those hands stroking her to awareness, even through the wet clothes molded to her body.

"What're you thinking about?"

Inhaling deeply, disturbed yet excited by the images running through her mind, Juliette blurted, "Making love in the rain." Surprised at herself, she caught a brief glimpse of his face, eyes wide, mouth open with astonishment, before she turned her head to stare blindly out the window. He started to speak, but began coughing instead, until he finally choked out, "I beg—your—pardon?"

"There was a couple back there..." Juliette was thinking at lightning speed, trying to salvage the situation "...standing in the rain making love." Of course, she couldn't tell him the couple was in her imagination, and that it was them.

"Making love?"

His question jerked her back to reality. *What am I doing here? If anyone ever finds out...* After all, it was one thing to fantasize about a passionate adventure with a stranger and another thing altogether to actually have one. Yet why was she here if she wasn't determined to live out her fantasies with this man? Not that she thought about having sex with him— exactly. Perhaps going just far enough to supply a warm memory for the long nights of chilly formality that her future promised. What was wrong with that?

He leaned forward to look past her out her window, then checked his rearview mirror. "I didn't see anyone making lo—"

Juliette interrupted, abruptly changing the subject. "You said no one would take me for a cop? Why is that? I could be on a special assignment or something."

Taking his time, he ran his eyes over her, then smiled. "You don't have the look."

With the back of her hand, she dashed away a trickle of water that was running from her hair into her eyes. "What look is that?"

"The disillusionment. You still look as if you believe in Santa Claus."

"Since when is believing in Santa Claus a problem?"

"He's a fantasy."

"What's wrong with fantasy?"

"Nothing, unless you let it get in the way of what's real."

Juliette shifted on the leather seat. "And if reality isn't the way you want it to be?"

"Then change it."

Juliette studied his intent expression as he peered through the windshield. With one sentence this man had given her confirmation that she was doing the right thing—rash or not. *This is fate—signed, sealed and delivered.* Her gaze touched on his firm lips. *This man.* It dawned on her that she didn't even know his name. Should she ask him? What if his name was totally unromantic, like Ferdy or Linus or something. But she couldn't call him Warrior King or Prince Charming—somehow she didn't think he'd go for that. She sat trying to match a name with his profile.

"Why're you looking at me so funny? Is my face on upside down?"

Juliette smiled. She'd never seen a face on better in her life. She loved the way his eyes crinkled at the corners when he was amused. "No, it looks fine to me."

"Then what?"

"I don't know your name."

The man threw her a startled glance. "I didn't tell you?"

"No."

"It's Shay."

"Shay?" The name fit him—short, to the point and intensely masculine.

"Shay—"

She stopped him before he could continue. "Shay's enough. It doesn't seem right for you to have two names when I can't even remember one." Besides, she thought, a complete name would make this episode too concrete to live forever in her memory, as it must. "Shay is what nationality, originally?"

"My family's as Irish as they come—shanty Irish, you know, the kind that kept the saloons in business? They came down the Ohio River during the potato famine and ran out of money in Cincinnati, so they stayed. At least that's how the family legend has it."

"There's nothing wrong with starting at the bottom of the ladder."

"And you'd know about that *how*, sweetheart?"

"What do you mean?"

He slid her a probing look. "You've never seen the bottom of a ladder in your life. You've got that high-class look that comes from centuries of good breeding—like some kind of royalty. Maybe I'll just call you Princess instead of Red. I kind of like that."

Princess. He was very observant, but she hated to be called that. Her father had always called her his little princess right before he issued some directive sure to choke her independent spirit. "You are a Yankee, then. I wondered about your accent."

He chuckled. "I'm not the one with the accent. Not when it takes you three times as long to say a sentence as it does me."

Juliette arched her brow, giving him her sauciest look. "We

don't see much need to rush in New Orleans. We like to take it slow and easy."

"Yeah, N'awlins—the Big Easy. They told me."

"Who did?"

His face tightened. "Just some people I work with , is all."

"What type of—"

"We're here." Shay pulled up to the curb in front of a charming, four-story house, an old family home that had obviously been converted into a series of apartments. An elaborate wrought-iron fence surrounded the gardens that embraced an aged brick facade. Window boxes spilling vines and flowers hugged the side of the building in the cool rain. He turned off the engine, but didn't move. "This is where I live."

Juliette peered through the side window. "It's lovely."

"It's a sublet. Just temporary."

"You aren't planning on staying in New Orleans, then?" She held her breath. It would be better for her peace of mind if he wasn't around to tempt her after tonight.

"I'm only here to wrap up some business and then I head back north."

"I see."

They sat in silence for a few more minutes, each was reluctant to make a move. Finally Shay said, "The rain looks as if it's letting up a bit. We'd better get inside before it changes its mind."

Juliette smiled. "Good idea." *Before I do, too,* she thought.

Shay slipped out the side door and came around to open hers, reaching down a hand to draw her from the car. "Careful, there's a big pud—" Juliette landed with both feet in a puddle that flooded over her shoes "—too late." Shay reached for her. "Ah damn, I'm sorry. I didn't see that when I pulled up."

Juliette laughed as his arms encircled her waist. "It could be worse. I could be drowning."

Shay grinned back. "Atta girl, that's the spirit."

At his words, Juliette felt as if she'd just been awarded the medal of honor. She could feel herself blushing, even though the rain was cool. "Thank—oohh!" He startled her as he yanked her from the puddle, swept her up into his arms without further conversation and headed for the iron gate. As if on cue, the skies opened, drenching them anew as Shay carried her up the sidewalk.

"Much more of this and we're both gonna drown," he muttered as he stepped onto the porch. He shouldered his way through the front door, then stopped in the vestibule, shifting Juliette in his arms and muttering under his breath.

Her arm went around his neck—for balance, she told herself, not because she wanted to get closer to him or anything. "Am I too heavy?" She'd said it automatically, praying he wouldn't release her yet. She could feel his strength, the hard muscles of his arms and chest tense against her body. All she had to do was turn slightly to touch his lips with hers. It was tempting, very tempting.

"Heavy?" Shay grinned down at her. "Since when are sprites heavy?"

"A sprite?" She was sure her eyes were starting to twinkle as she stared into his. His green eyes were glowing, and he tightened his arms as if he didn't want to let her go any more than she wanted him. "That's rather fanciful, isn't it? For a man who doesn't believe in fairy tales?" she teased, just to see what he would do.

Shay scowled as a stain of red slashed across his cheekbones. "I need my key to get in the other door," he said gruffly.

"Where is it? Did you leave it in the car?"

"No. It's in my pocket, but I can't reach it while I'm holding you."

"Then you'd better put me down." She hoped he didn't hear the disappointment in her voice.

"Yeah, maybe I should." Despite his statement he held her a bit tighter. "But it's not a heroic thing to do, not to a damsel in distress. Forget it—can't do it. Not when you're dripping from the knees down."

"I'm still wet, whether you're holding me or not," Juliette said in a reasonable tone.

"True. We could be stuck here till your shoes dry. Unless..." His brows lifted in a hopeful expression.

"Unless?"

His expression changed. A glint sparked in his eyes. "You wanna get it for me?"

"Get what? Your key?" Juliette gave him a suspicious look, warned by the challenging light in his eye. "That depends on where it is."

"Back pocket, right side."

"Back—" He was definitely up to something—something more than taking her mind off the "sprite" compliment that had embarrassed him. At least, she'd taken it as a compliment. Sprites were lovely, magical beings to her. She caught his lips twitching and glanced up quickly to see a teasing glint in his eyes. "Why don't you put me down? Then you can get it yourself."

"I can't. Your feet are soaking wet and this rug is practically an heirloom, my landlady said."

Juliette looked down at the faded Oriental carpet beneath Shay's feet. "This carpet? Well, it certainly looks old enough."

"We don't want to damage it."

"What about *your* feet? They're wet, too."

"I'm not dripping water the way you are." He pointed at the ornate pattern, which was now a bit darker than before. "See?"

Juliette decided he was not only teasing her, he was testing her. Why, she didn't know, unless he'd seen through her amnesia act. It probably wasn't the best role she could have chosen for her escapade—not that she'd consciously done so—but it was too late to backtrack now. Juliette looked him boldly in the eye and called his bluff.

"Back pocket, you said?"

She leaned around so she could slide her hand down his side, past his waist and over his tight butt. Her fingers hesitated at the top of his pocket, but his eyes held a challenge, and with a quick move she slipped her fingers inside his pocket and began grasping for the key. Her fingers slid over his firm buttocks as she explored the inside of the pocket quite thoroughly, then jerked her hand up and out. She wanted to blow on her fingertips to cool them off. "The key's not there," she announced in a tight voice.

His eyebrows shot up in astonishment. "It's not? I wonder what I...oh, how stupid. I remember now. I put in on my chain with my car keys this morning." He lifted his hand and revealed the key ring dangling from his little finger. "Sorry, Red. I forgot. Seems like you're not the only one with a bad memory." He leaned down and unlocked the door.

She stiffened and her voice dripped ice when she said, "You can put me down now." She knew he was suspicious of her story, and he'd just confirmed it. She'd have to watch it from now on, or run as if the hounds of hell were snapping at her heels.

"No can do, the same carpet is in the hallway." Clasping her high in his arms, he practically strolled down the hall toward the ornate caged elevator at the other end.

Annoyed, Juliette hissed like a wet kitten. She hated it when people patted her on the head and treated her like a fool. "I suppose you pulled that little trick to humiliate me? Right?" She raised her brows to their haughtiest level. "I demand that you put me down immediately."

He chuckled as he stepped inside the open elevator and slid the cage shut. He pressed the button for the third floor before he answered her. "Now, Princess—"

"Don't call me Princess."

"—don't lose your temper. You tell me what man could resist hanging on to an armful like you? I just wanted to see if you'd lost your spirit along with your memory."

Her spirit. He thought she had spirit? Was this man off track! If she had any spirit at all she'd tell her brother that she didn't intend to get married right now. Especially not to a man she didn't love and had known practically forever as another brother. *Spirit. That's a laugh.* The most spirited thing Juliette had ever done she was doing at this very moment. The only problem was, she wasn't sure what she was supposed to do next.

2

SHAY SET HER DOWN just outside the doorway to his apartment.

Juliette looked at her feet and dripping hem. "No heirloom carpets up here, I suppose?"

Shay laughed. "My landlady didn't mention the carpets up here at all."

Juliette shuddered as she stared at the huge red cabbage roses that sprawled across the moss-green background. "I don't blame her."

Sending her an amused glance, Shay fit his key into the lock and turned the knob. He shoved the door wide and said, "After you."

Juliette hesitated at the threshold. After all, the minute she stepped over it she was committed. Whatever happened for the rest of the evening was in her hands. Her breath quickened at the absolute knowledge that she was in control. Right now she could take what she wanted and the rest of the world be damned. No past, no future...only the present.

"If you're worried about the carpet," he said with a wink, "take my word for it—ain't no roses on this floor."

A small laugh gurgled in the back of Juliette's throat. "Thanks for telling me, but I'm not concerned about the rug."

Shay's expression sobered, his voice suddenly gruff, as if he was trying to allay her fears. "Don't be concerned about anything else, either. It's safe."

"Like a sanctuary, you mean?"

"Being a former altar boy, I wouldn't say anything so sacrilegious."

"Since when is safety a sacrilege?"

"When it's used to run away from things people should be facing."

Juliette froze. It was as if he could see into her soul. How did he know so much? Or was it merely a lucky guess? Lucky guess, she hoped. But he was right. She was running away, even if it was temporary. Instead of being here, she should be standing up to her brother right now, saying that although she loved him and wanted to help him, she had to consider what she wanted, too.

"Go on in, Red. I'll make some coffee to warm us up."

Juliette entered the short hallway, blinking when he reached around her and turned on a light. The soft glow illuminated the room beyond, beckoning to her, inviting her to leave the past behind and take temporary refuge. Regardless of what Shay had said, the thought relaxed her. She looked around the soft, rosy-peach-colored room. "This is very nice, so soothing."

Shay snorted behind her as he ducked into a doorway off the hallway and headed into the kitchen. "I might as well be living in a perpetual sunset."

"I like that. Don't you?"

Shay flung open the white shutters that separated the kitchen from the living area. "Not every minute, I don't. I'm more of a dark-chocolate-and-beige man."

Juliette chuckled. "Lots of leather, I suppose?"

Shay leaned through the cutout opening and winked at her. "Only on my women, Red."

"Oh—I forgot your coat. I left it in the car." She could still feel the weight of his leather jacket as it had engulfed her, still smell the masculine scents that lingered in the lining.

He gave her an airy wave. "I'll get it later. Come to think of it, that old leather looked pretty good on you."

She stared back at him. His face was perfectly charming when he relaxed and put all of his formidable nature behind him. Or maybe she was seeing something she wanted to see. After all, it would be much better for her if he was a pussycat instead of a tiger. It wouldn't be quite as threatening, or as damaging to her view of herself. Not that she didn't have the stomach for lion-taming. At least she hoped she did. It was hard to say. Most of the men she'd known had been rather tame beasts. Now that she looked at Shay again, the thought of him as a neutered house cat was laughable. If ever a man was tense and ready for action, it was this one.

She walked to the kitchen opening. "Need any help?" she asked.

"Nah. If there is one thing I know how to make, it's coffee."

"It smells delicious."

"That's because I grind my own beans." He indicated the coffeemaker. "I buy them special at the market and keep 'em in the fridge. You gotta do that so they stay fresh. You don't want stale beans."

"How did you become such a coffee connoisseur?"

"All co—" He stopped as if he'd shut off a switch.

"All what?"

"Uh, in my line of work I stay up late and do a lot of waiting for stuff, so a great cup of coffee really helps pass the time."

"What do you do?"

Shay turned slowly and looked at her. "It changes, depending on my assignment. Sometimes it's computers, sometimes it's people-oriented, so—"

"You're a temp, then?"

"A temp?"

"I mean a temporary employee, working for an employment agency?"

"Yeah. You could say I'm here on a temporary gig."

She smiled, thinking this type of independence suited him. "I always thought that would be an ideal way to work. You're constantly changing, going from place to place, job to job, learning something new, meeting different types of people. Not stuck in the same old rut."

"Are you stuck in the same old rut?"

"Yes..." Belatedly, she remembered she shouldn't remember. "At least I must have been—or do I mean must be? Why else would I forget everything? If I wanted to remember, wouldn't I remember?''

Shay shook his head and reached for two mugs hanging on pegs over the stove. ''It probably depends on what happened to make you forget. Amnesia's a funny thing, I've heard. It can be physical or psychological—last a few minutes, a few hours, or much longer. Trauma can bring it on. But the odd thing is, you don't forget everything. Somebody said you remember things that might not bear any relationship to your everyday life.''

Now Juliette was really feeling guilty. She liked it much better when he was questioning whether she could be faking. At least when he was skeptical she was better able to deal with deceiving him. But nice? Then she wanted to confess her lie.

''What I'm trying to say is, don't worry about the memory stuff. It'll come back. I'd bet my next paycheck on it.''

I should take that bet, Juliette thought, but she said nothing. ''Thank you for saying that. I appreciate it.'' She blinked, trying to keep at bay the tears that suddenly threatened. It had been a long time since a man had made her want to cry. The big hunk standing in the kitchen didn't have the vaguest idea that he was inspiring such thoughts, and Juliette didn't intend to enlighten him, but she wanted to...oh, how she wanted to. She stood there awkwardly, watching him pour steaming coffee into two mugs, then he turned and strolled out of the kitchen, around the corner and into the living room.

He extended his hand, a grave look upon his face. ''Here you go.'' He touched his mug to hers. ''To better times.''

''And drier clothing.''

''And drier...'' He shoved his hand through his hair as his gaze honed in on her dress, immediately dropping to focus on her chest. ''Ah hell, you're really soaked, aren't you? I mean everywhere, not just your feet.''

''Yes, but I'll—''

''It's hard to tell with a dark dress.'' He jerked his gaze from her breasts, and Juliette realized her nipples were suddenly standing at attention, practically begging for a salute from his lips.

Her breath caught for a moment, before she muttered, "I'll dry out. Besides, you're wet, too."

He shrugged. "Weather doesn't bother me much, but I don't want you to catch a cold."

"I'm not that delicate."

Shay's eyes darkened as his gaze skimmed over her. "Not true. I held you in my arms, remember."

"Yes," she said slowly, "I remember." Did she ever!

There was a heavy silence for a moment before he said, "I've got a robe in the bathroom over there. Why don't you put it on and I can hang up your dress to dry."

She froze and then warmed all over. *His robe. Should she...?*

"It's okay. You can trust me."

She met his gaze, his steady and reassuring, hers questioning not his motives as much as her own. She knew she could trust him. He was the type of man you depended on, even as he kept you guessing. Yes, she could trust him—damn it! Damn it all because that meant that if anything was going to happen tonight, she'd have to make it happen. For all her bold resolve, she was hoping he'd take the entire issue out of her hands. That way she wouldn't have to face her conscience tomorrow morning. She laced her fingers together, more to prevent herself from cupping his chin and pulling his face toward hers than to hide any distress.

"Red?"

"I know I can trust you. I wouldn't be here otherwise, Shay." For the first time she said his name aloud. *Shay.* She glanced up from under her lashes. The name suited his strong and cocky demeanor, his devilishly handsome looks. "Where's the bathroom?" she asked.

Shay seemed to relax for an instant, then as his eyes swept over her, he stiffened again. He jerked his hand puppetlike to a door off the living room. "Right through there. The robe's on the back of the door."

"Thank you." Juliette handed him her coffee cup. Turning

around, she managed to walk to the bathroom with some semblance of dignity. She stepped into a room the soft color of a summer morning, the clear blue walls and ceramic tile floor accented by porcelain as pure and white as fluffy clouds. She twisted around to reach her zipper, sliding it down until she could slip the straps off her shoulders. With one quick wiggle the straight sheath dropped to her feet, pooling against the white area rug like a black puddle. Juliette was relieved to be alone. She needed a few minutes to think. She glimpsed herself in the mirror. She'd worn nothing under the dress, her own tiny act of defiance, seizing the moment to prove she controlled her own destiny even though her brother was trying to arrange it otherwise. Not that anyone would have noticed if she'd been sitting at the restaurant table tonight as naked as a newborn babe; when they were talking business nothing else existed. But she'd known and marveled at her boldness. Provocative dress was not her usual attire—normally she wore chic business suits. But tonight she'd felt the sleek, smooth silk as it whispered against her skin like a lover, and she'd burned for the real thing. Now it seemed as if she might get the chance to experience that reality. If she could make him want her, that was.

Frowning, Juliette smoothed her hands over her small breasts and down her narrow hips. No wonder Shay had first taken her for a child. She might be petite and well-groomed, but she'd give her eyeteeth for statuesque and sexy. She gnawed at her bottom lip, wondering what to do. Unfortunately, nothing brilliant came to mind, so she'd just have to play the hand fate had dealt her. How fortunate that her father had taught her to love games of chance. She was about to play the biggest game of all, and risk everything if anyone ever found out.

Glancing around, Juliette spied Shay's robe hanging right where he'd said. She hesitated for a moment, then went over to lift it from the hook. The white terry cloth was worn thin and felt as soft as a baby's blanket. Juliette smiled and hugged it close. For some reason this tatty old robe made Shay even more appealing. No *GQ* look for this man, just clothes he felt comfortable with, Juliette bet. How long had it been since she'd been really comfortable with anything? Comfort meant accepting who you were, and she was having problems doing that at the moment. She wasn't sure why. It wasn't as if her life had taken a ninety-degree turn—at least not until she met Shay.

Shay. So unexpected. So different. So tempting. So perfect.

She'd been accustomed to the best of everything throughout her life, so she often took perfection for granted. Not that she meant to; it was just part of her existence. Recently, though, she was questioning her lifestyle overtly—not just as a passing thought. She slipped her arms into the sleeves of the robe, imagining the nubby fabric rubbing over his arms as he performed the same act time and time again. She settled the robe around her, feeling the weight on her shoulders, the soft fabric draping her like a familiar lover. She tied the sash, pulling it tight, and chuckled when she realized it practically circled her twice. Glancing in the mirror, she decided she looked rather like a lone potato in a large sack, so lost did she seem. Good God! She couldn't let him see her like this. Whatever made her think she could be a sex kitten? When he'd first mentioned his robe, her imagination had kindled erotic visions of herself in a sleek satin, wine-red number with a neckline that plunged to her toes and was guaranteed to drive any man crazy. She peeked at herself again, decked out in what resembled an oversize bath towel. Although she might find the terry cloth appealing, she doubted he'd feel the same way.

"What are you doing? I think you've really lost it, girl," she whispered to herself.

Juliette stood on her tiptoe and peeked at herself again. Her hair was tousled and her eyes were huge. It was an appealing look if you liked drowned rats or waifs. She swore under her breath and reached for a towel to dry her hair. Leaning over, she rubbed her head briskly, her mind scurrying in place like a hamster on a wheel as she tried to control her panic. *Ohmy-*

god, maybe there's a window I can climb through. She didn't get a chance to find out.

The door shuddered with the force of a fist knocking. "Red, hey Red, are you okay in there?"

Juliette whirled around and stared at the door as if it had spoken to her. "I—" Her voice emerged as a squeak. She cleared her throat and tried again. "I'm fine."

"You don't feel dizzy or anything, do you?"

Only when I think of coming out of here and what I want to happen next.

The doorknob jiggled, then turned. "I'm coming in."

"No, that's all right. I'm coming out." With a quick, despairing glance in the mirror, Juliette reached for the door and twisted the handle. She stepped from the bathroom, smacking into Shay, who was planted on the other side. Her face buried itself in his chest, which was exposed by the open shirt he wore. His rough hair tickled her nose, and her hands automatically came up to push herself away. However, she found them lingering on that chest, unwilling to move, her fingertips wantonly caressing his firm muscles, the sculpted perfection beneath her hands. She glanced up at him, only to find him staring down at her, his eyes sharp and intense.

"You changed your clothes," she said, for want of anything more.

"You weren't the only one who got wet."

Juliette's breath caught. He didn't know the half of it. She ached, needed, wanted, longed... "Oh yes," she whispered. "How stupid of me."

"Are you warmer now?"

"Definitely," she murmured. "How about you?"

"Me, too."

She knew she should step away from him, but she didn't want to. Couldn't make herself do so. She had wanted the consummate fantasy, the ultimate adventure, and it was standing right in front of her. The reality was right under her fingertips. She couldn't make herself move if she'd been standing on dynamite ready to blow. She felt his heated flesh practically scorching her fingertips.

Juliette smiled. "You seem very warm."

"I am." His hands lifted to cup her shoulders. "Matter of fact, it's downright hot in here."

She licked her lips. "Uh-huh."

"Ah, hell. Now you've done it."

She felt his hands tighten on her shoulders as she met his gaze. "Done what?"

Shaking his head, he muttered, "It's the mouth. I've always been a sucker for a mouth like yours."

Her lips felt as dry as a desert under the noonday sun. She licked her lips again, this time aware that his eyes followed the movement of her tongue. "A mouth like..." she let her words trail off, inviting his response. Maybe this seduction thing wouldn't be so hard, after all.

"Like yours." He leaned down, his lips touching hers with a gentle pressure, molding to her full contours.

Her lips tingled as they met his. She hadn't known a man's mouth could be so soft. She sighed. "Mmm..."

He drew back and looked at her, cupping her face with his hands. "They're as full and sweet tasting as a ripe berry. I love berries." He licked her lips, like a kid savoring a lollipop. "I could eat them up."

Her lips parted slightly as his tongue stroked over them. "What's stopping you?" She breathed the question into his mouth.

"You are."

"No, I'm not."

"I'm taking care of you. I can't take advantage."

"You wouldn't be taking advantage."

"Yes I would." He dropped his hands and stepped back from her.

"But—"

He turned and started for the living room. "Come on. The coffee's getting cold."

Stunned, Juliette stared at his retreating back. What had

happened? One minute the man was completely turned on, and the next he was sauntering away as if he were on his way to a garden party. Juliette's eyes narrowed as she considered his tight buttocks and long legs. Her temper started to simmer. If he thought he could taste her lips like a rich dessert, then walk away from her as if he'd decided it was too fattening, he'd better think again. If he hadn't kissed her, her senses might have returned. She might have decided this entire episode was best left as it was—charming, exciting, but ultimately unresolved. After all, part of her knew that was the smartest thing to do. But no, he'd thrown down the gauntlet. He had to kiss her and *walk away*. No woman could take that type of insouciant challenge lying down. If he thought this was over, he was sadly mistaken. Before the night was done she'd have him. Her family history dictated that the Fortiers fought for whatever they wanted, and she wasn't about to let her ancestors down.

She wanted Shay.

SHAY KNEW HE'D BEEN playing with fire. *Of all the stupid, unprofessional, brain-dead things to do!* He'd known better than to kiss her. It was bad enough that he'd carried her inside, even though it had served a purpose. He was trying to shock her and see if her memory would return. At least that was part of it. But the rest—ah, the rest... He couldn't resist the thought of getting his arms around her any way he could.

Shay could feel her eyes boring a tunnel through his back. He wondered what she was thinking, then decided he didn't want to know. Instead he walked over to the end table and picked up one of the coffee cups he'd set there a few moments before. He turned and held it out to her. That's when he got his first real view of her wearing his bathrobe.

"Son of a—" He choked down the rest of his words.

He would never be able to wear that robe again without imagining her in it. He'd almost thrown it out a few days before, but now that he'd seen it on this woman he might have to frame it. The thin terry caressed her curves, molding them and beckoning him closer. He wanted to hold her, to keep her safe from life's harm. What was she doing out on her own, anyway? Some man should have tucked her in his jacket pocket and not let her out of his sight. She looked slender and delicate, but not breakable. He took a closer look. No, definitely not breakable. There was something different about her, a glint in her eyes that put his senses on high alert. He didn't have the vaguest idea what was going on, but he suddenly knew that if he had any sense, he'd run for his life. He strove to get the situation back to normal. In other words, back under his control. After all, controlling events was what he did best.

"Here's your coffee, Red."

She walked toward him with a disturbing swish of her hips, reminding him of a cat on the prowl. Now that he thought about it, she had the look of an exotic feline, with those slightly tilted vivid blue eyes, winged black brows, high cheekbones and triangular face. He could only pray she wouldn't lick her lips like he was a saucer of cream, because that darting little tongue was what had set him off the last time. Her fingers touched his as she cupped the mug.

"Thank you," she said with a slight smile. Lifting the china to her lips, she took a tiny sip. "Mmm, that's delicious."

Shay had to look over her shoulder, resisting the temptation to crush her mouth under his. He thrust a hand through his hair. "I grind—"

"—your own beans. I remember."

Shay was positive his face was turning red. Either that or it was hotter in here than he'd thought. "Glad you remember something," he mumbled.

"I've also remembered that I really love coffee. Real New Orleans coffee, hot and so strong it could blast the top of your head off."

She said it with an innocent tone, but when he glanced at her, she looked anything but innocent. She looked as if she knew that his head was ready to blow any minute, and if she didn't knock it off he was going to haul her into his lap and make love to her until she didn't care if she ever remembered anything but him. Unable to think of a comeback, an unusual circumstance for a man in his line of work, Shay grabbed his own cup of coffee from the sofa table and indicated a chair.

"Make yourself comfortable."

Carefully he stepped around the table to sit on the sofa, only to jump up a moment later when she sat down next to him. With hasty steps he crossed to the bright colored armchair at right angles to the sofa and perched there like a confused parrot.

With an amused smile, Juliette curled up on the sofa, legs tucked under her, making herself right at home. "I won't bite."

"No. I know. I just didn't think..."

Man, was that the truth. If he'd thought at all, used even one-tenth of the brains God gave him, he would've minded his own business earlier this evening. Even though he suspected he'd been given a poor tip that wouldn't amount to anything at all, if he'd only used his brains he'd still be staking out the park where he could see the action...and possibly even glimpse his suspect. If he'd only used his *goddamn brains* he'd have left this lost waif—who was looking less lost by the minute—on the park bench instead of parked all nice and cozy on his living-room sofa.

He took a gulp of coffee and practically spat it back into the cup as the heat hit his mouth and tongue. He'd obviously underestimated the power of the reheat setting on his microwave. He swallowed, feeling as if his throat was on fire.

"Are you all right?"

Her concerned voice exacerbated his temper. When he could talk again, he said, "No, I'm not all right."

He glanced over at her, and her appealing look made him want to kick himself. What the hell was the matter with him? The woman had amnesia, for cryin' out loud; he couldn't have walked away from her. As a cop, he might be a real hard-ass, but as a man...well, he'd recently rescued a kitten from a Dumpster in Cincinnati and taken it home. So how could he live with himself if he didn't rescue, a two-legged creature? Especially one with such great legs, he thought as he caught a glimpse of bare skin showing through the robe as she adjusted her position on the sofa. *Whoa, boy—forget that. You're here to serve and protect.*

Juliette patted the sofa next to her. "Why don't you come sit with me?"

"That's not a good—"

"You're not afraid of me, are you?"

Shay's spine snapped to attention. "Of course not."

"Well then?"

She smiled, and Shay could swear he saw the remnants of an age-old Greek siren in that smile, the type of woman who lured sailors to death on the rocks. Somehow he was on his feet moving toward her without having any idea how he'd gotten there. He sat beside her, taking care to leave plenty of room so their bodies didn't touch. Pretending to be at ease, he leaned back, crossing his ankle over his knee, unwittingly exposing his ankle holster.

"Is that a gun?"

Ah hell, he'd forgotten about that. He'd automatically put it back on after he'd changed into dry jeans. "Yeah, but don't worry, it's legal. I have a license and everything."

"I've never known anyone who had a gun, except hunting rifles, of course." Obviously shaken, eyes round as doughnuts, she pointed at his ankle. "Do you still call it a handgun if you wear it on your foot?" She grimaced. "And why do you have a gun in the first place?"

Trying to relax her, he teased, "Well, I could be an escaped convict or some..." He stopped, realizing what a stupid thing he'd just said. Here she was, unable to remember anything, sitting in a stranger's house, wearing a bathrobe. He opened his mouth to reassure her when she tilted her head, saying thoughtfully, "You don't seem like a criminal."

"Why not? What do you think a criminal seems like?" God, he'd never known anyone so naïve. It scared the bejesus out of him.

She nibbled on her fingernail as she studied him. "I don't know, but not like you. You seem to have too many principles."

"Then maybe I'm a cop. Cops have principles." And he'd better remember them fast if he knew what was good for him. Never mix business with pleasure, remember?

"You're not a police officer."

"I'm not? Why not?" Not seeming like a cop was his stock in trade, so at least something was working right tonight.

She took a sip of her coffee, eyeing him over the rim for a long moment. "You could be, I suppose, but I can't quite see you as one. You don't appear that...that..."

"That what?"

She shrugged. "I don't know. Crude, or maybe I mean hardened."

"Not all cops are like that, sweetheart. Just the ones on TV. I could be a nice, sweet, sensitive cop who's in town on the trail of a criminal."

"What type of criminal?" From the expression on her face, she'd obviously fallen for his game and was playing along.

Shay grinned. "A real bad dude." The leader of a smuggling ring he was determined to nail. Failure wasn't an option in Shay O'Malley's book.

"Bad in what way?"

"Why do you want to know?"

"I'm curious. I've never known a cop. That is, if you're really a cop, which I doubt." She recoiled at the sharp glance he gave her. "What?"

"How do you know you don't know any cops? Is your memory returning?"

"No..." She paused. "It just doesn't feel familiar, is all."

He shrugged, automatically protecting his assignment. "Since I'm not a cop, I'm talking out of turn, but I'd guess cops are like everyone else."

From the way she looked at him, Shay had a feeling she was absorbing everything about him, from his untrimmed hair to his love for Irish poetry. "I suppose they could be, but—" she shrugged her shoulders "—I really wouldn't know."

"If you have no experience with cops, why were you so terrified that I'd take you to one?"

"I wasn't afraid of the police, but the publicity."

Shay frowned. "The publicity?"

She stared at the blank face of the TV and said, "You know how these things always end up in the news. Poor little person with no memory, found wandering alone. Then you have reporters poking and prying. Everyone making fun and asking questions."

"You sound as if you know something about the media."

She sent him a quick glance. "I don't know that, exactly. It just feels..."

"Familiar." He found himself transfixed at the way her blush enhanced her cheekbones.

"Yes."

"Anything else feel familiar?"

"Like what?"

He hesitated, then moved closer to her and took the coffee mug from her hand, placing it with his on the table in front of them. Then he turned back and gently pulled her against him, knowing it was insane, a total mistake, but doing it anyway, not wanting to know if he was trying to get to the truth of her situation or just trying to satisfy his need to have her in his arms again.

She snuggled against him. "This doesn't feel familiar, if that's what you're asking."

His fingers caressed her shoulder. "This doesn't remind you of any special man in your life?"

Smiling, she shook her head. "But it does remind me of being warm and cozy." The old windows in the building rattled and rain pelted the glass. "I'm glad I'm in here," she whispered.

"There must be someone," he persisted, sticking to the subject like a bulldog with lockjaw. "You're too beautiful not to be involved with someone."

"You think I'm beautiful?"

"Yes." His breath caught in his throat as she looked at him as though he was the only man in the world. He'd never experienced that before, never felt the keen desire to protect and ravish at the same time. "Very beautiful."

She smiled and pulled his arm closer. "This doesn't remind me of any other man. At the moment, all I can remember is you."

Shay had to touch her. He couldn't help himself. It was as if a goddess had come to life and offered him his heart's desire—innocence mixed with a bit of vixen and a touch of spice. He tucked her hair behind her ear, his fingertip lingering there before descending slowly to her earlobe.

"Ears are funny things, you know," he mused. "On some people they look as if they've been stuck on with no thought for what the face looks like, but on you, everything matches...."

Her breath rushed out of her mouth as she whispered, "You've made quite a study of ears."

His fingertip moved down to trace her jawline. "I make a study of everything about every person I meet."

"That sounds like work."

He ignored the little jolt to his conscience. "I like it. I like looking at a person and wondering what they're thinking. Wondering if they know what I'm thinking."

"It's hard to tell what people want to keep hidden."

"Sooner or later most people slip up."

"Even if they're very good liars?"

"Good liars are harder to read, but if you're patient..." His fingertip traced her full bottom lip. "I can be incredibly patient."

"And if I don't want patience?"

"Ah, sweetheart..." He outlined her top lip with his finger. "Patience is a virtue."

"And if I don't want virtue?"

"Then you've come to the right place. Virtue's overrated. I'll take sin every time."

She sucked his fingertip into her mouth, then released it to smile up at him. "Especially during Mardi Gras, when sin is a way of life."

Shay's heart needed restarting after she released his finger. He'd felt the tug of her mouth through his entire body. His mind drifted, wondering what her lips and tongue would feel like on more sensitive parts of his anatomy. He forced himself to reply, "Then it's our duty to uphold tradition, wouldn't you say?"

"Most definitely."

"Besides, who knows what you might remember once you relax."

"I don't think this is the way to relaxation."

No lie there, Shay agreed. If he got any more wound up, he'd shoot into outer space. Her lips beckoned him, but no more than the soft little moan of anticipation she made. What red-blooded male could resist that sound? *He* certainly couldn't. He bent his head and kissed her, softly at first, then settling into it. His lips stroked over hers, again and again as he coaxed her to open to him. Not that she needed much urging. Her parted lips beckoned him inside, and he was never a man to resist something he really wanted. And he really wanted her.

He deepened the kiss, knowing he couldn't have left her if he'd tried. He should, he knew, but his blood was starting to run hot. He could no more stop his emotions than he could a runaway train. She was on track with him, keeping pace as their tongues lunged and dueled, her body pressing against his, warming him in a way he'd not known before. Oh, he had known passion, a great deal of it, but he hadn't known passion mixed with such sweetness and soul-deep desire.

The thought went briefly through his mind that, regardless of what happened, this would be a night he'd remember for the rest of his life. It wasn't every day a man fell in love with a stranger.

3

"MAKE LOVE TO ME." Her words whispered into his mouth.

For an instant he couldn't move. He heard her spoken request with every part of his body. Her plea slipped into his mind and settled down to stay. Shay's reawakened sense of duty and honor insisted he say no, this would be a mistake, but it was hard to resist something this strong. A feeling rose from his gut to tell him that this moment was what his life was about. This was the missing key to who he was. All philosophical and romantic bullcrap, of course, but it felt so right that it soon overcame his inner warnings. In the grip of intense masculine need, but with a lack of romantic finesse, he muttered, "You got it."

Clasping her tightly, he wrenched his lips from hers, rolled to his side and sat up, taking her with him. In one fluid movement he shifted her in his arms and rose to his feet, holding her against his chest. Her gaze, frosted with passion, locked with his. She smiled, a slow sensuous lift of her lips that curled his toes.

"I want to make a memory, Shay." She smoothed a lock of hair from his forehead with her fingertip. "A memory that will last..." *a lifetime.*

"Sweetheart, the way you're talking is—"

She pulled his head down to hers and slanted her mouth across his. "This is the only thing that's real. This. Here and now."

Here and now. Shay lifted his mouth a scant inch from hers. "Then we shouldn't waste it." With renewed purpose he strode across the room to the bedroom. He shouldered open the door and stepped over the threshold. Taking her to the bed, he gently placed her upon the quilted spread, then followed her down. Kneeling beside her, he gave the sash of the robe a brief tug. The terry cloth slipped free of its loose tie and fell away. Hands trembling he spread the robe, then sat back on his heels and filled his eyes with her.

Her skin was like marble, fine and almost translucent, but with a glow that invited a man to explore the vitality beneath. She lay, her arms raised slightly over her head, and let him look his fill. She seemed slightly apprehensive, but when a small whistle escaped from his lips she blushed, then chuckled. It was the chuckle that got him. That small gurgle of sound lifted his heart.

He couldn't remember ever wanting anything this much. He wanted to take, but he wanted to give, too. His hands explored her, starting with the shape of her face and working their way down, over her long elegant neck to her small shoulders, to her perfectly shaped breasts with their high tight buds. "You are so perfect."

"No, I'm not."

"Hey, I know what I'm talking about. I love beautiful things, so when I say you're perfect, you're perfect." He continued his exploration, running his hands down her slender waist, down over her hips.

"Ah—" she caught her breath as his hands traversed her hipbones "—a connoisseur. I'm impressed."

"You should be. Connoisseurs are very picky."

"Meaning this isn't a common occurrence with you?"

His fingers brushed her cleft, delving deeper to find the treasure. "There's nothing common about *this* experience, sweetheart."

"I wouldn't know."

"You're gonna find out." He smiled and dipped his head to her breast. "Don't worry. It's like riding a bike. It all comes back to you."

Her only response was a moan. Then she gasped and arched as his fingers sought her. "Please," she whispered.

"I will," he whispered back as he stretched out beside her,

ready to give her all the pleasure he was capable of giving. His index finger and thumb spread her velvet opening for his caress.

She shifted restlessly as he made lazy circles on her sensitive skin, getting nearer and nearer his goal. "I ache."

"I know, sweetheart, I know. I'll make it all better."

His mouth touched her breasts and lingered, laving first one, then the other, pulling and tugging her nipples to an erection that nearly matched his own. Her hands fisted in his hair and pulled his busy mouth up to hers. He needed no urging to take everything her lips had to offer. Mouths open, they did battle, tongues dueling with fierce abandon—advance and retreat, then advance again. His fingers followed the same pace until finally, hips gyrating, she thrust upward.

Frantic to join her now, to revel in her heat, Shay tore off his shirt and unsnapped his jeans, helped by her eager hands. She yanked the denim down, but the fabric stopped at his ankles, caught on his gun.

Shay swore. He sat up and made quick work of his loafers and holster. Yanking his jeans off, he threw them across the room, followed by his briefs, before turning back to her. He was so hard he was afraid he'd break if she touched him. She was staring at him as if she'd never seen a man in full arousal before. There was something in her eyes that checked him for a moment, an awkwardness that he found enchanting. She was like a barely opened flower offering its face to the morning dew and warming sun. He hated the thought that someone might mishandle this woman. He didn't know why that thought leaped into his mind. He had no reason to think she might be in any danger, other than the memory loss that could be a result of—of what? He had no chance to follow up on his thoughts.

She put her hands on him, her fingers sliding up his manhood to gently squeeze the sensitive head. "You're so soft. I didn't know a man could be so soft." Wonder colored her voice.

Shay groaned as her fingers slipped up and down his length. "I'm so hard I'm gonna explode."

"Now that would be something to see."

He stilled her hand with his. "No, sweetheart. It's better you should feel it."

She smiled, anticipation sharpening the angles of her face. "Then what are you waiting for?"

Shay came up on his elbows and reached toward the nightstand. Opening a drawer, he withdrew a small foil packet and quickly protected them both before reaching for her again. "Not a damn thing."

He took his time, bringing her up to fever pitch again, until she cried with the wanting. Then and only then did he slip inside her. He pressed forward, inch by inch, stunned by the tightness of her body, by the barrier he felt. Alarmed for a moment, he stopped and tried to pull back, but her legs clamped him in place, heels urging him on. Clarity faded, leaving only the crimson flame of desire. He gave...and he took...until finally they shuddered to a climax together.

Afterward he smoothed her hair back from her face.

"Thank you," she said.

Shay grinned. "No, thank you."

She met his grin with a wistful expression, her eyes serious. "I'll never forget this moment."

He yawned and settled her comfortably against his side. "There'll be a lot more to remember, I promise. I just need to close my eyes for a minute." Sexual satisfaction combined with an early rising and a long, frustrating day were taking their toll. His eyelids drifted shut for a moment before he jerked them open to look at her face. He smiled again, then pressed a kiss on her forehead. "Rest, sweetheart—" he interrupted himself with a jaw-popping yawn. "—'cause pretty soon you're gonna need all your strength again."

She blew on his eyelids. "Go to sleep."

"Right," he mumbled.

Her voice caressed him as he slid into sleep. "Sweet dreams...Prince Charming."

Shay woke just before dawn. Arms aching and empty, he reached for her, just as he'd reached for her a few hours before to make love with her again. This time the bed beside him was empty. There was no trace of the woman with no memory. No trace except for his inevitable erection, her evocative scent on the pillow next to him, and her memory burned into his mind.

AT FOUR IN THE MORNING, Juliette had been lucky to find an empty taxi still cruising the streets looking for Mardi Gras stragglers. Agreeing to let her send him his fee and a big tip for the inconvenience of bringing her home, which was much farther from town than he usually ventured, the cab driver dropped her off at the wrought-iron gates that spanned the entrance to La Belle Rivière des Fleurs. Juliette walked up the magnolia-lined driveway that led to her family home, taking care to stay in the shadows so as not to be observed.

The plantation had been in their family for a very long time, passed from father to son. Heritage, tradition—this was the way of life revered by her ancestors since the beginning. Her privileged family heritage went all the way back to 1807, when her titled Spanish great-great-great-great-grandmother married a bastard French prince who'd been awarded land in New Orleans in addition to his French estates. Each generation sacrificed and struggled to add to the family fortunes, to the family luster. It was just unfortunate, Juliette thought, that she could be the latest sacrifice.

She stopped in the shadow of a weeping willow tree and stared at her home, taking in the classic columns that accented the mansion, supporting the second-story gallery and creating the wide veranda that wrapped around the perfect example of Greek Revival plantation architecture. Or so the guidebooks said. She wondered what Shay would make of it. Would he be impressed? He hadn't seemed the type of man to be overly impressed with things. People either, for that matter. He took them as he found them, Juliette believed. How did he find her? Would he care that she'd left? Or would he be convinced that she'd made a fool of him, and write her off?

Of course that's what he'd do.

Her romantic stranger wasn't really a warrior prince. He was just a normal man who'd had a brief affair that would fade from his memory in a week, while it would last forever in hers. Juliette glanced up at her home again. Much as she'd always loved it, home had begun to feel like a prison.

She crept around to the back of the house and slipped inside the kitchen door. The room was dark, lit only by strips of moonlight spilling through the windows. She tiptoed over to a corner and opened a door to the servants' stairs. This wasn't the first time she'd used them, but it was certainly the first time she'd used them after an experience like this. Taking care to avoid the last step, which always creaked, Juliette emerged into the second-story hallway. Leaning against the wall for a moment, she looked down the corridor, focusing on the rich, ruby-red carpeting and the crystal lamps that accented the damask wallpaper. The effect was opulent, yet tasteful—two adjectives that adequately described her life. Not for the first time that evening, she wanted to scream at the confining nature of her existence. However, her upbringing held sway. Screaming was discouraged. It wasn't appropriate behavior. Although she'd recently screamed her head off in Shay's arms as she'd succumbed to her first night of passion—loving every minute of it.

With a quick glimpse around to be sure she was unobserved, Juliette sped over the thick carpet to her room, which occupied an end suite off the corridor. She let herself in with a minimum of noise, then leaned back to relish her triumph. She'd managed to experience a true adventure—one even more exciting than she could have dreamed—and no one would ever be the wiser. Her brother would have assumed she'd gone to bed early, as she'd indicated she would when she left the restaurant. And there would have been no one to tell him differently, as her father had left last month for the family's estate in France to personally handle a crisis involving his vineyards. With no one at home that evening, she'd followed her usual practice and even given the servants the night off. So her secret was safe.

Juliette walked over to her four-poster bed, the bed she'd occupied ever since she was a child. She ran her fingertips over the carved upright posts that stretched to the ceiling, and fingered the ivory silk quilt that spilled over the mattress to pool onto the carpet beneath. It looked different to her now. The last time she'd slept in this bed, she'd been an innocent. Well, she was innocent no longer. She was no longer a virgin, but a full-fledged woman, who'd not only experienced passion, but reveled in it.

Her body still sang with the force of Shay's lovemaking. It had killed her to leave him as she did. He'd lain with one arm thrown over his head, as relaxed as a boy abandoned to slumber. With his eyes closed, Juliette realized that his thick eyelashes were the longest she'd ever seen on a man, seemingly incongruous with his intense masculinity. Yet it only added to his male beauty. She'd been tempted to press a kiss on his lips, soft with sleep, but feared to wake him. She hated to deceive him. He didn't deserve that type of treatment. She felt very guilty about that, but had been unable to tell him the truth. Juliette gave a deep, unhappy sigh. It was better this way. Shay wasn't the type of man who'd be happy to be used as a plaything or an escape.

She stripped off her clothing. With each movement she remembered Shay's touch, his fingers here, his tongue there. She reached for her nightgown and pulled it over her head, letting the silk whisper past her knees. She got into bed and nestled down under the cover, staring up at the delicate, crocheted lace draping the arches of the canopy. The pattern above her had as many holes as the story she'd told Shay tonight. Yet he'd fallen for it, or pretended he had. Now that she considered it, she wasn't sure why he hadn't marched her to the nearest health clinic or police station. For the first time, she really considered the situation and wondered why. Why, beyond the obvious—that she'd seemed in need this evening.

Juliette remembered the vulnerable expression that came into his eyes right before they'd made love, when he'd relaxed and really looked at her. What was she to him? A casual experience, or was he searching for something himself? Was that what tonight was really about—two people with needs, instead of just one? She hoped so. She wouldn't feel as guilty if that was the case.

She let her mind drift as she relived her night with Shay. From the moment she'd emerged, wearing only his robe, to discover him with his shirt hanging open and the top button of his jeans unsnapped, she'd been lost. Funny how that had happened. One moment she was an innocent, uncertain about her appeal. The next moment she was a siren who couldn't sing her temptation song fast or loud enough. With this man, she'd discovered a side of herself she hadn't known existed. Oh, she had imagined the sensual side was there, but had seriously doubted she'd ever be the type of woman to inspire a man's hunger. She'd been amazed to discover her own hunger was as strong as his. She could still see him, his face tight with desire as he made love to her. Her sensitive body still sang from his lovemaking.

Shay.

She grew hot just thinking of him. She closed her eyes and drifted, smoothing her hands down her body, much as he had done. *This is madness. I'll never see him again.* He would remain what he was destined to be—a memory to take into the future with her. But oh, how she wanted to see him again!

Her body moving restlessly, she tried desperately to refocus her thoughts. It was no use. She ached to see him. Make love with him again. She moaned, the ache intensifying as he continued to invade her mind as surely as he had invaded her body. She closed her eyes. *Shay, please don't hate me.*

THREE DAYS LATER, Shay O'Malley strode into the first district house of the New Orleans Police Department. He blew past the uniformed sergeant at the front desk and attacked the stairs, climbing two at a time to the second floor, where he slammed through a door into an open room that looked like a bad stage set on a television show. The desks were old and unmatched, scarred with cigarette burns and gouges, stained with coffee rings. The walls were the institutional green that only the government could love, and the floor was linoleum that had been scuffed so often the janitors had obviously given up on it. The room resembled most of the other departments Shay had worked in with one difference. For all the bustle of ordinary police activity, there was a different feeling—one more laidback and easy. It drove him nuts—especially today. His temper was already short because he'd spent the past few days trying to track down his mystery woman. He'd run into dead ends everywhere, almost as dead as his line of questioning with the case that had brought him to New Orleans in the first place. Of course, the entire investigation wasn't helped by the pace of life in New Orleans, which was dead slow. It was a thought echoed by the laidback drawl of a female voice behind him.

"Land sakes, Yankee, if you aren't some kinda busy man today. You're bustling around like you're the whole Northern army hell-bent on capturing N'awlins before noon."

He snapped a glance over his shoulder, taking in the amused attitude of the tall, statuesque, blond-haired woman standing behind him. "I am a Yankee."

With a casual gesture, she pushed back her hair, then smiled. "I know, sugar, but I don't think it plays real well down here."

Turning to face Detective Lucille Monteverde, Shay hitched a hip onto the corner of his temporary desk. "Excuse me?"

The woman adjusted the badge clipped onto the lapel of her well-cut beige jacket. "What I mean is, I don't think your Northern attitude and way of doing things will get you a lot of cooperation down here."

"What do you mean by that?"

She shrugged. "Just some of the stories I'm hearing, is all."

"Such as?"

"Such as, I hear y'all are in town investigating one of our most illustrious families."

"Yeah? So?"

"So...some people aren't too happy about the way you're going about it."

Shay folded his arms across his chest. "I'm listening."

"Well, now, far be it from me to make any suggestions to a visitor to our fair city, but in this town, you'll catch more flies with honey than all your vinegar."

"What the hell are you talking about? The only way I know to do my job is to 'do my job.'"

"Well, now, if you don't mind a teeny bit of advice...I'd suggest you smile a bit more if you're trying to shake down a bank secretary for the financial records of Louis Fortier's shipping association."

Shay could feel his neck turning red. He had gotten a bit short with that woman, who was as resilient and homely as one of Louis Fortier's tugboats. "I tried to play nice, but when she didn't hand over the information, I played the odds that she'd cooperate if I came on like a jerk." He leaned forward, his most intimidating scowl in place. "I didn't think I had a choice. I made a decision. I followed through."

Lucille leaned right back. "Maybe so, but I don't think offering to have some police friends throw her in the pokey was the best way to get her cooperation."

Shay rubbed his chin with a rueful hand. "It didn't have the desired effect."

Lucille barked a short, sharp laugh. "You don't know the half of it, sugar. Seems this lady complained to her manager about some stranger pretending to be a representative from Fortier Shipping threatening her, then the manager scurried over to the bank president, who is a very good friend of the mayor, and of Louis Fortier and his son Michael, I might add. Not to mention that the mayor is also very fond of keeping his campaign coffers full, since there is an election coming up this fall and he's already running full-tilt toward the vote, and the bank president and the Fortiers are all prominent members of the same political party. So you see, it gets a mite sticky. Perhaps your hit-'em-over-the-head method isn't the best way to go about getting some results here."

"Are you giving me a warning to back off, Lucille?"

"Nope, I'm giving you only one thing—me."

Stunned, Shay stared at her. Then he grinned. "You?"

"Not in the biblical sense, you understand, Yankee, although you are ever so tempting to this Southern flower..." She heaved a great, theatrical sigh. "But I'm afraid that's out, as I am engaged to a perfectly yummy man. As of this morning, I am your newly assigned partner."

"I don't need a partner."

"Our captain begs to differ. He says you need help."

"How are you going to help me?"

She put her finger on his nose and wiggled it. "For starters, sugar, I'm going to get you close to your suspects without them suspecting you so you can nose around and see what you're up against."

Shay lightly slapped her finger away. "How're you gonna do that, Detective? From what you're saying, if I try to get near these people, society will close ranks."

Lucille reached into her pocket and withdrew a pair of elaborately printed envelopes. "I have two very sought-after invitations to the annual masked ball given at the plantation home of Louis Fortier. It's the crowning event of Mardi Gras. Everyone who is anyone in New Orleans society will be there."

Shay reached for one envelope and pulled out the folded card. "Including Stephen St. James?"

"Now why wouldn't the Fortiers invite their partner to the family ball? Especially since St. James has run tame in that house since he was a child. He's not only Michael's best friend, but his and Michael's fathers were very close, too." Lucille pursed her lips and considered Shay.

"You say everyone who's anyone will be there?" He remembered his mystery woman, her aristocratic accent, her high-class appearance, and wondered if he'd find her there. If he did...

"My, my, my...you look like some big ole dawg just peed in your Wheaties." Lucille examined her ruby-red nail polish. "If I weren't such a brave little detective, I'd be running for home right about now."

Shay looked up. "Huh?"

"Who is she?"

He blinked. "Who is who?"

"The woman who put that look on your face, of course."

"What makes you think a woman put this look on my face?"

"Trust me, only a woman could be responsible." Lucille bumped him over, so she could perch on the desk next to him. She grinned. "I know 'cause I've been responsible for any number of men looking just like you, including my fiancé just the other night after an itty-bitty spat."

Attempting to hide his amusement, Shay commented, "He has my sympathies."

"He doesn't need it, sugar. We make up *real* well...."

His grin escaped, despite his attempt to keep it hidden. "If that sentence had gotten any longer, Lucille, I could have driven a truck through it."

She waggled a finger under his nose. "So you sit right here and tell little Lucille all about it. We're going to be partners, after all. Your pain is my pain."

Shay slid her a look. "I have a feeling *you* are gonna be my pain." It was just his luck that he'd have to partner up with a woman who could see through his veneer. He hadn't met a woman yet who could mind her own business.

"Where'd you meet her?"

He didn't intend to answer, but he found himself saying, "In a park down in the French Quarter, a few nights ago during one of the parades. She was just sitting on a bench, and I..." His voice trailed off as he remembered his first sight of her, the way his nerves had hummed as he'd stared at her. Lord, he could still feel her with every part of his body.

"Umm...then what?"

Shay glanced away from Lucille's probing look. "Then nothing."

"Nothing? You don't mean to tell me a big ole rampaging Yankee like yourself didn't scoop her up and carry her off?"

"What makes you think I'd do anything like that?"

Lucille laughed. "The expression on your face."

Shay attempted to preserve his dignity, saying in a careful tone, "I did ask her if she needed any help and—"

"Did she?"

"Yeah, she did. She couldn't remember anything and I—"

Lucille hooted with laughter. "Go on—that's the oldest trick in the book. Especially during Mardi Gras, when everybody is out to party and would rather not remember it the next day."

"I don't think it was a trick."

"Sugar, some of the best hookers use it." She sent him a sympathetic look. "She didn't roll you afterward, did she?"

"No, I still had my wallet and all my money."

"You're lucky."

"Yeah, but I don't think she was a hooker." Not this woman. Every instinct he had rebelled at the thought.

Lucille lifted a brow, then whistled. "Let me guess. You've been trying to find her?"

"Not—" He quit trying to lie when he caught sight of her knowing look. Ah, the hell with it. "I haven't had any luck."

"No place is better for disappearing than New Orleans."

Shay shoved an errant lock of hair off his brow. "If you say so—partner."

Lucille patted him on the hand. "Don't you worry, sugar. I'm going to introduce you to some high-society belles at the ball this Friday. You'll forget all about your little ole mystery woman."

Shay prayed she was right. As it was, half of his attention was focused on finding the key to his criminal case, while the other half was fixated on a woman who smelled like rain-damp jasmine and had skin as soft as a rose petal. At the moment, he wasn't sure who he wanted to find more.

"We have to go in costume, sugar."

He shook his head. "Go where in costume?"

"To the Fortier Mardi Gras ball. It's one of the most elaborate costume parties in New Orleans, even given what usually happens at Mardi Gras events. It's wonderful. I'm surprised Louis Fortier left for France before the ball."

"He's gone?" What the hell...how had Shay missed this?

"He spends half the year on his French estates, anyway, but he loves showing off at the ball, so something must have taken him back out of town in one heck of a hurry."

"What about Michael Fortier? Did he go with him?"

"Of course not. This ball is one of the premier social events. It's a Fortier tradition. What's a Fortier tradition without a Fortier?" Lucille eyed him, pursing her lips as she gave him an intense once-over. "Now let's see...what type of costume should—"

"No costume." Shay sent Lucille a look guaranteed to freeze her to the floor. "Forget it, there's no way I'm going to dress up like some—"

"Pirate. I think you'd be a great pirate." Lucille patted his hand again and jumped off the desk. "Don't you worry, I'll take care of everything. Besides, what's the big deal? You work undercover most of the time, don't you? I don't suppose you do it in your best suit?"

"No, but I don't do it in one of those shirts that look like a sail at full mast and a stupid cape, either."

Lucille eyed his legs. "I bet you'd look good in tights."

"No tights. Pirates don't wear tights."

"How do you know?"

"Because if they do, you can forget the whole idea."

Lucille laughed. "Don't worry, sugar, I'll make sure you look manly, and modest, and dangerous. No woman will be able to resist you. All the New Orleans belles will be falling all over themselves to find out who you are."

"That could be useful." He smiled, then snapped his fingers. "Wait a minute. If it's so hard to get an invitation to this fancy society ball, how'd you get *two?*"

"I get 'em every single year, sugar. I grew up with Juliette Fortier. My father had a house right up the road."

"Hold it, Lucille. If that's so, you can't work this case. You wouldn't be able to—"

"You know, Detective O'Malley, I understand your reasoning, but I don't mind telling you that I am a might offended by that remark. I'm a cop, a damn good one. I have one goal and one goal only—to see justice done. Now, I happen to think you're barkin' up the wrong tree here with the Fortiers but—" she shrugged "—if you aren't, then who better to be involved than someone who knows the ins and outs of New Orleans society?"

"And what if I'm right about Michael Fortier and Stephen St. James being involved in this smuggling activity?"

"Then who better to be there at the end than an old friend who can help Juliette pick up the pieces?"

Shay met her level stare. "Okay, I'll give you a chance."

"No, sweetie, I'm the one giving *you* a chance. Don't blow it." With that, Lucille marched out of the squad room, stopping at the door to issue one final ultimatum. "I'll have your costume by Friday. Don't shave between now and then. You'll look more in character that way."

Shay stared at her as she sailed through the door. *Goddamn all women.* Every time one of them came sneaking into his life, he regretted it. Instantly his mystery woman's face crystallized in his mind—okay, so mostly he regretted it. He couldn't stop dreaming about her. Every time he closed his eyes, she was there. He could still see her dark hair splayed across his pillow, feel her limbs tangling with his....

He rubbed his smooth-shaven chin. *A pirate.* Well, why not? No one had ever accused him of hanging back when a job needed doing. Besides, he loved being undercover, the opportunity to indulge himself and be another character. It was the Irish in him, he figured. It wasn't because he was running away from the reality of his life. Nah, it was the adventure. He lived for adventure. With any luck at all, this Mardi Gras ball might change the game, net him some hard evidence.

A pirate? Bold, adventurous, unscrupulous…greedy. Yeah, that was a role he could get into. And he was great at improvisation, ruthless enough to play this game and win. He had no intention of leaving New Orleans without getting the job done to his satisfaction. He didn't start anything unless he was sure he'd come out on top. Until recently…

He should've tied her to the bedpost. Then she wouldn't have run out on him.

Slapping his palm against his thigh, he got to his feet. He couldn't stand here dreaming about finding a woman who didn't want to be found; he had a crook to catch.

4

SHAY PAUSED on the stone path that led to the Fortiers' front entrance. To his appreciative eyes, La Belle Rivière des Fleurs, or the "Beautiful River of Flowers," as Lucille had translated a few days before, was just as lovely as its name. Beds of blooms lined the wide approach to the plantation house and nestled against the wide veranda. The air was heavy with the intoxicating scent of magnolia and jasmine blossoms. Century old oaks and pecan trees, festooned with Spanish moss that stirred in the breeze, and adorned with thousands upon thousands of twinkling white fairy lights, created a fanciful impression, while the welcoming glow from the floor-to-ceiling windows of the house completed the picture.

A smiling couple attired in colorful costumes of brocade and satin brushed by Shay as he took stock of his surroundings. The woman turned to look at him. "Well, Yankee," Lucille drawled, as she took a better grip on her fiancé's arm, "are y'all just going to stand out here all night, or come on inside and give all these Southern women a chance to goggle over your dashing pirate self?"

Shay could feel himself blush, which was something that hadn't happened in a very long time. "Damn you, Lucille," he muttered looking down at his costume. "At least I've got pants—" even if they did fit tighter than he liked "—but I almost choked myself sitting on my cape, and I got my sleeve caught in the car window when I rolled it up."

"Now, now, don't let's be testy." Lucille reached to adjust his hat, tilting it to a more rakish angle. "I declare, if I didn't have my Preston here, I'd jump you myself. That's how dark and dangerous you look. A woman's fantasy come to life, sugar."

Lucille's fiancé chuckled. "My advice is don't listen to her. Don't take the bait, 'cause the minute you do, you're deader than a frog sitting in the fast lane."

Shay grinned at the tall, good-looking blond man, whose relaxed attitude and Southern charm could give Lucille a run for her money, and probably did. "I've noticed that already."

"Well—" Preston smiled "—since you're obviously a quick study, you don't need any help from me."

Shay eyed Lucille, who was pretending to study her flawless manicure. "I can handle her. She's not that tough."

Lucille sent him a flirtatious look. "I'm not the one you have to handle, remember, sugar? I suspect you're going to be a mite busy this evening."

Shay frowned. "Tonight is strictly business, Lucille." He'd gotten in enough trouble the last time he'd decided to mix business with pleasure. He hadn't had a good night's sleep ever since.

"Of course it is. Now, what's your name going to be again?"

"Shay Mallory, instead of Shay O'Malley." He shrugged. "It's cleaner if you don't get too elaborate when you're undercover."

"Well, Mr. Mallory, what do you say we go to the ball?"

"You and Preston go in first. I don't want anyone to connect us."

Preston hesitated for a moment, then stuck out his hand. "Good luck, with whatever you're doing tonight, Shay."

Shay sent Lucille a questioning glance. "Thanks."

"Don't worry, sugar. I only tell Preston the bare bones of things." She sent her fiancé a megawatt smile. "Don't I, darlin'?"

"Generally not even that. I've discovered being engaged to a police detective could be a bit uncomfortable if we didn't set up some ground rules. Ignorance can be bliss."

Shay nodded as he took in the man's whimsical expression

and his serious eyes. "You're very wise. Sometimes it's better not to know."

Laying a proprietary hand on Preston's shoulder, Lucille glanced at Shay. "My feeling exactly, sugar."

He lowered his voice. "Keep your eyes and ears open, partner. We'll compare notes later."

"Ohh, I can't wait." Lucille winked before tugging on Preston's arm. "Come on, darlin', I'm just dying to dance."

Shay watched them as they sauntered up the path. *Sometimes it's better not to know.* Easier said than done. He frowned. As it was, his Red Riding Hood was continually in front of him, her image lurking in his mind. She'd disappeared as if she'd never existed. But she did exist! He still had the ache to prove it. It started deep in his gut and gnawed at his insides like a hunger. What he needed was something to shake him up, get his mind off *her* and back onto this case, where it belonged.

"To hell with it," Shay said, setting his jaw. Stephen St. James would be here tonight. Shay had enough clues to link St. James with the mob connection that had first brought him onto the case in Cincinnati. Now it was time to bait the trap. He adjusted his half mask and his attitude. "Time to stir things up."

He set off for the house, taking the steps to the veranda two at a time, to the surprise of the welcoming committee, who stood right inside the double doors, accepting invitations. After handing his over, Shay stepped inside the marble foyer and noted the Fortier ball was in full swing. Music floated over the laughter and murmurs of conversation.

Shay stepped to his right, leaned back against the wall and took a moment to get his bearings. He was used to being in unfamiliar situations, but this venue was certainly one of the most decorative he'd ever experienced. The sight of men and women clad in colorful, sumptuous costumes and elaborate masks transported him from the modern world to a past era of sophisticated decadence.

Whoever had told him New Orleans was a party town

wasn't just whistling Dixie. And where there was a party, there was bound to be a bit of sin somewhere. What a perfect setting for upper-class villains such as Stephen St. James and Michael Fortier.

Shay surveyed the crowd, pausing to examine each man before moving on to the next—categorizing, calculating, mentally comparing them to the pictures in his file. The crowd parted for a moment, giving him a glimpse of a small group of people standing near the far end of the room. As he stared, he suddenly felt as if someone had just clubbed him in the gut, then given him an uppercut to the chin.

She was here.

He narrowed his eyes to peer even more sharply through the slits of his mask. His amnesiac, one-night lover was standing across the room, bold as polished brass, smiling and conversing with some of the guests. Even though she was draped in a Grecian gown of the purest, most virginal ivory, holding an elaborate mask casually in her hand to obscure her face, he'd have known her anywhere. He scanned her from top to bottom, then up again. *Oh yes, it was her.* He'd know her body—the sweep of her neck, where it met the sweet curve of her shoulder; her delicate ears and luxurious black hair—anywhere. He could be six-feet under and blind and he'd still recognize her.

What had Lucille said? "Anyone who matters will be at the Fortiers' ball." It looked as if she'd been right. For an instant, relief swept over him as he stared at his lost waif. *Alive.* He could put his vivid imaginings behind him. She was alive and obviously kicking, judging by the smiles and laughter that emerged from her companions. And here he'd been keeping himself awake at night with visions of her body being violated, then dumped into the Mississippi, or buried in some landfill—everyday coplike images that had been a part of his waking and sleeping life for the past nine years.

Instead, there she stood, elegant, smiling, flirting. He gritted his teeth, fighting the wave of sexual frustration she'd been able to arouse since the moment he'd met her, a wave made stronger by relief. *She was alive—goddamn it!* He adjusted his hat, pulling it a bit lower over his brow, the rakish plume almost brushing his shoulder. When he got finished with her, she'd wish she wasn't.

Hand anchored on the short sword at his hip, he launched himself from the wall and swaggered toward her feeling every inch the bold buccaneer out to plunder treasure. And he knew how precious this treasure was—knew intimately. She glanced in his direction, then froze, lowering her mask to reveal a face that was suddenly as white as her dress. Her lips parted and he could almost hear her gasp for air.

Never taking his eyes from her, he moved closer, watching as she pulled herself together, pretended to turn aside to begin another conversation, when every instinct must have urged her to run. Shay could almost admire that—at least, he could have if his vision hadn't been blurred by hurt and anger. He reached her side, stepping closer until he could catch her scent, that intoxicating jasmine fragrance that he swore still hovered in the air of his bedroom. He took her hand, feeling it ice-cold in his. Leaning down he whispered, "Memory returned, did it?"

She snapped him a wary look, then glanced at the people standing nearby. "I beg your pardon, sir?" she said under her breath.

"I said—" he raised his voice a bit "—your memory's returned."

She pulled her hand from his. "I...I don't understand."

He took her wrist in a firm grasp and started to back up, taking her with him. "I'll explain it to you."

She attempted a gracious smile and a lighthearted tone. "I think you've made a mistake, Mr. Pirate."

"I don't think so, Princess."

"I told you not to call me Prin—" She swallowed the rest of the word, her eyes wide and panicked behind the mask she now held stiffly in front of her like a shield. Her body tensed as she stared at him, ready to take flight at the first opportunity.

Shay smiled, a terse stretch of the lips, as he cupped her elbow with his palm. Princess was only one of the many names he'd like to call her at the moment. "Come on. Let's have a little talk."

He took a firmer grasp on her arm as he pulled her from the crowd and headed determinedly for one of the French doors that opened off the rear of the ballroom. When he got this little witch outside he was going to... To what? He stared straight ahead. He wasn't sure what he was going to do.

They emerged into the night, the woman at his side now silent as the grave, their only communication the pressure of his fingers against her skin, the brush of her gown against his leg. Shay glanced around, then chose some stone steps that led down off the veranda into a lush garden. He ushered her along the walkway, only to turn onto another charming path that wound through a carefully conceived wilderness, until he came to a clearing. Looking around, he discovered a statue of Cupid there, surrounded by vines. Heavy with blooms, the spot provided a secluded nest for Cupid's targets.

Shay took the woman by her shoulders and whirled her around until she faced him, her back pressed flat against the stone wall behind her. The mask she clutched dropped into the grass at her side, and he stared down into her face. Ripping off his own mask, he muttered, "All right, *Princess*, what's going on? What kind of game is this?"

Her voice, when she finally found it, was hoarse. "No...no game."

"Don't give me that. What was it? A little bet with your society friends, huh? Life a bit boring, maybe? You just decided you'd go screw the first guy who was sucker enough to fall for your big blue eyes and lame story?"

Streaks of red slashed her cheeks. "No, no, God no. You don't understand. I didn't plan to—"

"I understand you played me for fun." The words fell from his lips, dagger sharp, as sharp as the wounds she'd left in his heart. "Played me, then left."

"No. No I didn't." Then she bit her lip. "I mean, I did, but I didn't mean to—"

"To what? To drive me nuts?" He hid his hurt, concentrating on his anger instead. "Do you know what you put me through this week? Imagining you were lost, maybe hurt... God knows what I thought." Grabbing her elbows, he shook her. "Why'd you leave that way?"

"I remembered everything," she said, a desperate tone in her voice. "I suddenly remembered everything, and you were asleep and...I thought..."

"You thought...?"

"I *didn't* think. It was too...I panicked." She licked her lips. "I decided it would be better if I didn't have anything more to do with you."

"Just like that, huh?" He snapped his finger under her nose. "I'm nothing—never happened. Is that what you're saying?"

For just a moment Shay saw a crack in her veneer as her gaze wavered, revealing a longing that she attempted to cover with another cool, controlled statement. "It's better if we just forget what happened."

"Yeah, sure," he agreed, his instincts telling him now was the time to push for the truth. He trailed a finger over her jawline, feeling her shudder as he touched her lips. He smiled when they opened in wordless invitation. "You can forget this?"

"Yes," she breathed.

He moved his fingers down her throat, then followed them with his lips. "Can you forget this?"

"*Yes,*" she hissed.

He continued to explore with both hands as he pressed kisses on the round swell of her breasts. "And this?"

"Yes."

His hands slid down her hips, cupped against her thighs, thumbs pressing upward against her, moving with sure, slow strokes. "Don't you remember my mouth on you?"

"I...please."

"You screamed when you came."

"Oh, please, don't—" She moaned, head moving side to side as his tongue laved the valley between her breasts.

"Don't what? Don't remember?" His fingers continued their seductive rhythm. "Or don't stop?"

"I can't!"

"Sure, you can. All you have to do is open that lying little mouth and say 'make another memory with me' and I'll get right to it."

Her eyes met his, dark and disturbed, turbulent with emotion—and need. "Why are you doing this?"

"Doing what? Torturing you or pleasuring you?" He pulled her bodice down, revealing her nipples. "Which?"

Grabbing his hair, she pulled his mouth down to hers. "Both, damn you, both."

At that moment, all of the erotic scents of a New Orleans night combined into one overwhelming seduction. Everywhere his fingers and lips touched, another shock of sensation awaited, and the night swirled around them, alive, hungry, waiting for the satisfaction the seductive shadows promised.

She pulled his shirt from his breeches and stroked her palms over his chest, leaning forward to rub her sensitive breasts against the coarse hair on his chest. She gasped, giving back her excitement in the form of a kiss that raised his blood to the boiling point.

He loosened the tie of her gown and the draped bodice dropped to her waist, freeing her to the warm, moist night air and his hot mouth. Rocking back, she cradled his head in her arms, thrusting her breasts toward him. "Shay," she breathed, the sound of his name soft as a sigh on the breeze.

He was unable to respond for a moment; she overwhelmed him. First her denial, then the fierceness of her response. Which was he to believe? Damn the woman. She was tying him up in knots! Him, the cool, oh so cool, veteran. He'd seen more of life than most men his age, and been in and out of more temporary relationships than he could count. He was far too savvy to be taken in by this...this—

"Shay." Her voice lingered in his ear, wistful, promising him delights he could only imagine as heaven's ultimate reward.

He lifted his head, meeting her eyes. "What?" he whispered.

"I haven't been able to stop thinking of you, wanting you. Let's make a memory one more time, please. One more time."

Shay hesitated, feeling his anger fade, only to be replaced by a yearning such as he'd never known. Shame engulfed him for a moment; he'd been trying to punish her; but if he took her now... Taking her now, under these circumstances, would become his punishment instead of hers. He was torn. Every logical cell he possessed urged him to retreat, just as every instinct urged him to advance. Ultimately, the woman in his arms took matters into her own hands.

Unbuckling his wide leather belt, then unhooking his breeches, she reached inside to find him, hard and heavy. She closed her hands around him and caressed him, until finally, with an urgent moan, she dropped to her knees to take him in her mouth.

Shay was lost.

Any feelings of remorse disappeared as her tongue worked magic. All denial fled as his system shifted into high gear. He could only feel. Ready to explode, he lifted her up and parted her draped skirt, to find a teeny pair of bikini underpants that revealed more than they concealed. He practically ripped them aside, cupping her hips and lifting her to settle her on his shaft. Her legs gripped him hard around the waist as he leaned her back against the wall and the cushioning vines.

Then he started to move. Rocking slowly, he envisioned her closing around him with each thrust, overflowing with sweetness, slick with passion as she gripped him and held him tight. Waves of emotion washed over him, the waves crashing higher with each passing moment. He grasped her hips, thrusting harder, deeper, feeling her grabbing him in return. He groaned. "It's even better than before."

She trembled in his arms, whispering fiercely, "Don't stop."

Stop? It would be easier to stop a freight train. Furnace flaming, throttle wide open, he raced toward the summit, with her stoking the fire every step of the way. Desperation and desire proved a volatile combination. It made the ordinary unordinary. The act of making love took on a whole new dimension.

Greedy beyond control, her lips devoured his. "More. I want more."

"Everything I've got...I promise." He was as good as his word. Moments later, he tightened his hold on her, and she on him, as their tension built to a release.

Slowly, reality returned—bodies cooled, vision cleared, the night once again took on form and dimension. Shay held her in his arms, not wanting to let her go, positive that once he did, he'd wake up and discover it had all been a dream, that he was once again alone with the scent of jasmine on his pillow.

"All right, Princess?" he breathed into her ear.

Her answer came, still dreamy with passion as she tightened her legs, reluctant to let him go. "Perfect. But you don't need to call me Princess. I don't use the title."

"What title?"

Her eyes popped open.

Confused, he stared at her. "What title?" he insisted.

She met his gaze for an instant, then looked away, focusing behind him. She released her grip on his body so suddenly that he grabbed her hips to readjust her weight before lowering her to the ground.

She tried to break free of his arms. "How could I...? No, how could you have...?" her voice trailed off as she glanced from side to side in obvious distress. "What have I done?"

He let her go, momentary guilt making him demand, "Do you want me to say I'm sorry?" This was one of those times, he thought, when a woman's mind was incomprehensible to a man. He certainly had no remorse, not really. He'd found her again, so that was enough for him.

Busy trying to rearrange her clothing, she didn't answer him.

"Is that it? 'Cause if it is, you'll wait a long time." He grabbed her arms, sliding his palms up and down. "I'm not sorry about making love to you. Not when I intend to make love to you every chance I get." He'd had no intention of making love to her when he'd brought her outside; at least he didn't think he had. But now that it had happened, he had no intention of stopping. She'd gotten under his skin, so he'd just have to try to work her out of his system, he reasoned. He was sure something was missing in his logic, but was reluctant to question it more closely.

She moaned. "Don't talk like that. Please don't talk like that."

He stared down at her. "Why not?"

"You and I can't... It's no good."

He chuckled. "I don't agree. I think we're very good together."

"It's impossible at the moment," she insisted, her eyes filling with regret.

"Nothing's impossible." As he said that, reality intruded in the form of a man's voice calling.

"Juliette? Juliette?"

Shay glanced over his shoulder toward the voice, then turned back. "Let me guess. You're Juliette."

Her breath came in shallow pants, as if she'd been running too hard and too long. "It's my brother," she gasped. "Oh my God, it's my brother."

"Your brother?"

"Yes, he's... I must be out of my mind. We're in the garden, for heaven's sake!" She yanked her bodice back up, slapping away Shay's hands when he tried to help. "I have to go."

Shay grabbed her as she tried to dash past him. "Wait a minute. I'll walk you back. I'd like to meet your brother."

"Are you mad? You can't." She swept a lock of hair back into place. "He'd take one look at us and know what we were—"

Shay chuckled and let her go. "You're probably right."

Juliette stepped around him and onto the path. She hesitated, then turned. "I'm so sorry. I shouldn't have let it go this far, but I couldn't— I can't see you again, Shay. It's not good for either of us."

Shay smiled and tucked his shirt into his trousers. "Not true, Red. I think it's very good for both of us."

Her face flushed as she met his gaze. She opened her mouth to speak, but her brother's voice interrupted again. "Juliette, where are you?"

She sent one more hunted glance over her shoulder, then lifted her skirt and ran lightly up the path toward the sound of the party. Shay watched her go.

Juliette. It suited her, romantic, innocent—frowning, he stopped in mid-thought, the name slamming into his gut. *Juliette Fortier. Damn it!*

JULIETTE SLOWED DOWN when she got to the main garden path. She stood for a moment, hand resting against the trunk of a tree, trying to gain her composure. Right now, she was positive a jury would find her certifiably insane. What other explanation could there be for her recent behavior? If it wasn't insanity, then it was her hormones, and she wasn't sure which would engender more sympathy in a jury. No question, the minute she'd laid eyes on Shay, her rational mind had taken a vacation. She'd simply reacted—saw what she wanted and went after it. Royalty's right, or so her ancestors would say. She supposed it was reassuring to know that she could be as single-minded as a man in the same situation, but somehow she didn't think her family would see it that way.

She could hear her brother, his tone now impatient and demanding, calling her name. She was amazed at how close she'd come to being caught. How could she have made passionate love to a virtual stranger, in her own garden, practically under the feet of hundreds of guests, the crème de la crème of New Orleans society? Not to mention the important guests from out of town. Wouldn't they have loved to get a sight of her a few minutes ago? The oh-so-proper Juliette Fortier with her legs clamped tight around a man's waist as he pleasured her among the flowers.

Pleasured?

What a weak, old-fashioned word for what she'd just experienced. For a few minutes in Shay's arms, with his hot mouth on hers and his hungry passion exploding inside her, she'd glimpsed paradise before she'd fallen back to earth and reality.

"Juliette!"

A reality that was becoming more impatient by the moment, judging by the tone of her brother's voice. Juliette fanned her cheeks, attempting to make all thoughts of Shay go away, so she could at least try to get through the rest of the evening with the poise that had been the stock in trade of generations of Fortiers. As the hostess of the ball, she had duties that couldn't be shirked. And at the moment she had to come up with a good story for her brother. He was sure to question her absence from the ball. She swallowed her nervousness and continued up the path to the veranda, where Michael was pacing.

At the sound of her footsteps, Michael Fortier whirled around, his short cape billowing. "Where the hell have you been?"

"In the garden."

"We have guests, remember."

"Of course I do, Michael. I hand-lettered the invitations."

Michael scowled. "You know better than to run out like this. People have been asking for you."

Thinking fast, Juliette pretended to adjust her diamond-and-pearl earring. "I lost one of my earrings out here earlier. It must have been when I was showing your Washington guests the garden. You know our great-great-grandmother would turn over in her grave, or even get right out of it and haunt me, if I lost the 'earbobs' she got from the king of Spain. So I came out to retrace my steps, and sure enough, it had dropped into the bougainvillea."

"Next time be more careful," he scolded.

She stepped over to him and placed her hand on his arm. "Michael, I was absolutely panicked, I tell you. Why, somebody might have run off with it, or a crow could have found it and taken it to its nest or something." Juliette continued to chatter on about nothing until she felt Michael relax. Inwardly she breathed a sigh of relief, hoping Shay had the good sense to stay hidden until she got inside.

"You need to be more careful, Juliette. We hired guards for tonight, but the wrong sort of people could still get onto the grounds."

Nervously, Juliette searched the shadows, praying Shay was nowhere to be seen. At the same time, she was wondering how he'd gotten in here. How on earth had he found her? She'd been so stunned to see him she hadn't questioned his appearance. But now that she thought about it, she knew the name "Shay" had not been on the guest list.

"Something could have happened to you," Michael intoned as he opened one of the French doors to usher her inside.

Juliette swallowed the lump that rose in her throat. *Something did. Something so thrilling, so satisfying. I'll never be the same again.*

"Ah, there's Stephen." Juliette followed her brother's gaze. "He makes a splendid Harlequin, doesn't he, Juliette?"

Stephen's tall, slender body did justice to the costume, suggesting both athleticism and grace, but her attention was transfixed by his mask. The only visible part of his face was his mouth, his thin patrician lips smiling down at the older woman clasping his arm. He looked like a devious satyr. Suddenly, with the sharp awareness of a fox, he looked up and locked eyes with her. Juliette shivered at the intensity of his gaze, then immediately told herself not to be foolish. This was

Stephen. She'd known him her entire life. He was Michael's best friend.

"I should have worn a more interesting costume," Michael muttered in her ear.

Juliette glanced at her brother. "Not true. You look like what you are—a dashing, romantic prince."

"A bastard prince," Michael grumbled, "with no kingdom and no power."

Juliette lifted her mask, saying in a light tone, "Better than a pauper, isn't it?"

"Not when I have to beg Father for every scrap."

"Oh, Michael, you're exaggerating as usual."

"No, I'm not. I'm his only son. I'm the future. Who the hell does he think is going to take over our business interests someday—you?"

Juliette couldn't help but bristle at his comment. "If I were interested I don't see why—" Truth be told, she'd never had any desire for direct participation in that part of the family business. But still...

"If you were interested, which you've always indicated you're not. So I'm it, and the old man isn't going to live forever, regardless of what he thinks."

"Michael. Let's face it, you haven't always been the most dependable..."

"That's history."

"I know," she said placating him, "but maybe Father just needs a bit more time to be certain that—"

Michael's lips twitched. "I don't have any more time."

"Why not? You're not even thirty yet."

"That's not what I meant. I've got some deals cooking—Stephen and I do, that is—deals that depend on fast decisions. Stephen's going to present the details to Father, since I can't get him to listen to me."

Because Michael avoided looking at her, Juliette became suspicious. "What type of deals?"

"Nothing you'd be interested in. Just shipping some cargo for people Stephen knows." Michael guided her around the edge of the ballroom, heading for the front of the room. "Besides, I need some quick cash for my campaign coffers, and this deal would give it to me."

"So you've definitely decided to run for the state legislature?"

"Yes. Dad's political cronies were very persuasive." Her brother gave her a surprisingly shy, sweet smile. "You know the routine—they need young blood from an excellent family, someone they can groom for a national run someday."

Juliette stopped and hugged her brother. "Michael, how exciting. I'm so proud of you."

"Juliette," Michael protested, trying to remain dignified. "What will people think?"

"That I love my brother?" Juliette teased with a saucy grin.

Dropping his pose for a moment, Michael hugged her back and chuckled. "They might. Or they might think you've completely lost your mind and just thrown yourself at a stranger. Everyone knows Fortiers never act this way in public."

Juliette caught her breath. Her brother's comment struck too close to home for comfort. She glanced over her shoulder, and let out her breath in a whoosh when no wild, sexy pirate appeared. All she saw were the colorful, swirling shapes of people dancing and enjoying themselves. How stupid to feel disappointed. She ought to be relieved.

"Come on, Juliette." Michael grasped her elbow. "Stephen's waving for us to join him."

Juliette was tempted to tell him to go on ahead so she could take a moment to gather her composure, but she knew Michael wouldn't agree, not with his jaw set in that mulish line. "We wouldn't want Stephen to wait, would we," she murmured.

Michael sent her a sharp glance. "Don't you like Stephen?"

"Of course I like him, Michael."

"Good, because he's very fond of you."

Fond. She didn't want fond. She wanted a man who could jump-start her heart with one glance. A man who could heat her blood with a simple touch of his hand. A man who—

"He wants to marry you, Juliette."

"Michael, please don't start this again. Not now."

Her brother hesitated for a moment, then said in a soft tone, "Please understand, I mean this for the best."

He swept her the few remaining yards to where Stephen was standing near the ballroom stage, his mother hanging on his arm. Juliette had no opportunity to question Michael further once Mrs. St. James gave her a tepid hug and an airy society kiss.

"How lovely you look, Juliette."

"So do you, Mrs. St. James."

Stephen's mother reached up and patted his cheek. "That's because my son helped me pick out my costume. He has such good taste."

Juliette smiled. "Yes, I know."

"Mama," Stephen interrupted with a smile. "Isn't that Guy LaMont over there with your friend Veronica?"

Helena St. James turned, her eyes narrowing as she patted her solidly lacquered hair. "Yes. Perhaps I should say a tiny hello." With the elderly bachelor clearly in her sights, she nodded farewell and set sail.

Juliette felt a wave of sympathy for the unsuspecting male, a sentiment she knew her brother would share. She turned toward him, only to have her attention diverted by Shay strolling into the ballroom.

He looked so cool and collected, she'd swear this wasn't the man who'd been making passionate love to her barely twenty minutes ago. Then his eyes met hers and she changed her mind. Behind the black half mask his eyes were hot, alive and full of the devil. She felt as if she were naked, laid bare to his gaze. The thought excited her, even as it alarmed her.

She watched as he wove his way across the ballroom through the crowd of dancers, his intention to reach her absolutely clear. She caught her breath at the way his costume enhanced his virility, the close-fitting trousers calling bold attention to his trim hips and long legs, the billowing shirt outlining his wide shoulders and strong chest. She wasn't the only woman noticing him, either. Juliette slid a sidelong glance at a group of interested ladies, some of whom were practically drooling. Jealousy flooded her. She wanted to tear off his mask, fasten her lips to his and show all these women that he belonged to her, and her alone.

"Are you all right, Juliette?" Stephen's solicitous voice broke into her thoughts.

"I'm fine," she snapped, earning herself a censorious look from her brother and a surprised look from Stephen. "I'm fine," she repeated, softening her voice. "It's a bit hot in here, that's all."

"Yes, it is," Stephen agreed.

Juliette pasted a smile on her face and returned her attention to the ballroom. She saw Shay laughing with Lucille Monteverde, one of her best friends.

"Michael, why don't we make the announcement now?" Stephen suggested, leaving Juliette to wonder what announcement was being made.

"Yes, I guess," Michael murmured. "Yes, all right, now's good. He abruptly grabbed Juliette's hand and pulled her toward the stage.

"Ouch, Michael, you're squeezing my fingers."

Her brother relaxed his grip. "Sorry. I'm a bit nervous."

Juliette smiled. "This isn't the first time you've welcomed people to this ball in place of Father."

"I know."

"So what's the problem?"

"This time it's different."

Juliette looked out over the crowd, seeing the same faces she always saw. "Different how?"

"You'll understand in a minute."

She noticed Stephen ascending the steps on the other side of the stage, watched as he crossed the expanse to stand next to Michael. This was unusual. Never had anyone but a Fortier officially opened the Fortier Mardi Gras ball.

At a nod from Michael, the band fell silent and the crowd followed suite. "Ladies and gentlemen and honored guests.

Tonight is a very special occasion for the Fortier family. Not only are we welcoming you to the *true* new millennium ball this evening, but we also have the great joy of making a very special announcement."

Juliette stared at her brother. He was going to announce his candidacy. She hadn't realized he was definitely running when he'd mentioned it earlier.

Michael adjusted the microphone. "As you may know, the Fortier family and the St. James family have strong ties going back to the friendship and business partnership of our fathers, Stephen's and mine. Tonight, I take great pleasure in announcing that those ties are about to become even stronger."

A horrible realization gripped Juliette as Michael reached for her hand. Her mouth opened, but no words emerged when Michael said, "It is my honor to announce the engagement of my sister, Juliette Liane Fortier, to a man who is like my brother, and will soon be one in actuality—Stephen Richard St. James."

Stunned, Juliette allowed Michael to place her hand in Stephen's, but she whispered "No" so softly only Michael could hear. "You can't do this."

"I have no choice," Michael whispered back, leaving her standing beside Stephen.

Fully aware of all the eyes upon her, Juliette attempted to swallow her anger for the moment. She said nothing as Stephen stepped to the microphone, answering the crowd's applause with a message of his own.

Juliette barely heard what he was saying over the roaring in her ears. "...loved her forever...joining our families in more than just..."

Just get through this, she thought, as he slid a ring onto her finger. She'd sort this out later, in private. She glanced out over the ballroom. Then her eyes met Shay's and her world tilted. He stood at the front edge of the crowd, not far from the stage. If she'd realized earlier that he was there she might have gotten the courage to... She dismissed that thought.

She'd already told him it was a bad idea to see him again. Now...now it was completely impossible. As his eyes hardened and his lip curled, she could swear her heart was breaking into little pieces.

Somehow she got off the stage, and people immediately began surrounding her and Stephen, separating the two of them as they offered their best wishes. Juliette smiled and nodded automatically, a perfect product of her social upbringing, but there was a fog where her emotions should have been—a deep blanketing fog that pressed down on her until she wanted to gasp for air. Although her brother had been pushing hard for the past six months, never in her wildest dreams would she have thought he'd do such a thing to her. He'd hinted there was a problem and that he needed her help to get out of it, but never, never would she have believed— Turning sharply to look at her brother, she stumbled and would have fallen had it not been for a strong arm that suddenly slipped around her waist.

"Well, well, well," a husky Yankee voice growled softly in her ear as he hauled her close, "now here's an interesting situation. Lover to the right, fiancé to the left. Which door will the lady choose?"

Shocked, she stared up into Shay's snapping eyes. "Please," she whispered.

His words slashed her like sharp knives. "I've already done that, remember? Or has another bout of amnesia struck?"

Before Juliette could answer, Stephen appeared at her side, giving Shay's encircling arms a hard stare. "Juliette, are you all right?"

Shay released her and answered before she could draw breath. "She just turned her ankle. She would've toppled right over if I hadn't been standing next to her."

Stephen placed his arm tenderly around Juliette's shoulders. "Would you like to sit down, darling?"

"No. No, thank you." Being completely removed from the universe sounded much better to her.

After giving her a searching look, Stephen nodded and extended his hand to Shay. "Thank you so much, Mr... Sorry, I didn't catch your name."

Smiling, Shay shook hands. "Shay Mallory. I'm a friend of Henry Sabin's, Mr. St. James. He suggested I look you up while I was in New Orleans."

Stephen snapped to attention. "Henry Sabin?"

"That's right."

"Ah-ha," Stephen said, "and are you planning on spending much time in our fair city, Mr. Mallory?"

"Only until my business is done. Henry thought you might be able to help me with that."

"I see." Stephen nodded. "I'd be delighted to help a friend of Henry's. Why don't you come to my office on Monday? It's at 13 rue de Palais. Say, ten o'clock?"

"Sounds good."

"Anything else I can do to repay your kindness to my fiancée, please let me know."

"How about a dance?"

"I beg your pardon?"

"What—" Juliette was certain her expression was just as comical as Stephen's.

Shay reached for Juliette, effectively shutting her up. "I'd like to dance with this lovely lady, before she's completely off the market."

Stephen's eyes narrowed. "She's off the market now."

Shay laughed as he folded Juliette in his arms, taking care to hold her at a respectable distance. "Then no harm done, right?"

5

SHAY SWEPT HER into the dance before she had a chance to complain, "Off the market! You make me sound like a breeding cow."

"A cow? No. I'm thinking about another female animal. One that barks."

"Go ahead," Juliette said, trying to maintain her dignity. "I'm sure you have reason to feel as if I'm a...a—"

"A bitch?" Shay said, making sure his sweetest, most helpful expression flitted over the part of his face revealed by his mask.

"Yes," she hissed, drawing the word out as if it hurt to say it. He swung her around until they reached the edge of the dance floor. "So tell me, Princess Juliette, how long have you been planning this trick? Trapping some dumb son of a bitch so you could make an idiot of him two times in a row?"

"I didn't plan any of this. Not last week, not tonight. How could I plan something like this? I'm not that type of person, for one thing. For another, how would I know you'd be here? I didn't even know your last name, and I certainly don't recall addressing any party invitation to a 'Shay Question Mark.' I'd have to be the best clairvoyant in New Orleans to plan this in order to humiliate you."

Shay was silent for a moment. She was right. Of course she was right. It was his temper that made him think otherwise. She'd have had no more idea of who he was than he would have been able to connect Juliette Fortier with the woman he'd rescued the other night. The only photos he'd seen of Juliette were taken when she was much younger, when she had long hair and still carried quite a bit of baby fat—nothing remotely like the woman in his arms. They danced in silence for a moment before he whirled her out into the deserted conservatory. He pulled her into the shadows, dropping his arms from around her. Touching her was almost painful, bringing up too many unspoken hopes, stirring too much desire.

She touched his arm. "Shay, please believe me. I didn't know what my brother was planning to do tonight. It took me by surprise as much as it did you."

He wanted to believe her—God knows he hungered to—but it was impossible. He'd already fallen for her innocent act once; there was no way he was doing it again. "You've lied to me ever since I met you. Why should I believe you now?"

Her lips trembled for a moment. "I don't know why you would, except...because it's the truth?"

He shook off her hand. "You wouldn't know the truth if it hit you in the face and whistled Dixie."

She winced. "I don't blame you for being angry, but that's not fair."

"The truth is, what? Someone without a pedigree isn't good enough for a real-life princess?"

"That has nothing to do with it. I told you I don't use the—"

The anger roiling in his gut exploded as he spat the words at her. "Oh, right. You just use *people*, right?"

Juliette reared back and slapped his face, a short stinging blow the sound of which was covered by music from the ballroom. From between clenched teeth she said, "How dare you!"

Shay winced, then grabbed her trembling hand to prevent her from slapping him again. "Oh, I dare. I dare a lot. That's part of my problem." He dared to take her home, to try to be a knight in shining armor for her, and look where it got him.

"Your problem is you're too arrogant to believe you could be wrong about me."

"That's because I'm not."

"You are."

"No. From what I see, you wanted some fun before tying yourself down, and I was handy."

"You're right." Her face was full of pain as she acknowledged the truth. "I did want...but I didn't plan to—"

"Won't wash, Princess. I think you're in this dirty little charade up to your beautiful neck."

"What charade?"

He grimaced, his tirade arrested as her question brought up his guard, the guard that a cop never really dropped for long if he wanted to live. "Never mind."

"What are you talking about?"

"Nothing." He waved her away, wishing he could dismiss her as easily from his thoughts. The way he opened up and responded to this woman astounded him. It wouldn't happen again. His lips twisted as he said in his most sarcastic tone, "You'd better get going before your beloved Stephen comes looking for you."

"He's not my beloved."

"You could have fooled me."

She bit her lip at that, hesitating for a moment before asking, "What type of business do you have with Stephen?"

"That has nothing to do with you." *Liar,* he thought. Like it or not, now it had everything to do with the woman standing in front of him. The only question was how much did she know about her brother's and Stephen's activities?

Juliette tilted her head, a hint of wariness in her eyes. "Did you know who I was and try to meet me to gain some kind of edge with Stephen? Or with my brother, perhaps? Is that what this is really about?"

Shay was speechless. He hadn't expected her to turn the tables on him so neatly. It wasn't true, but still...her theory sounded almost plausible, even given the fact that Juliette Fortier had rarely sought the spotlight, leaving the role to her brother and father. Finally, Shay's brain kicked into gear so he could answer her. "Don't try to put this back on me, Princess."

She glanced over her shoulder. "The music is stopping. Someone will be looking for me."

"Lucky you. Rescued in the nick of time."

She hesitated, then blurted out, "Shay, I want to see you. Can you meet—"

"You've seen all there is to see of me already," he snapped. His gut clenched as he realized he'd never again view her face tense with yearning, her eyes dark with wanting.

"I could say the same."

Stalemate. She was right. In this instance they both had a lot to lose. He sure as hell didn't want Stephen St. James looking at his cover too closely. Even if his fake background was set up to look solid, you never knew what might go wrong. Because of that, and because he didn't quite trust himself around Juliette, he decided he'd better take a different approach. The approach he should have taken when he first met her. "I'm here to set up a business deal with your fiancé, period. I don't believe in mixing business with pleasure." He forced a leer. "Even though it sure was a pleasure, Princess."

She went dead white, then gasped and flushed a deep scarlet. "That's that, then. But look, Shay, I'm worried about my brother. You have to meet me and let me explain."

Shay stared at Juliette. *Agitated* was too soft a word to describe how she looked at the moment. If anyone saw them right now, they'd never believe they'd just met. He realized he'd have to put his emotions aside and quit provoking her so he didn't jeopardize his investigation. He forced his mind back into cool-calculating-investigative mode as he studied her. Besides, he had a job to do, and she could prove helpful. "All right," he agreed, "tomorrow, three o'clock, St. Louis Cathedral."

She gave him a surprised look.

His brows rose. "What better place for a liar to tell the truth than in a holy place?"

She lifted a haughty chin and her lips thinned into a taut, angry line. "Before this is done, you're going to end up on your knees apologizing, begging me to speak to you again, you...you *cretin.*"

Shay stared into her blue eyes, satisfied to see his words had hit their mark. Those eyes might haunt him for the rest of his life, he thought, even as he let cutting words drip lightly from his lips. "*Cretin!* Why, Princess, how you do talk to us poor, pitiful peasants."

A flash of temper replaced the hurt and confusion in her eyes. "You're running that princess angle into the ground, aren't you?"

He had to admire her spunk. Just when he imagined she'd be ready to swoon, she found that spirit he'd glimpsed when he first met her. "Are you denying you're a princess?"

"Not at all. I just don't want to be treated like your warped idea of one."

He almost smiled. "How do you want me to treat you?"

"Like a woman."

"I did that and look where it got us."

Hesitantly, Juliette laid her hand on his arm. "Shay, I know you don't want to believe this, but I had no intention of hurting you. I really am sorry."

He stared down at her hand, so slender and delicate, then he focused on the diamond adorning her left ring finger. His jaw tightened until he thought it would shatter like glass. "Sure you are," he muttered through his clenched teeth. He jerked his head toward the ballroom. "Go on, get back to your fiancé."

Juliette hesitated, then turned and walked slowly away. Shay watched until she was swallowed up by the crowd.

As he lost sight of her, Shay slowly moved out of the shadows, emerging like a man who'd aged fifty years. He stepped from the relative calm of the conservatory into the brilliant light and gaiety of the ball, feeling like a complete outcast. Never in his life had he had such a sense of not belonging, which was ridiculous given his job. Working undercover, you never belonged. Even then, though, he'd been able to make himself comfortable, make himself seem to fit in. But not now.

Now, with the reality of Juliette and her situation, all he needed was a dirty cap to tip and a shuffling gait to complete his sudden feeling of unworthy peasant standing before a great lady. It had nothing to do with any actual royal pedigree she possessed. After all, those things didn't make a person better than anyone else—at least, not according to his staunch American beliefs. But it did have everything to do with the reality of his job and family circumstances. Irish crofters' blood and blue blood didn't mix any more than did a cop's and a criminal's. And like it or not, he couldn't rule out the possibility that Juliette was a criminal.

What does she know? Now that his mind was somewhat clearer, this became a primary question, even though his heart hated to consider it.

Shay hugged the wall at the edge of the ballroom. He searched the crowd, looking for any face that struck a wrong note—an exercise in futility, considering the masks, but you never knew. A cop didn't just study faces; mannerisms were just as important. A way of walking, a specific gesture, a tilt of the head—all could set off an alarm. Surely, though, Stephen or Michael wouldn't be stupid enough to invite their associates to this ball? Nonetheless, Shay watched Stephen carefully as he moved across the room, smiling and welcoming guests as if he were already firmly ensconced in the Fortier heritage. He kept Juliette clamped to his side. Shay could see her face, a bit pale but still composed, her perfect-hostess act firmly in place. Michael Fortier was nowhere to be seen, which Shay found odd. Until now, he'd been playing his role as host and head of the Fortier family to the hilt.

"I think my brother's in trouble." Juliette's words came back to him. His lips curled. *Princess*, he thought, *you don't know the half of it.* The clock was ticking now. In only one week the rumored shipment of illegal immigrants and smuggled goods from South America would move through New Orleans, then up the Mississippi to the drop-off point in Ohio. This he and his superiors in Cincinnati had learned after they'd captured Henry Sabin a few weeks ago. The arrival of the "goods"

would be timed to coincide with the elaborate confusion created by the final gasp of Mardi Gras gaiety—a very smart move, in Shay's view. But then, he'd always known Stephen St. James was smart. What he wasn't sure about was how Michael Fortier was involved.

No time like the present to find out.

Keeping an eye on the crowd, Shay continued to prowl along the fringes until he located a door in the back wall of the ballroom. He felt behind him for the handle, then slipped backward through the open door. He turned around, finding himself in a servants' hallway at the back of the house. He stood quietly for a moment, trying to get his bearings. He could hear the clink of dishes and the hum of conversation that indicated the kitchen area was somewhere down the hall to his right. Which meant to his left must be other areas of the house, areas in which he had more interest. With any luck he'd find a study or an office that might yield some information.

He glanced around, seeing no one. *Nothing ventured,* he thought. With a flare of excitement in his gut he moved over the serviceable carpet with soft, sure footsteps.

He crept up the dark hall, stopping every few feet to listen for sounds other than those that emanated from the ballroom. At an intersecting hallway, he turned to his right, moving farther away from the front of the house. The faint murmur of two male voices stopped him as he tried to determine where they were coming from. He continued down the hall, until he heard a door open and the voices became clearer.

Shay paused, senses alert, eyes watchful as he recognized Michael Fortier's well-educated Southern accent saying, ''Thank you for coming.''

Caught in the open, Shay just had time to glance around before they emerged. To his left, he located an alcove and quickly ducked behind some heavy velvet curtains. He found himself in a storage space, boxed in by floor-to-ceiling shelves stuffed with linens and other dining items. Obviously this hallway led to the formal dining room.

Shay held his breath, hoping he hadn't been spotted. Long moments passed before he lifted an edge of the drape with a careful movement, letting his breath rush out when he saw Michael Fortier escorting a man down the hall in the other direction, away from his hiding place.

Their voices drifted back to him as Michael clasped the man's shoulder. "I appreciate your help, *señor*."

Señor? South American, maybe?

"It was my pleasure. Naturally, any friend of my dear friend Stephen's..."

"How kind of you."

The man with Michael was of medium height, black-haired, tanned and impeccably dressed in a well-cut business suit. Someone who wasn't attending the ball, Shay thought. The man turned, offering Shay a brief glimpse of his face. Though he looked familiar, Shay couldn't quite place him. But he'd swear the suave *señor* wasn't the legitimate businessman he pretended to be.

"Don't worry, Felipe, I'll give him your message," Michael said, as the two men turned a corner and disappeared.

Shay figured they were heading for a side door that would enable the man to leave the house without using the front entrance. He must have come in that way, too, because without a costume in the middle of the throng of party guests, he'd stand out like a tiger with a toothache. Now why would someone go to all that trouble not to be seen? To make sure he wouldn't run into Michael returning, Shay waited a few more minutes, then emerged thinking about what he'd just seen.

Felipe who? Common enough name—definitely not American. So we've got a man from south of the border who knows both Stephen and Michael. Grinning, Shay retraced his steps to the ballroom. *What a stroke of luck.*

He slipped in the same way he'd left. Moving away from the door, still keeping to the edge of the dance floor, he looked for the blond head of his partner, Lucille. Unable to see her on the dance floor, he continued on, hoping to find her in the dining room at the buffet tables, or else outside on the veranda. Eyes alert, body tense under his pose of nonchalance, Shay nodded and smiled as he made his way through the glittering throng. He'd just stepped into the main hallway when a peal of husky laughter attracted his attention. He wandered through the archway into the dining room and spotted Lucille, who was carrying on an animated discussion with her fiancé. Shay watched her for a moment, waiting until she realized he was there before he moved to the buffet, as other guests were doing.

Astonished, he surveyed the table, so loaded with dishes it seemed to sag in the middle like a swaybacked horse. He'd been to elegant restaurants and parties before, but he'd never seen such an impressive display of food, seemingly chosen as much for the color and presentation value as for edibility. Yet more evidence of the social status that set the Fortiers apart from most of the people Shay had ever known. He grabbed a plate, then haphazardly nabbed something that looked like raw vegetables mixed into a batter, then a crawfish recognizable only by its size and its claws, which held tiny red tomatoes. He finished with a few pillowy cheese rounds, then backed away from the table before he had to make more decisions. Turning on his heel, he approached Lucille and Preston, making sure it seemed as if he was moving casually around the room so he wouldn't call attention to their relationship.

Lucille smiled, a well practiced society smile designed to make everyone forget her profession. "So, how's it going, pirate man?"

"Just peachy." Shay jerked his head toward the tables across the room. "Swell party. Lots of food."

"The buffet is always one of the jewels of the Fortier ball. It represents the best of New Orleans cooking, from Cajun to Creole to French."

Shay stared at his plate as if he'd just discovered an alien being. "That explains why nothing looks familiar."

Chuckling, Lucille pointed to his plate. "Is that an artichoke quiche?"

"How the hell would I know?" Shay popped it in his mouth. "It's pretty tasty."

Lucille grinned. "I should hope so. They've used the same caterer for years. Everyone is always vying to get Georges for their party, but he gives the Fortiers first choice of the party date, then keeps busy for weeks in preparation."

"The Fortiers must pay some bucks if he's turning down other work."

"Fortiers don't hesitate to spend money. At least Michael doesn't." Lucille gave the room an approving glance. "This is one of the most elaborate parties I've seen them throw. I guess he figured that since his father was out of town he'd do it the way he wanted."

"It's a success, from what I'm hearing," Preston said.

"Did they have any of those little ole puffed-up shrimps over there?"

Shay stared at Lucille as if she'd gone mad. "Fat shrimp? I don't know if I saw anything with tails, besides these little suckers." He indicated his crawfish.

Preston laughed. "I know what you mean. Give me a good old, juicy steak any day."

Shay nodded. "You got it."

"Unfortunately," Preston continued, with a smooth grin, "I have to attend enough of these things that I have no choice but to recognize the food on the buffet." He turned to Lucille. "Would you like me to get you something, darling?"

"Mm, you sweet sweet man. I'm just dying for a bit of nourishment so we can dance some more."

"Your wish is my command." Preston dropped a kiss on her nose, then nodded at Shay. "I'm sure y'all can find something to talk about in the meantime."

Shay watched him walk away. "Nice guy you've got there. And he knows when to make himself scarce."

Lucille sighed. "Yes, he is just the yummiest, most delicious man I've ever met. And I've met quite a few."

Shay lifted a brow. "Ever been tempted by Michael Fortier? He's a good-looking guy."

Shrugging, Lucille waved her hand. "I dated him a few times, but he wasn't my type."

"Why not?"

Looking around at the guests, Lucille fanned herself gently and nodded ever so slightly at the French doors that led outside. "I declare it is so close in here."

Picking up on her cue, Shay put down his plate, lightly grasped her arm and strolled to the corner of the room. "Let's get some air."

"That sounds nice. It's a pleasant evening and the view is lovely. I'm sure you'll enjoy it."

Shay escorted her through the doors and onto the veranda, casually moving out of view and earshot of the crowd inside. "Why weren't you tempted by Michael Fortier? He's got everything—money and a title to go with it." The better Shay understood Michael's personality, the easier it would be to arrive at the truth.

"Michael was always too anxious to prove himself. It turned me off, I guess. That's the problem when children have a strong parent who controls the purse strings. They either try too hard, or they don't try at all."

"His father's tightfisted?"

Lucille snorted. "What an understatement! My father used to say that Louis Fortier could squeeze every last drop of ink out of a dollar."

Shay glanced around. "This place doesn't seem to be suffering."

"Oh, it's not. Louis is more than willing to spend on the things he feels are important, but he demands a strict accounting from everyone else, I hear."

"Including his son?"

"Michael has always been a bit of a dilettante in his father's eyes. At least that's the rumor."

"You mean he spends too much time and money on the wrong things? Or are we talking about women?"

"There have always been women. But I know he always needed cash, too. When we were teenagers, Juliette used to say her brother was always coming up with schemes to make money. Or else he was trying to hit her up for spending money when his allowance ran short."

"She had available cash?"

"She's always been careful with her finances, as far as I know."

"And what about Daddy? Does Michael hit him up, too?"

Lucille arched her brows. "Could be, but Daddy is very reluctant to relinquish control, of anything. He's a shrewd businessman. His only weakness seems to be his vineyard in France."

"Not his children?"

"He's a rather cold fish. Very very charming and elegant and all, but when you get right to the heart of him...I always thought of him as a block of ice."

"So Michael was always coming up with schemes to get money."

Lucille placed her hand on Shay's arm. "Don't misunderstand me, Shay, I don't think Michael would do anything illegal. With a father and a family like his, he wouldn't dare. That's why I think you're following the wrong hound. So, you're going to have to convince me otherwise."

Shay glanced around to make sure they were alone before he asked the next question. He softened his voice, his technique honed by years of hushed undercover detail. "I ran across somebody tonight with Michael and I wondered if you'd know him. The guy's a real slick character—dark hair, early forties, foreign accent, sounded Spanish. His first name's Felipe—"

"It could be one of Michael's political cronies. They come from all over the place, both inside and outside the U.S., I hear."

"Why would he be meeting with someone like that in the middle of the ball?"

"Simple, sugar. I just heard a very strong rumor tonight that Michael might run for office. You know politicians.

They're always looking for two things—influential support-
ers and—"

"Money," Shay muttered.

Lucille tapped his arm with her fan. "That's right, but even
so, I still think you're chasing a lost dog."

Shay didn't agree. If Michael was interested in politics, that
added a twist to the situation. With the media scrutiny political candidates now faced, it was even more imperative that
any secrets the Fortiers might have remain *secret*. Where
would that leave Juliette? Especially if she was telling the
truth when she'd said she hadn't known anything about the
engagement before this evening? All of a sudden the issue became a lot more personal than his commitment to law and order. If, *just if*, Juliette didn't know anything about her
brother's activities—and Shay realized this was wishful
thinking—then she was sitting on a keg of dynamite with a
very short fuse. Some men put ambition and personal gain
above all else. Shay hoped Michael Fortier wasn't one of
them.

"Hate to disappoint you, Lucille, but I don't think the man
I saw was a political supporter."

"Then who is he?"

Sliding her a teasing glance, Shay said, "If I knew that we'd
be home free, wouldn't we?"

"I hate smug Yankees, did I ever tell you that?"

Shay chuckled. "Nope."

Lucille tossed her head in a haughty manner. "Consider
yourself told."

Pretending to grab his chest, Shay grinned. "You've cut
this black heart right out of me, fair lady."

Lucille gave him a wry look, then returned to the subject.
"You're thinking your mystery man is from the South American cartel, aren't you?"

"My gut tells me he is. We know the cartel has its fingers in
smuggling and in gambling. We know New Orleans is a port
of entry, a direct transportation route to the center of the

country—it's perfect. Plus our guest mentioned Stephen's name."

"But Shay, I haven't gotten any other information tonight that would indicate they'd be involved in an operation like the one you're suggesting. Why would either of them take such a risk? These are two men born with silver spoons in their mouths."

"That doesn't always matter, Lucille. You know that as well as I do. Sometimes it's just the thrill of the game." God, he wanted to link this mystery man to Stephen St. James! More than to Michael Fortier, Shay realized—a thought he didn't want to explore too closely. "Come on, we'd better get inside before Preston thinks I've kidnapped you."

They walked back into the dining room from the veranda just as Juliette Fortier walked in from the hall. Shay focused on her hand resting lightly on Stephen's arm. He gritted his teeth. He had to admit that nailing St. James wasn't just a professional issue anymore, it was personal.

Shay knew the moment Juliette became aware of him. He met her eyes across the room. Hers were wary and defensive, the angry flash almost covering the hurt and betrayal there. *Don't blame me for ruining your fairy tale, Red. Blame your brother and his sleazeball friend.*

Just then, he saw Stephen's hand slide down her back in a proprietary gesture. Jealousy lit a fire in him, practically burning a hole right through his heart. Shay didn't want anyone else touching Juliette, and the thought of Stephen actually making love to her was more than he could bear. Shay turned away abruptly. "Gotta go. I've seen enough."

Lucille looked surprised, but covered her reaction quickly as she saw Juliette and Stephen glance in their direction. Under her breath, she said, "Want me to help you search the computer files for your mystery guest? I could meet you downtown at noon tomorrow."

"Sounds good."

"Oh, by the way..." she plastered a flirtatious look on her face and tapped Shay's arm with her fan "how'd the costume work? Did you find yourself a lovely Southern belle tonight to replace the one you lost?"

Shay hesitated, feeling Lucille's innocent question pierce his heart for real, unlike her joking comment of a few moments ago. "No," he finally said, trying to avoid looking at Juliette. "Just a lot of flirtatious women looking for a quick thrill."

Lucille spread her fan, saying with a languid wave, "Better luck next time."

Shay swallowed a groan. *Next time?* There wouldn't be any next time. Once was enough to be taken for a fool, to be treated like a scroungy mutt trying to make up to a pureblood Afghan. Next time? No way. Next time, he'd leave the damn woman sitting on a park bench. He whirled on his heel and stalked across the room, scarcely registering all of the admiring female glances thrown his way.

JULIETTE NOTICED and wanted to scratch out the eyes of all the other women who had the nerve to look at Shay. Not that she had any right to feel that way, but that didn't temper her response. She could feel the weight of Stephen's palm against her back, searing into her like a branding iron. Suddenly she wanted to slap Stephen's hand away, then run to find Shay and beg him to take her with him. But of course, she couldn't do that. She was Princess Juliette Fortier and as such had to give everyone a charming smile, nod graciously, carry on a polite conversation, even laugh with a lighthearted trill, all of which was giving her the headache from hell!

When Preston Royden walked over to say hello, Juliette grabbed the opportunity to escape, excusing herself to visit with Lucille.

She forced herself to move slowly across the room toward her friend, when what she really wanted to do was fling Lucille up against a wall and demand to know what she thought she was doing making eyes at Shay. Her indignation died as she realized she couldn't lay claim to Shay, no matter how much she wanted to, not with Stephen hanging around her neck like a millstone. She glanced at her clenched left hand. Stephen's ring glinted possessively on her finger.

"Hi, stranger," Lucille said. "I couldn't get near you after the big announcement. Glad you broke away before I had to track you down."

"Yes, it's been nonstop kissing and hugging for the past hour or so." Juliette smiled, wondering how she'd get Lucille to tell her what she and Shay had been talking about. "Who were you talking to before?"

Lucille wrinkled her nose. "When?"

"That pirate. I, uh, met him briefly. He said he was here to see Stephen and..."

"Oh, you mean Shay Malone? No, Mallory, I think it was." Lucille shrugged her bare shoulders. "I'm not sure."

"Have you known him long?" Juliette was trying to appear casual, failing miserably.

"I don't really know him at all. Preston and I met him out front when we got here. Why?"

Juliette shrugged, but her voice was tight when she said, "You seemed pretty interested."

"Well, good gracious, girl, where are your eyes? What a hunk! The man is as sexy as they come. That pirate costume was designed to give women shivers, I swear."

"You were flirting with him." Juliette knew she sounded as if she was accusing Lucille of stealing the heritage silver, so she attempted a smile and tried to soften her approach. "At least you looked like it, you wench. That's fine behavior for an upstanding officer of the law." And all the time she'd wished she was in Lucille's place.

"Of course I was. But then, I flirt with everyone. You know that." Lucille grinned. "Don't you remember that time in the tenth grade when I flirted with your boyfriend and you didn't speak to me for three whole weeks?"

"Philip Casteneer. He wasn't worth the trouble."

Lucille pursed her lips. "Cute, though, with a great butt."

Juliette looked at her friend and laughed. She couldn't help it. Lucille was Lucille, and Juliette envied her. Lucille, too, was from a socially prominent family but she'd been allowed, even encouraged, to have a life beyond the confines of duty, family responsibility and moral rectitude. Juliette had craved the freedom of her friend's life, but life and circumstances took them in opposite directions.

"You never change, Lucille."

"Sure I do," Lucille said, her expression turning serious. "You just haven't been close enough to notice for quite a while."

Juliette met her gaze. "I've been very busy, trying to get my bearings as new head of the Foundation. And with Father out of the country as much as he is, I've started taking over a lot of his social duties and—"

"I wasn't criticizing you, Juliette."

"Oh." Juliette gripped her hands together, flinching as the engagement ring bit into her flesh. "But I don't want you to think…" *Think what? That I don't know who I am and I'm miserable? That I slept with a man I'd never met before and then made love with him in the garden right under the noses of my guests, and then said nothing when my brother practically auctioned me off to his best friend?*

"Juliette." Lucille's gentle voice and the touch of her hand as it stroked her arm brought her back to reality. "Honey lamb, are you all right? Is there anything you want to talk about?"

Juliette glanced at the floor, blinking back tears that threatened at her friend's gentle questions. She wanted so much to confide in Lucille. When she could, she glanced up and smiled. "Everything is fine. It's just been a rather difficult evening."

"Difficult?"

Juliette evaded Lucille's suddenly sharp gaze. "Difficult emotionally."

"Well, of course it is. Good heavens, you just got engaged. That's enough to trigger all types of displays." Lucille's eyes gleamed with mischief. "After Preston asked me to marry him, I lip-locked him for so long my parents told me they were going to call the fire department to separate us."

Juliette chuckled. "That sort of thing would never happen in the Fortier household," she said with mock hauteur.

"Naturally not." Lucille grabbed Juliette's hand. "That's quite a rock, by the way."

"Yes, it is."

"You looked stunned when he put it on your finger."

"I was."

"We've all been expecting it."

"You have?"

"Absolutely. Do you remember David Dupree? A friend of Preston's? Anyway, he was back in New Orleans and said he'd asked Michael about you, hinting that he wanted to ask you out, but Michael said you were already spoken for, promised to Stephen. David was surprised because of the way Michael said it."

"How was that?"

"He said you had no choice, that you and Stephen are inevitable."

Juliette fell silent. No choice was right. Not after Michael pulled that dirty trick tonight. She'd gone along with his charade in order to avoid a scene, but she wouldn't let him get away with it.

They were both silent for a long moment, then Juliette decided to change the subject before her friend started prying in earnest. "So what were you and Shay What's-his-name talking about?"

"Casual stuff—New Orleans and this ball. Oh, and then he asked for directions back to town. He said he'd made the wrong turn on the way out here." Lucille heaved a sigh. "If only there wasn't a Preston, I would have taken him to town myself. He had such broad shoulders and one of those I'll-bet-I-know-what-you'd-look-like-naked smiles."

Juliette snapped to attention. "But there is a Preston and you're engaged, remember?"

Lucille chuckled. "That doesn't stop me from looking, does it?"

"I suppose not."

She wondered if Lucille knew how painful it was to look and know you'd never be able to touch again. To experience ecstasy and realize that it would have to be locked away in a special memory box forever, revisited only when she was alone. Juliette fought to keep her expression under control, but could feel Lucille examining her as if she was a specimen in the police lab. Funny how she always forgot her friend's profession until something happened to remind her.

There was another long moment of silence before Lucille said, "Oh, here comes Preston. With more food, bless his heart."

"And Stephen is waving to me." They touched cheeks, Juliette trying to resist the urge to clasp her friend tight, as if she might not see her again. She walked across the room to Stephen, who lightly grasped her arm. As his fingers tightened she could almost hear the sound of a cell door slamming shut. She gritted her teeth.

Somehow, Juliette got through the rest of the ball—counting the minutes until she could corner her brother alone.

THE CLOCK WAS CHIMING three when Juliette finally waved the last guest from the premises. She'd managed to close the door behind Stephen St. James and her stepmother-to-be a bit earlier, watching as he'd turned and run down the steps like a man without a care in the world. Why should he have? He'd achieved what he'd always wanted to achieve. Or so he'd indicated. Juliette didn't doubt him, exactly. But there was something about his attitude that made her wonder. She wasn't sure what it was beyond a faint smugness that didn't seem to fit with her vision of an overjoyed suitor.

There in the spacious hallway that had seen the troubles and triumphs of so many generations of Fortiers, Juliette gathered her courage. Michael had made himself scarce in the past hour, but it wouldn't do him any good. She smiled at the few servants wearily clearing the mess, then dismissed them, asking them to finish in the morning. Then she took a deep revitalizing breath, rearming herself with the anger that had been simmering all evening, and set off to find her brother. If she knew him, he'd be hiding in his study, hoping she'd be too solicitous of his privacy to barge in on him. Fat chance!

Juliette marched up to the closed, ornately carved door—Michael's fortress, barred against intruders. She hesitated for a moment, then without a word, or even a knock, she flung open the door and stepped inside.

"Michael?"

Startled, Michael spilled the tumbler of whiskey he'd been holding to his lips. "Juliette! God, you scared the hell out of me."

"I hope so. I really hope so."

Michael frowned and brushed at his shirtfront, trying to stop the dribbles from becoming puddles. "Ah, look. Now I'll have to have the dry cleaner special treat this for spots before I can get it back to the costumer." He continued fussing with his outfit, until Juliette thought she would explode.

"Michael, you can rub those spots until the material disappears, but you're not going to get out of facing me like a man."

At that Michael lifted his head, torn between offering her an expression of confusion frosted with guilt and one of haughty defiance. Defiance won. "I beg your pardon?"

"You heard me." She advanced into the room. "How could you do that to me?"

Michael's eyes widened. "Do what?" It was a look Juliette recognized from their childhood. He'd used the same expression every time he tried to evade responsibility for one of his harebrained actions.

"Don't play innocent. You know very well what—announcing my engagement to Stephen!" She pointed her finger at her brother. "I'm not engaged to Stephen."

"On the contrary."

"I never wanted to be engaged to Stephen, and if you'd asked me I would have told you that."

"Juliette, Juliette..."

She waved her hand and started to pace. "But no, you didn't ask me, you just went your normal high-handed way and arranged my life to suit your needs, didn't you?"

Michael poured another drink. "Juliette, you know Stephen's been in love with you forever."

Juliette whirled around and faced him. "No, I don't know that. I know you and Stephen's father and ours thought it would be great, but I know nothing about Stephen's feelings, and as sure as I am standing here he knows nothing about mine."

Gulping, Michael attempted to soothe her. "I know. You've been confused and depressed lately. That's why I—"

"Confused? I think that's the wrong word. How about pushed, prodded, shoved, annoyed..."

He sipped again, watching her over the rim of his glass. "You're letting your emotions run away with you, Juliette."

"I have good reason after your little show tonight."

"I did it for you."

"Oh, you did? How do you figure that?"

"You need a man like Stephen, steady and reliable, able to move in the same social circles, not too excitable to counteract that volatile nature of yours."

"The one thing I am not is volatile. No Fortier is allowed to be volatile. It's bad form."

Michael went on as if he hadn't heard her, his voice beginning to slow a bit as he finished his drink. "You need someone to guide you and help keep you in line. Since you couldn't see what was best for you, I stepped in."

"And you decided just like that that Stephen was right for me. Without asking my opinion? Without even asking whether or not I could stomach the man?"

He poured another tot of whiskey. "Stephen is a loyal friend to this family."

Juliette took a wide stance in front of his desk and folded

her arms. "So is the cook's cocker spaniel, but I don't want to marry Sparky, either."

Michael sighed. "You see? This is a prime example of what I mean. Sometimes you say things that—"

"Get off it, Michael. You're not the head of the family, no matter what you believe. Does Father know about this?"

"He's delighted."

"What?"

Her brother leaned back and contemplated her. "He agrees this is a good match for you."

"For God's sake, a good match?" She leaned forward, spreading her hands, and demanded, "What's the matter with you? It's the twenty-first century! I'm not even twenty-five yet, hardly left on the shelf, begging to be married to anyone who uses a men's room."

Michael winced at what he obviously considered her crudity. "We all agreed it's good for you to be settled at an early age."

"You mean, you've been convincing Father of that, don't you?"

He sipped his drink. "You'll thank me for this one day, you'll see."

"Don't count on it, because there isn't going to be any reason I should. I'm not going through with this engagement, Michael. I have no intention of marrying a man I don't love."

"Love! Oh, for— Love can grow."

"So can weeds. And believe me when I say Stephen St. James is not the man for me." Shay's face swam into her consciousness—piercing green eyes stormy with passion, mouth harsh with desire. He'd shaken her to her soul and made her realize what she'd be missing if she settled for anything less. Granted, he didn't love her, and she didn't love him, of course, but just the experience of Shay was enough to last a lifetime. At least that's what she tried to convince herself.

"You're wrong. Stephen is exactly the man for you." Michael drained his glass once more. "But you haven't been allowing him to state his case, which he's been trying to do for the past couple of months."

"So you've helped out by telling everyone around town that I'm off-limits. That I'm destined for Stephen, like some kind of—of virgin sacrifice." She thumped her fist on his desk. "Don't deny it. I've heard the rumors from a very good source."

"Juliette," Michael sighed, refilling his tumbler yet again from the cut glass decanter standing on his desk. "If I've been hinting to people, it's only because you and Stephen just weren't getting the job done. He needed help, and he's helped me so much that I—" he took a gulp of whiskey, then shrugged "—I took some action."

She reached out and took the glass from him, thumping it on the desk with such force that a drop slopped over onto the blotter. Michael didn't even notice. "Whose idea was this little surprise announcement, yours or Stephen's?"

"What makes you think it was Stephen's idea?"

"Because high-handed though you are, even you wouldn't pull this stunt if you weren't forced to do it."

"Forced? Don't be ridiculous."

She stared at her brother, noticing how weary he suddenly looked. "Yes, forced. Michael, you can be a grade A bastard, but tonight was really out of character for you." She grew uneasy. What was he up to?

He grabbed his glass with both hands. "My only thought was for your happiness."

"Then you should have refused to announce my engagement, or at least warned me about what was coming so I could have put a stop to it."

He swirled the liquor in his glass, watching the motion as he said in a quiet tone, "You can't put a stop to it. It's too late."

"I most certainly can. I'm not engaged to Stephen, regardless of that sham tonight, and I intend to announce that in my own way as soon as possible. I'll just tell everyone that we made a mistake. That we decided it was best to stay longtime family friends and—"

He looked up, alarmed. "You can't do that."

"Of course I can. Don't worry, I'll keep you out of it."

He rose from his chair and reached out for her arm. "Damn it, listen to me. You have to marry Stephen."

"What do you mean, I have to marry Stephen?"

He adjusted his grip, stumbling a bit as he rounded the desk. "It's all arranged. That was the deal. I can't go back on it now."

Grabbing his hand, Juliette demanded, "What do you mean, deal?"

"Nothing. Forget it. Talk later, okay? Head hurts...not making any sense." He let go of her arm and chugged the rest of his whiskey, practically dropping the glass onto the desk. "It'll be clearer...tomorrow."

"Michael, how much have you had to drink?"

He drew himself up with dignity, or attempted to. She watched as he stood there, swaying and unsteady. "Don't worry 'bout it," he declared. "Fortiers...can handle their... liquor. And I'm...Michael Fortier, born of the seed... sprung from the...loins of a king...once upon a time." He rubbed his forehead and chuckled—a strangely mirthless sound.

She gazed after him as he turned and began weaving toward the door, carefully placing one foot in front of the other like a tightrope walker. "Tonight isn't the end of this, Michael."

"...right there, little sis," he muttered. "It'll never... end...it's just beginning."

Juliette watched him go, resisting her instinct to run after him and help him to his room. He was the big brother she'd always looked up to. Until tonight. Tonight, she saw a frightened man. Or was it only her overwrought imagination? Maybe it was the stress of seeing Shay, and the lateness of the hour. Whatever it was, she'd never seen her brother like this before, never felt such mixed messages coming from him. It confused and worried her.

The house was still—too still, Juliette thought. As if it waited for something that was better left alone. Michael's comments still hung in the room. His barely disguised fear still hovered in the air, waiting to work its spell, ready to invade her and confuse her until she couldn't breathe. The atmosphere thickened, and even the insects outside had hushed. Juliette could feel the house closing in around her, like a family with too many secrets. She shivered. Call it women's intuition, subliminal messages, spirit talk, whatever you wanted—she had a very bad feeling.

6

SHAY STOOD IN THE SQUARE outside the cathedral, feeling as if elephants had been trampling him in his sleep. At least he didn't have a hangover—or not much of one. The coffee he'd consumed at the squad house with Lucille a little while before hadn't really helped. He ran his tongue around his dry mouth, wishing he'd brought another cup with him. He could use it.

After he left the Fortier home last night he'd driven toward town as if the devils were at his heels, ready to herd him to hell. Not that it made much difference to him. As far as he was concerned the hellfire had heated up when he'd discovered Juliette Fortier was his mysterious little park waif. But it really began burning when her engagement to Stephen St. James was announced. At home, he'd belted back a few drinks to douse the flames.

St. James, of all people. He rubbed his forehead. *Damn, Red, what the hell have you gotten yourself mixed up in?*

He'd met some bad dudes in his time, but the ones who made a profit from other people's hopes and dreams were the worst. This type of smuggler was at the bottom of the food chain as far as Shay was concerned. And they usually believed they were above the law. A belief Shay couldn't wait to disprove. He was going to nail St. James and his organization so hard that the air in New Orleans wouldn't settle down until next Mardi Gras!

But now there was Juliette.

His mind spun as he thought of how shocked he'd been to see her the night before. But no, he had to put her out of his mind. He'd spent his life so far pursuing justice and truth. He couldn't ignore his goals now just because of a voice like music, deep blue eyes, a mouth to die for and a small, sexy body.

Entering the cool sanctuary of the church, Shay automatically bowed his head in reverence for a moment before looking around for the entrance to the gardens. A woman who was leaving pointed the way. He thanked her and walked toward the door, his footsteps hushed and reluctant. He wished he could remain here and avoid seeing Juliette. The only way he could exorcise her would be to stay away from her. Unfortunately, that was impossible.

He stepped through the door and onto a stone path. He hesitated when he saw her seated in a secluded corner of the garden. Drawing back behind some of the plantings, he watched her for a moment, hoping to regain his composure. Every time he saw her she took his breath away, she was such a tantalizing mixture of innocence and sin.

Peering through the leaves, he studied her. She was wearing a tidy navy-blue suit with a tasteful decorative pin, a finely knit turtleneck sweater that effectively allowed no skin to show, and serviceable heels. She'd added minimal makeup and pulled her hair back in a no-nonsense style that revealed her ears and the simple pearl studs that matched her brooch. Shay smiled. Obviously, Juliette was wearing her armor, dressing as if she was going to an audience with a church bishop. Was it to give herself courage?

He sobered, becoming grim. She was going to need that courage before all this was over, regardless of the level of her involvement. No matter how she'd treated him, as he saw her sitting among the flowers and plants, he suddenly realized that he'd give almost anything to keep her safe. But for his own self-protection, he couldn't reveal his thoughts. He'd have to play this scene with his head, not his heart—much as it might kill him.

He had a job to do. It was just his bad luck that Juliette sat square in the middle of it. One way or another he had to bring this entire affair to a conclusion, and if he needed to use her to do so… He gritted his teeth as his conscience twinged. *You're a cop, O'Malley. Gotta do what you gotta do.*

Realizing he'd have to use every card in his deck to get the information he wanted, he stepped out onto the path and headed toward his destiny.

JULIETTE SAT ON A BENCH in the gardens of the cathedral. She'd gotten there early—too early, as a matter of fact. She'd been waiting for about twenty minutes, trying to glean some composure from the serenity of the orderly plantings and from the watery sunshine that peeked out from around fluffy clouds. It wasn't working. She was just as tense as she'd been when she arrived. She tried to breathe, wondering what she would say to the man who'd been haunting her, both waking and sleeping.

She'd been sitting on another bench when she first met him, she thought, wishing she could go back to that time. Was it only four or five days ago? A lifetime had passed since then. She felt old and weary, exhausted from trying to understand what was happening to her and her family. She wished her father was in town so she could try to talk him around. Perhaps if he'd been here consistently for the past six months, things wouldn't have progressed to such a state.

A slight noise made her glance up. Shay stood on the path watching her—much as he'd watched her the night they met. The night she'd leaped into what she'd thought would be a one-night stand with a man straight from a tale of bold knights and fierce dragons. Instead her brief adventure had spawned a constant hunger that gnawed at her, and now the breath hitched in her throat as her gaze roamed over his body. He was dressed in jeans, a T-shirt and his old leather jacket. Had he worn the same outfit deliberately to remind her of their time together? To tease and torment her? She met his piercing green gaze, and wished she could see those eyes grow deep emerald with passion once again. As it was, they were distant and analytical, his mouth was drawn into a straight line, his arms were held stiffly at his sides. Those arms where she'd felt so safe, so welcome...and so loved. Loved? Yes, that was how it had felt.

Love?

She couldn't love this man. She'd just met him. Met him and betrayed him in a way no man would forgive. Not that the betrayal had been her fault. At least the engagement part hadn't been. But the rest—yes, the rest resided firmly on her shoulders and in her heart. She swallowed, aware that he'd come closer. He said nothing, just watched her almost warily. She licked her lips, searching for something to say to break the tension.

"I see your jacket dried out."

"Yeah. This is a tough old piece of leather."

She tried to smile. "Like its owner, I suppose."

"Except for the old part, I'd say that's right."

"Would you...would you like to sit down?" She indicated the bench.

"No, thanks. I'm comfortable here."

She looked up at him, a long way up, it seemed. Or was that just because her guilty conscience made her imagine him ten feet tall? "You're giving me a crick in my neck. Please sit down." She moved as far as she could to her right, leaving a large expanse for him. She couldn't risk having him touch her, no matter how accidentally. "Please."

Shay shrugged and to her surprise straddled the bench. "If you insist."

She tried not to look at his spread legs, at the heavy bulge of his masculinity that beckoned her to touch. She tried not to remember how he'd felt inside her, how he had stretched her, then satisfied her until she'd never be able to remember another man. Feeling the heat rush to her cheeks, she jerked her gaze away. "Must you sit like that," she muttered.

"What do you care how I sit?"

"Never mind. I don't." Hunching a shoulder, she let the silence lengthen, wondering why she'd ever wanted to see him. How could he help her figure out what was going on with Michael when he wouldn't even let her explain about their night together? His attitude wasn't exactly encouraging. Not that she blamed him, under the circumstances.

"Look, Shay," she said in a soft voice, "I don't blame you for being angry. I deserve it. But you have to believe me when I tell you that I never wanted to deceive you."

"Come on!" he retorted. "'I don't remember anything'— doesn't that sound familiar?"

She turned to him, looking straight into his angry eyes, willing him to believe her. "I didn't do it maliciously. Never maliciously."

"Tell me another story, lady."

"All I can tell you is the truth."

His mouth twisted. "Do you even know what that is?"

She flushed, but kept her eyes steady on his. "I was having dinner with my brother and Stephen, and some of their business associates at a restaurant not far from where I met you."

His gaze sharpened. "What associates?"

"A married couple I know, and some businessmen whose names I can't even remember. I was only half listening when they were introduced." Shaking her head, she looked down at her hands and brushed some imaginary dirt from her skirt. "I was in a strange mood. All I could see was my carefully scripted life stretching endlessly before me. I told them I had to leave, that I had a headache and would get a cab. My brother followed me to the door, going on and on about fulfilling my duties as a hostess."

As if she hadn't been doing her social duty all her life, she thought, still indignant over Michael's lecture. "I couldn't listen anymore. I just walked out." She still couldn't believe she'd done it, that she'd put her responsibilities aside so easily.

She peeked up at Shay, relieved that he was now listening to her instead of trying to bait her. "I started wandering. Before I knew it I was in that park. I sat down and wished for an adventure, and you appeared."

"Lucky me," Shay muttered.

"I know I shouldn't have lied to you, but I saw you and all

of a sudden I thought, what if I had no history, no ties? What if I could do anything I wanted to do? What if I just let go and—"

Shay waved his hand. "I get the picture."

"I couldn't let you take me to the police. Someone could have recognized me. I've avoided publicity for years, but the rest of my family maintained a very high profile. I couldn't take a chance that my name would end up in the paper. Not only would my family have been mortified, but bad publicity isn't good for the Foundation. So I asked you to take me home with you."

"You only wanted me to keep you out of the news?"

She twisted to face him. "No. I asked you to take me home because I wanted to make love with you."

Shay remained silent, unmoved.

"I knew you wanted me, or could want me. I saw it in your eyes. So I grabbed the opportunity. And I'm not sorry about it, either."

Shay reached out and clasped her shoulders. "Damn you, Red, why are you doing this?"

"Because I don't want you to think I'm a—a conniving little bitch. I lied to you, yes. I left you, yes. But I swear on everything I hold sacred that I didn't intend to become engaged last night."

Shay's fingers tightened. "Then why are you engaged?"

"My brother has been at me about this for months. He mentioned it in passing a long time ago, but then suddenly it was serious. There were subtle hints at first, from him and from Stephen. When I didn't cooperate, the hints became nudges, the nudges became full-blown arguments. I couldn't get away from it."

"Where was your father in all this?"

"Father has been preoccupied with other matters." She felt bereft when Shay removed his hands from her shoulders. For a moment she'd thought he would take her in his arms, tell her not to worry. Foolish hope. She was beginning to see the only person she could really depend on was herself.

"Does he know about your engagement?"

She nodded. "Michael said he does. I haven't spoken with him yet."

"Why didn't he come back for your announcement?"

"First, I don't know if he realized what Michael intended to do at the ball, and second, he's having trouble with his vineyards. Some type of blight, I think he said." She smiled. "Knowing my father, he'd never consider leaving his vines under those circumstances. He takes his vineyards very seriously."

"More than his children?"

Juliette gave him a sad smile. "Sometimes."

"What about your mother?"

"Living in the south of France with her latest conquest. He's about twenty-six, I believe."

Shay looked at her. "Your parents are divorced?"

"Don't look so surprised. It happens, even in *royal* families. They've been divorced since I was three."

"You and your brother—"

"Stayed with my father. He had custody."

"That's unusual."

"He had better lawyers and a lot more money. Anyway, I love my mother, but no one in her right mind would say she was a maternal woman."

"So you and your brother...?"

"Had each other. That's what makes it so hard, despising him." She could feel tears well in the corners of her eyes, and blinked furiously. She wouldn't cry in front of this man. "This isn't the brother I grew up with. I don't know what he's done to make him act like this." She clasped her hands together, gripping so tightly she could see her knuckles turn white. "First Michael said, 'I'm only thinking of your happiness.' Then, 'This is the way to insure the future.' Then, 'It's expected, has been since you were little. You have to, our family depends on it.' Finally, last night, he took matters out of my hands and announced the engagement. He knew I wouldn't

The Harlequin Reader Service® — Here's how it works:

Accepting your 2 free books and gift places you under no obligation to buy anything. You may keep the books and gift and return the shipping statement marked "cancel." If you do not cancel, about a month later we'll send you 4 additional books and bill you just $3.34 each in the U.S., or $3.80 each in Canada, plus 25¢ shipping & handling per book and applicable taxes if any.* That's the complete price and — compared to cover prices of $3.99 each in the U.S. and $4.50 each in Canada — it's quite a bargain! You may cancel at any time, but if you choose to continue, every month we'll send you 4 more books, which you may either purchase at the discount price or return to us and cancel your subscription.

*Terms and prices subject to change without notice. Sales tax applicable in N.Y. Canadian residents will be charged applicable provincial taxes and GST.

If offer card is missing write to: Harlequin Reader Service, 3010 Walden Ave., P.O. Box 1867, Buffalo NY 14240-1867

NO POSTAGE
NECESSARY
IF MAILED
IN THE
UNITED STATES

BUSINESS REPLY MAIL
FIRST-CLASS MAIL   PERMIT NO. 717-003   BUFFALO, NY

POSTAGE WILL BE PAID BY ADDRESSEE

HARLEQUIN READER SERVICE
3010 WALDEN AVE
PO BOX 1867
BUFFALO NY 14240-9952

Play The Lucky Hearts Game

and get... FREE BOOKS & a FREE GIFT... YOURS to KEEP!

Yes! I have scratched off the silver card. Please send me my **2 FREE BOOKS** and **FREE GIFT**. I understand that I am under no obligation to purchase any books as explained on the back of this card.

Scratch Here! then look below to see what your cards get you...

DETACH AND MAIL CARD TODAY! (H-T-02/02)

© 1998 HARLEQUIN ENTERPRISES LTD. ® and TM are trademarks owned by Harlequin Enterprises Limited.

342 HDL DH33   **142 HDL DH32**

NAME   (PLEASE PRINT CLEARLY)

ADDRESS

APT.#   CITY

STATE/PROV.   ZIP/POSTAL CODE

Twenty-one gets you **2 FREE BOOKS** and a **FREE GIFT!**

Twenty gets you **2 FREE BOOKS!**

Nineteen gets you **1 FREE BOOK!**

TRY AGAIN!

Offer limited to one per household and not valid to current Harlequin Temptation® subscribers. All orders subject to approval.

Visit us online at

www.eHarlequin.com

go along with it, so he just did it. Without caring about me, or my feelings! He just did it."

"Did you talk to him about it later?"

Juliette snorted, her eyes kindling with remembered fire. "What do *you* think?"

A tiny grin lifted the corner of his mouth. "I think I'm glad I wasn't Michael."

Juliette flashed him a small smile. "I don't know who Michael is at the moment." She was quiet as she remembered her brother's face, blurry with drink, his eyes avoiding hers, his mouth weak. "Last night, all he could say was, 'You have to do this. We have no choice.'"

"What did he mean by that?"

"I don't know." She folded her hands, trying to keep from flying into outer space. "I'm scared Michael has done something stupid. I'm afraid he's in over his head."

"And you don't know how or why." Shay paused to give her a skeptical look. "And I thought you and Michael were so close."

"We were, up until a few years ago. Then things began changing. I thought it was because I was growing up and focusing on my own life. I'd established the Fortier Foundation and was working to make it a success and—"

"What does the Fortier Foundation do, exactly?"

"We help people who need help—everyone from ill children to artists looking for funding."

"It's a family trust only?"

"Well, we started it. Of course, we're hoping that people will begin donating or adding us into their wills. That's how this type of thing works."

"But currently only family members have access to the money?"

"That's right."

"So your brother has full access?"

"No one can touch the principle."

"But the interest is fair game?"

Juliette stared at him. "What are you trying to say? Why are you asking all these questions?"

Shay shrugged. "Curiosity."

She was silent for a moment as she studied him. He looked the same, yet different to her. There was an intensity about him that she hadn't seen before. Not the same intensity he'd brought to his lovemaking, but harder and sharper. It put her on the defensive. "Who are you? Are you with the police?"

"I promise you I'm not NOPD," he replied truthfully.

She gave him a suspicious stare, but before she could respond, he smiled and said, "Where are my manners? I'm Shay Mallory. We were introduced last night, remember?" His voice deepened as his gaze roamed over her. "You do remember last night?"

Juliette tried to ignore the burning his words sparked, tried to ignore the memory of being with him in the garden, his body fitting so perfectly with hers she'd lost total control of herself. She licked her lips, attempting to get the conversation back on track. "What I *don't* remember is how you got into an invitation-only event."

With a shrug and a casual smile, Shay said, "No big deal. A business acquaintance had a few unused invitations."

"Who? The same acquaintance you mentioned to Stephen?"

"No, a different one."

"Not Lucille?" That just popped out. By his surprised look, she knew the sharp rasp of jealousy had come through in her tone.

"Lucille?"

"Lucille Monteverde. The woman you were speaking with in the dining room last night."

"Oh, Lucille and her fiancé, uh…"

"Preston," she prompted.

"Right, Preston. Nice couple."

"Have you known her long?"

"Who? Lucille? No, I met them on the front porch."

"So you didn't know her before last night?" Juliette stared

at him, wondering if he and Lucille could somehow still be professional acquaintances. His pointed questions a few moments before had smacked of a prosecution, although she wasn't well acquainted with investigative techniques beyond what she saw in films or read about in books. Lucille kept that part of her life away from her friends.

Shay met Juliette's stare with an open one of his own. One that promised no secrets were hiding behind his eyes, or in his heart. "No, I didn't. Is she a good friend of yours?"

"We've lost touch recently, but she was my best friend all the way through high school."

"Friends are good."

"Yes." Juliette studied him, looking for a clue as to who this man who'd moved into her life and claimed her thoughts might actually be. But all she saw was an overwhelmingly sexy man with a guileless look in his eyes and an interested expression on his face. Still, something was nagging at her and she had to push. "Lucille's a police officer."

"She's a cop? That woman who looks as if she could be headlining a society column is a cop? You're putting me on, right?"

Juliette relaxed. That dropped-jaw look was the standard reaction people had when learning Lucille's profession. Perhaps Juliette had just let her imagination run away with her when she thought they knew each other well. "No. It seems unusual, but it's true. Lucille was always a risk taker. Besides, her father started as a prosecutor and ended up a judge, so you could say it runs in the family. You both seemed so intimate last night...so at ease with each other, I mean...that I must have jumped to the wrong conclusion. Unless you have some business with her or something?"

"Business with a cop? The only business a cop has is putting away criminals." He grinned, his voice light and joking. "What are you suggesting? That since I'm not a cop I'm a crook?"

"You do carry a gun."

"A lot of people carry guns."

"Except for Lucille, I don't know anyone who does. I didn't lie about that."

Shay smiled. "You'd be surprised. Sometimes the people you don't suspect are the people who do. Take your fiancé."

"Stephen carries a gun? How do you know that?"

"I didn't say he carried a gun. I said he could, and you probably wouldn't be aware of it unless he wanted you to know."

"Oh." She frowned. There was something illogical about his comment, but she couldn't quite figure out what it was. This man had the rare ability to twist her up in knots. She forced herself to return to her probing. "You set up an appointment to speak with Stephen tomorrow, didn't you?"

"Yeah, I did. A guy I know recommended I talk to him. He thought Stephen's contacts might be able to help me out."

"Help you out with what? I thought you did some type of temporary work. Isn't that what you said?"

"Yes, I do, but I have projects that generally have special needs."

"Such as?"

"Such as...sometimes I'm hired to make sure things get to the right people without someone else trying to take it away. That's why I've got the gun." He smiled. "It's just a precaution. I use it to scare people off more than anything."

"Have you ever used it?"

Shay laughed. "Questions, questions, questions. Are you sure *you're* not a cop?"

Juliette flushed and smoothed her hair back behind her ears. "Lord, I'm so confused. I don't know what to think of you. I don't know what to think of anything at the moment."

"You're not supposed to think of me at all, remember? You've got a fiancé."

"But I told you I don't intend to—"

His hand on hers stilled her agitated movements. "Look, Red, I was asking questions because I'm interested in you. Because, engaged or not, I want to know everything about you. I have no right, especially now. But there it is."

"You already know the most important things," Juliette whispered, looking away. "You know more about me than anyone ever has."

Shay cupped her chin and turned her back to face him. "That night. Were you a virgin?"

"Yes." At his look of horror she decided that her decision to change her virgin status was her own private business, and she saw no reason to explain or excuse it. So she changed her story. "I mean…virginal as in I didn't have a lot of experience. There was a boyfriend in college, but…" She cleared her throat. "Anyway, there's been no one since him."

"Why not?"

"I'm picky. Besides, it's not so easy when you belong to my family. I've tried not to give anyone reason to think I've followed in my mother's footsteps, because New Orleans society just loves to serve good gossip with their appetizers."

Shay outlined her lips with his thumb and moved a bit closer, saying in a husky voice, "Yet you gave yourself to me."

"I couldn't help it."

Shay sighed and pressed his lips against hers, the touch gentle and heartbreaking as he lingered. "Ah, damn it, Red, what am I going to do with you?" He caressed her face, running his fingertips over her brows, stroking her skin with his fist. "I want to lock you in a castle tower and keep you there until it's safe."

She moved her cheek against his knuckles. "That would be lonely."

"You wouldn't be lonely. I'd be there with you."

Juliette shivered. What this man could do to her with a few words delivered in that rasping sensual voice, his Northern intonations so different from the honeyed drawl of the men she knew. Finally she whispered, "Why?"

Shay just smiled, that sexy smile that raised goose bumps all over her body. "I have no idea." He bent his head again and kissed her, and Juliette could feel herself melting at the taste of his lips, at the warmth of him as he gathered her in his arms to pull her closer. The scent of his tangy aftershave took her back to the night they'd met. He'd been wearing the same scent then. Abandoning herself to his embrace, she plunged into the moment, caressing his shoulders, sliding her hands into his hair as he deepened his kiss. She drew back, nipped his bottom lip and thrilled at his response; there was a gentleness, a sweetness about it that took her by surprise and made her want him even more. She could spend her life with this man, she thought. It made no sense, but then sometimes things didn't. Sometimes you just had to go with what felt right. Shay Mallory felt right.

He lifted his head, looking down at her—looking for an answer to an unasked question, perhaps? She had no answers to give him. That thrilling, bone-deep desire he drew from her every time he touched her was all she had to give. Shivering with emotion, she placed her hands on his face. Just then a small ray of sunshine caught the facets of her ring and drew her attention.

She froze for a moment before groaning. "What am I doing?"

"Making love." His husky response again left goose bumps in its wake.

She rested her forehead against his. "I keep making things worse. I see you and all I can think about is the last time we were together."

Tipping her head back, he met her gaze with a fiery one of his own. "You think you're the only one, Red? You're in my mind. I close my eyes and replay every minute since we met. I hear a soft Southern drawl and I hear you. I look at other women and all I can see is your face."

"Oh, Shay, don't, please." Juliette's thoughts were whirling. All she wanted was for Shay to take her in his arms again and make her whole. That was impossible. She was a Fortier. She knew what she had to do. She took a deep breath. "Until I can sort this situation out, we...we can't see each other any more, so don't even try."

"Wait a minute." His expression grew tight and closed. "You asked to see *me* today, remember?"

"I know I did. I had to explain. I couldn't let you keep hating me."

Shay sighed. "I can't hate you. I've been trying, but it isn't working. You're like a drug. One taste and I'm hooked."

She grasped at the only thing that could put the brakes on her emotions. "That doesn't change anything. I'm engaged."

His face sharpened with a mixture of accusation and pain. "I thought you said that meant nothing to you."

"It doesn't. But I can't just forget about it."

"Even though you were tricked into it?"

Juliette pulled back from him, preparing herself for what she had to do. "Yes. Even though I was tricked into it."

Shay's mouth twisted. "How noble."

Flushing at his caustic tone, she rose to her feet, praying for strength as she looked at him. "I have to deal with this situation in my own way, and in my own time. Until that happens, I don't want to see you again."

"New Orleans isn't that big a town, sweetheart."

"I doubt we move in the same circles."

"Oh, right, I forgot. You're an aristocrat, a real-life princess. A member of the almighty Fortier family."

She lifted her chin in a gesture perfected by centuries of her ancestors. "That's right, I am. And as such, I have to think of my family honor."

Shay laughed. "That's rich. Were you thinking about honor when I saw you on that park bench? I doubt it."

His words pierced her heart. "We all make mistakes," she said.

"Yes, we do." His expression had changed from determination to regret, which puzzled her.

"I don't intend to make any more of them."

He stood up, towering over her. "Join the club, Red."

They looked at each other for a moment before Shay said, "What about your brother? Think he won't make any more mistakes, either?"

The worry that had propelled her to this meeting came back full force. "I won't let him." With that, she turned and walked away.

SHAY O'MALLEY, dressed in a nicely cut sports jacket and trousers, a custom-fit shirt and shoes polished to a brilliant shine, walked into the elegant lobby of Stephen St. James's offices armed with nothing more than his wits and his determination.

On the way to the elevator, Shay noticed the equipment of a first-class security system, wall-mounted minicameras, a sophisticated visual monitoring system built into the security guard's desk, probably accessorized with a vast network of audio alarms and restricted-access corridors. Shay grinned to himself as the elevator doors slid open with an expensive hush and he stepped inside. *Nothing too good for our boy, Stephen.*

Shay's pulse raced, not with fear, but with excitement. There was no better rush than getting right in the middle of the danger and playing the game for all it was worth. There was a point when all the background information, all the security and all the planning fell by the wayside. After that, it was just him and the crook. The rush was one of the things that kept Shay a cop. And it was one of the reasons he was delighted to be back undercover.

The elevator slid to a smooth, graceful stop and the door whispered open. Shay stepped out to be met by an attractive woman smiling at him, gesturing him to follow her. She ushered him into a room that featured an entire wall of floor-to-ceiling windows and the most impressive view of New Orleans and the Mississippi River he'd seen to date. After a quick check of the area, he focused on his quarry sitting erect and composed behind a magnificent carved desk on the right side of the room.

Stephen St. James rose, offering his hand and a pleasant smile. His voice seemed to roll across the room, his Southern tones rich, full and as mellow as aged brandy. "Mr. Mallory, welcome." He waved his arm at the view. "What do you think of our little city?"

Shay knew he was expected to admire and fawn, so he said, "It's great, and that view...you've got the best seat in the house."

"I do. I sure do." Coming around the desk, Stephen clapped Shay on the shoulder and led him to the other side of the room, toward an arrangement of leather chairs and antique tables. "We'll be more comfortable over here. I had my secretary order some chicory coffee—y'all haven't tasted a New Orleans brew until you taste it this way."

"Sounds great to me, Mr. St. James."

"Stephen, please. Any friend of Henry Sabin's is a friend of mine, I'm sure." Stephen sat down in the power position— the light and view behind him so Shay had to squint to see him. "So fortuitous your knowing Henry, isn't it?"

Head up, O'Malley. Shay went on red alert. His adrenaline was pumping. Had Stephen heard something about Henry's arrest? About Henry cutting a deal to save himself from prosecution? Nah, he wouldn't dare. Just in case, Shay gave Stephen his most eager, innocent look. "I sure hope it turns out that way."

Stephen poured their drinks, then handed a cup to Shay. "How is Henry?" he asked. "I haven't seen him for quite a while. Is he still a skinny runt with a ponytail?"

This was what Shay loved, matching wits with the opponent, narrowly avoiding disaster. "Not quite. The man I know is six foot four and built like an overstuffed sofa." Smooth confirmation, Shay thought. No fuss, just quick and efficient. *Man, this is gonna be fun.*

Stephen nodded, the chill in his eyes now overlaid with a welcoming warmth. "Ah, I see we do know the same person, after all."

Shay relaxed. For a few moments, he sipped in silence, trying to determine how best to approach the subject of his visit. He half hoped Stephen would take the lead, but instead, the man waited him out, not opening the conversation to anything that could be misconstrued in any way. Finally, Shay plunged in. "I have some merchandise that I need to move."

Stephen took another small sip from his cup. "Do you?"

"I have a deal that means some very big profits to anybody concerned. That is, if I can find a way to get it out of Bolivia, and get some additional funding to smooth the way." Since he suspected that Stephen's role with the cartel encompassed both financial securities and cargo shipping, Shay figured he'd jump at the chance to make a double profit.

"Bolivia? Interesting country, Bolivia." St. James crossed one creased trouser leg over the other. The fanciful thought raced across Shay's mind that if Stephen had lived in old New Orleans he would have been called a dandy, classified as one of the fashionable dudes concerned only with pleasure, and who lived very well on the labors of others. "Have you a time frame in mind for your little project?"

"Next week."

"Hmm." Stephen sipped at his drink. "That's not much time."

"No, but it's worth it." Shay waited tensely, hoping Stephen would say more and snap up the bait he was dangling.

"There are logistics to work out, and we are rather busy at the moment." Stephen leaned forward, offering Shay more coffee before refilling his own cup. Leisurely, he leaned back in his chair and let a small smile lift his lips. "How do you like New Orleans coffee?"

The hell with the coffee, let's get to the meat of the matter. Of course Shay couldn't say that aloud, so he smiled back and said, "Different taste. Not for the weak-kneed, I'd say." The coffee was only one of the things he would miss when he left this place. The other didn't bear thinking about.

"Like other things in New Orleans, it grows on you," Stephen replied. "It's a wonderful city for excess." Shay was wondering where to go next when he continued, "Tell me a little more about this 'shipment' of yours. Do you have any special needs to consider?"

Closer, Shay thought. *Come a little closer.* "The buyer's willing to pay, and pay big. All I have to do is deliver it 'alive and kicking,' so to speak, and with all the accompanying valuables intact."

Stephen stared at him, his eyes going from blue to an opaque gray. "I see."

"Which could mean very big bucks to you and to me."

"I see," Stephen said again, his tone noncommittal, his body posture perfectly relaxed.

"What do you think?" *This guy is good,* Shay mused, as he studied him, seeking a clue to his thoughts. The game was always so much more enjoyable with a worthy opponent. He had a feeling that St. James would give him a good run for his money. He just wondered where Michael fit into all of this. Did he know exactly what he was involved in here?

"I think I'll mull it over," Stephen said, with another small, urbane smile.

"Mull it over?" Shay feigned surprise. After all, that would be the correct reaction if his deal was for real. From this point on, Shay couldn't afford to make any mistakes. He had the prey close to the line, now he just had to keep making the bait as tempting as possible.

"Yes, I make it a practice to think things over very carefully before I commit my resources."

"That's smart, I agree, but I have a deadline to consider."

"Ah." Stephen raised his index finger. His expression was friendly, but there was a coldness in his eyes as he stared at Shay. "But this is N'awlins, and it's Mardi Gras."

Shay gazed at the man opposite him, careful to hide his annoyance at having to play the mouse to this cat waiting to pounce. "And besides, you like to take your time, right?"

Stephen smiled, a smile that Shay felt was deliberately mocking, even though it appeared warm and gracious. "Of course."

Shay realized that he might have been a bit overeager, so he leaned back and set about correcting his impression. "I want the job done right. And from what I've been told, that means by you. So maybe taking a bit of time would be good. Besides, it'll give me a chance to acquaint myself with your fair city."

"Did you enjoy the ball the other night?"

"Absolutely." Shay grinned. "I met a number of beautiful women."

"Yes, New Orleans is known for beautiful women."

"Your fiancé is one of them. You're a lucky man." Juliette's image swam before his eyes for a moment, before he pushed it away. *Don't think about her,* he thought. *Not now. Keep your eye on the ball, damn it.*

Stephen nodded. "I'd agree with that. Juliette is stunning."

"Have you known her long?" Shay wanted to knock St. James's teeth down his throat for even speaking Juliette's name aloud, but he had to play the game.

"All my life," Stephen replied. "Our fathers were best friends. They'd always envisioned our families uniting. Now, I'm happy to say, Juliette and I are going to make that wish come true."

"Your marriage is advantageous on all fronts then."

"Pardon?"

"You'll get a beautiful wife, plus..." Shay let the pause draw out for a few moments, then added softly, "the Fortiers' ships." St. James could run the goods with no interference from anyone. Shay gave Stephen an admiring look. "It seems the perfect scenario for expanding your business interests."

Stephen appeared watchful and remote. "Any connection is good for that."

Come on, let go. Open up. Just a crack, a tiny crack I can use—that's all I want.

Shay was getting impatient with their thrust-and-parry match. He wanted to pull his sword out and start slashing. He knew he couldn't. Stephen St. James was a wily character and Shay would have to hold back his aggression and play the game for as long as it took, if he wanted to get anywhere. He chuckled. "Isn't that the truth? You never know where you'll find a customer."

Stephen smiled. "Spoken like an entrepreneur."

Leaning forward, Shay nodded. "Money matters to me. It matters a lot. And I don't care what I have to do to get it."

"A man after my own heart, I believe."

"I hope so." *Not just the heart, pal. I want the whole body.*

"You'll have to be careful not to overreach your ambitions."

Shay smiled. Another warning, smoothly delivered. "You don't need to worry about that. I know what I can accomplish...with your help, of course."

Stephen considered him for a long moment before placing his cup and saucer on the table and rising to his feet. "Do you have plans for this evening?"

Shay placed his own cup down on the shining wood surface. "No. No plans."

"I've always found it pleasant to get to know my business partners socially as well as professionally. So civilized. Don't you agree?"

"Sounds good."

"I'm having a small dinner party tonight. Perhaps you'd like to join me and my fiancée, and some other associates?"

Shay stood up. "I'll look forward to it."

Stephen showed him to the door. "My secretary will give you directions."

In the elevator a few minutes later, Shay leaned back against the paneling and replayed the dinner invitation in his mind. All in all, he thought this was a hopeful sign. His appearance, or something he'd said or done, had gotten him past the first stage. But had he been accepted so easily? The hairs on his neck lifted. Somehow he didn't think so.

Three questions were troubling his mind. One, was it the illegal shipment he'd been tracing that was jamming the shipping schedule? Two, when would Stephen take the hook Shay had dangled and commit to the job? And three—Shay grinned as the third question popped into his mind—what in holy hell was Juliette Fortier going to say when she sat down to dinner next to the man she never wanted to see again?

7

"I LIKE THAT DRESS ON YOU, Juliette. It's charming," Michael said, as they headed into the city on the way to Stephen's that evening.

"Thank you." Juliette could barely squeeze the words through her lips. This was the first time she'd been alone with her brother since their conversation the evening after the ball. He was obviously avoiding her.

"I bet Stephen will like it."

"Michael, I want—"

"You look beautiful in that color. Dark pink, is it?" he interrupted. Michael either didn't notice her tone, or pretended not to. He made it a habit of not noticing things that made him uncomfortable, Juliette knew.

"Rose. It's called rose." She closed her eyes for a moment. The slight headache that had been stalking her since she'd cried herself to sleep after leaving Shay the day before was fast becoming worse.

"Rose, such a delightful—"

"Oh for heaven's sake. If you're going to talk to me, talk to me about something meaningful."

"Such as?"

Juliette glanced at him, seeing by the appalled expression that slipped over his face that Michael had asked the question before realizing where it could lead. She decided to take the opening. "Such as what's going on with you, Michael?"

"With me? Well, let's see. This morning I had a meeting with the political party's nominating committee, with some of the movers and shakers who've been talking to me about—"

"That's not what I mean and you know it."

Michael tried to take refuge in his older-brother role. "Were you asking about my afternoon?"

She gave him a disdainful look. "You know very well I wasn't."

"No, I guess you weren't. However, for the record—"

"I want to know exactly what kind of trouble you're in." She wouldn't have thought he'd even heard her except for the whiteness of his knuckles as his hands tightened on the steering wheel.

Smiling, he focused on the road ahead. "No trouble, except for trying to reconcile our financial accounts, which is simply beyond me at the moment."

"You told me I have no choice about an engagement to Stephen."

Michael gave a lighthearted chuckle. "It's been in the stars since you were a little girl. You know that."

"No. This didn't happen to fulfill family expectations. How naïve do you think I am?"

"Well, really, Juliette. I don't think it's my place to inquire into your love life."

"Damn it, Michael!" Juliette exploded, slapping her hand on the leather dashboard in front of her, the sound sharp in the quiet, luxurious Mercedes. "I don't know what kind of games you're playing—"

Startled, Michael glanced at her. "I'm not playing games. I gave Father my word that I wouldn't—"

"What? What are you talking about?"

Michael stared at her for a moment, then licked his lips, trying to recapture his lighthearted smile. "Obviously, we aren't talking about the same thing."

"Were you talking about gambling?"

He gave her a cool smile. "Of course not. That little problem is in the past. What I meant was…I gave Father my word that I wouldn't," he said again, emphasizing every word, "let any harm come to you while he was gone. That I'd watch out for you as well as he would. So I wouldn't consider your happiness a game."

Juliette tossed her head. "I don't need anyone to watch out for me." When were the men in her family going to realize that? They both had this archaic idea that she needed to be guided, so that she didn't accidentally make the same mistakes as her mother. She'd generally considered it loving and thoughtful, a sign of how much they cared. Now she wondered if it was their need to control, rather than real concern for her welfare.

"Father wanted this engagement to happen. He often said so."

"He wouldn't want it to happen if he knew I was against it."

"Come on, you're talking as if Stephen is an ax murderer. Half the women in New Orleans would love to be in your shoes. The man's good-looking, charming, rich, polite, amusing—"

Folding her arms, she stated firmly, "I don't love him."

Astonished, Michael threw her a look. "Love him? What the hell does that have to do with it? If you're lucky, love comes later. It grows, along with the relationship and the success of the partnership." He sounded as if he was speaking to a three-year-old.

"We're not talking about a merger. We're talking about my life."

Michael laughed. "Oh, Juliette, how melodramatic. Next thing I know you'll be telling me you've fallen madly in love with our neighborhood butcher and intend to live happily ever after."

"You make love sound so absurd and plebeian. Love stories happen. They happen every day. You see someone and without knowing how it happened or why..." Shay's face appeared in her mind. Not as she'd last seen him, but as he'd looked when he made love to her.

"And you know this how? You've met someone?"

"What? No. Why?" All Juliette's alarm bells went off at his comment.

"Well, you do sound as if you're speaking personally."

She shook her head, further warned by his speculative glance. "I'm talking about what's happening with my friends."

"What friends?"

"Lucille and Preston, for example."

His eyebrows lifted as he wryly commented, "Lucille has known Preston since she was in high school, and if I remember right, she refused his first two proposals. I wouldn't call that love at first sight."

"Our parents, then." The minute she said it she knew it was a ridiculous suggestion, especially given her brother's hostile feelings about their mother.

Michael's laugh was bitter. "Oh, there's a good example." He turned onto a side street in the French Quarter. "Granted, they married for love, but one man's love was never enough for our dear mama. Definitely a relationship to emulate."

"You're right, that was a bad example, but that doesn't change anything. You used me." She waited for a moment, but he said nothing, just continued to drive with a frozen look on his face. "I don't know how it all fits with this engagement, but I think you did it to get yourself out of trouble."

"Juliette—"

She galloped on, her breath coming faster as she focused on the consequences. "It must be very bad if you needed to offer me up as the sacrifice."

"Juliette, calm down—"

"I am calm."

He reached to pat her hand. "We're almost there, and you're going to be all flushed and agitated. Everyone will notice."

She jerked away. "Don't try to treat me as if I'm a Victorian maiden."

"Then stop behaving like one," Michael snapped as he pulled his car into a small cul de sac behind tall iron gates. "I'd rather we kept our tiresome family disagreements to ourselves."

Juliette stared at him. "I'm not your adoring little sister

anymore, ready to kiss your toes whenever you open your mouth. I'm going to find out what's going on and put a stop to it." She got out of the car, deliberately slamming the door, hearing it echo in the courtyard.

Michael gave his Mercedes a pained glance. "You really don't need to slam the door like that. It's not a pickup truck."

"Sorry."

For a moment longer they stared at each other, one seeking and one avoiding. Finally, Michael glanced at his watch and said, in his most urbane tone, "Shall we go in? It would be rude to make everyone wait for dinner while we shout at each other like rival street vendors."

Juliette nodded toward the door. "Yes, a Fortier can never be rude—only high-handed."

In silence they made their way up the brick walk to the door of Stephen's classic mid-1800s town house. They waited in the shadow of the ornate second-story balcony for the door to open. A slight breeze brought a chill and the misty hint of rain. As a few isolated droplets hit her face, Juliette drew the shawl that matched her dress closer around her shoulders.

It had been raining when she'd met Shay, she remembered. Then she sighed. Shay might as well have been a lifetime ago, so lost did he seem to her at the moment. She felt as if she were in a maze, with doors shutting behind her to close off her retreat. She wished she could talk to someone, but as she went through her small list of confidants, she rejected each for one reason or another. Ideally, she would speak with Lucille, but under the circumstances it was impossible. Until she knew what Michael was mixed up in, she couldn't risk speaking to anyone connected with the police, regardless of how old their friendship.

The door opened and the maid welcomed them. "Mr. Michael, Miss Juliette, come right on in. Mr. Stephen and his other guests are waiting for you in the parlor."

"Thank you, Beulah. Been keeping yourself out of trouble?" Michael asked.

Beulah giggled, her wizened face puckering up with pleasure like a young girl's. "Oh, go on with you, Mr. Michael. I'm too old to be gettin' in trouble."

Michael dropped all his society pretenses and winked at her. "You're never too old, Beulah."

With a flash of her gold tooth, Beulah grinned. "Ain't it the truth, boy, ain't it the truth."

Juliette watched Michael slip an arm around the St. Jameses' long-time housekeeper to give her a hug. This was the brother she loved, this charming mischievous scamp. Where had he gone? When had the joy left him? She had no answer, and quite honestly, she was almost afraid to find out. The truth could mean she would no longer know the man whose blood and history she shared. And that loss would be unbearable. Not for the first time, she felt an enormous tug between her own desires and family loyalty.

Pulling her gaze from her brother, Juliette concentrated on the elegant foyer. Memories engulfed her. She'd been in and out of this home as if it was her own both as a child, and later as an adult. The privileged atmosphere here was similar to the type of environment in which she'd been raised. It was a milieu her royal family and heritage had raised her to expect, and to embrace. Which she probably could have done eventually if she hadn't slipped her leash and met Shay.

Shay had changed everything.

She wasn't the same woman she'd been last week. With Shay had come confusion and doubts—doubts about herself, about her future, about all she thought she knew.

As her brother turned to offer her his arm, his smile so genuine, so loving, she suddenly wondered if she was imagining everything. Michael's problems might be perfectly innocuous, and the engagement announcement a way to fulfill what he saw as his obligation to their father, misguided though it might have been.

In a moment of crystal-clear awareness, she realized it didn't matter. Any consideration of Stephen she might entertain in the face of family pressure was out of the question now that she'd experienced Shay Mallory and gotten a peek at the possibilities love could offer. She might have to wait until all the Mardi Gras festivities were over, but she was determined to speak with Stephen and break off this charade as soon as possible. Then she'd find a way to help Michael, if he needed it. All easier said than done.

Her headache pounded a bit more fiercely as she allowed her brother to lead her into the parlor. Leaving him, she walked forward with her eyes focused on her supposed fiancé.

"Juliette," Stephen said, seeming so happy to see her that Juliette found herself smiling back at him almost naturally. Again there was a moment of unreality as she stared up at him.

This was Stephen, after all. She'd known him forever. Known his sleek, shining helmet of blond hair, his cool blue eyes that could crinkle at the corners when he was really amused. His lithe body and elegant manner of dressing, his suave conversation and economy of movement—this was Stephen, her brother's best friend, son of her father's best friend.

"Darling, I'd like you to meet a guest of mine..."

Her eyes automatically slid to the left encountering a firm chin and an intriguing mouth with just the slightest tilt of a smile. The man was slightly taller than Stephen, and she lifted her gaze, to meet bright green eyes gleaming as if the devil himself lived inside.

"...Shay Mallory. You remember him, of course—the pirate who danced with you at the ball?"

Juliette's world stopped turning. Her eyes blurred, her ears filled with a great rushing sound and her mouth went dry. Images raced through her mind, some erotic, some tender, all riveting. How could she ever forget Shay? Her eyes stayed on his, seeking an answer. In his gaze, she read humor, concern and a warning all at the same time. *Pull yourself together, Red*—that much she understood. Juliette tried to swallow, tried to find her voice through vocal cords that had become brittle. Somehow she managed to say, "Of course I remember. How could I forget a pirate?" *How indeed!*

"And I didn't even make you walk the plank to remember me."

Automatically her lips formed a word. "True." *Liar.* She'd been walking on a narrow ledge since she'd first met him. Trying to keep the longing out of her expression, she ran her gaze over him.

"Are you all right, Juliette? You look a bit pale." Stephen's solicitous voice at her elbow forced her back to reality.

"It's—it's starting to rain. I think I have a bit of a chill." And how! Suddenly she was frozen as an icy grave.

"Come over by the fire, darling, and let me get you a drink."

She automatically set one foot in front of the other, walking toward the marble mantel. "Thank you. That would be nice."

"Some sherry?"

She sent a sharp glance toward Shay, then focused on Stephen. "Whiskey. Neat."

Stephen's eyebrows raised. "Whis—all right. I have a very smooth Irish blend you might try." He walked across the room and returned with a small crystal tumbler that contained a moderate tot of whiskey.

The amber liquid caught the light from the fire as Juliette lifted the glass to her mouth. She took a sip and shuddered, then glanced at Stephen, seeing the humorous expression in his eyes as he waited for her to change her mind. Then a large hand folded around hers to help her out.

"You might just want to toss that first one back as fast as you can. That's the best way to fire up your insides."

Juliette gasped. "A fire." Lord, his hand on hers was producing all the fire she needed.

"The Irish know how to make a flame that goes down as smooth as water," he said, raising the crystal to her lips. "Just relax and let it slide down your throat. That's it."

She closed her eyes as tears threatened to well up, but the chill had gone. In its place was a roaring inferno. She opened her eyes, her vision clearer now, and focused on Shay. With a rock steady voice, she said, "Thanks for sharing your wisdom. I'm sure you had a fine time gathering it."

He chuckled and removed his hand from hers. "You're right."

"Another one, darling?"

Juliette turned to Stephen and found the humor lingering in his eyes now overlaid with a quizzical gleam. She handed him the glass. "No. One was enough, thank you."

Stephen's eyes met Shay's, and they shared one of those looks most men use when comparing notes about an incomprehensible female. "I thought it might be." Then, before he could say more, Beulah ushered a few more people into the room.

"Excuse me," Stephen said, walking across the room to greet his new guests.

Shay used the moments to whisper, "Surprised?"

Juliette let out the breath she didn't even know she'd been holding. "What are you doing here? I told you I—"

"Your fiancé invited me."

"For God's sake, why?"

Shrugging his shoulders, Shay said whimsically, "Maybe he likes me."

She scowled. "He doesn't know you."

He gave her a small smile that directly touched her heart. "No. There you have the advantage."

"Will you be quiet? Someone might hear you."

"Afraid?" he teased.

Afraid? Yes. But of herself or him? Juliette wasn't sure.

They had no chance to say more as Stephen brought the other guests over for introductions. For the next half hour, Juliette smiled and chatted with two pleasant couples, whom she knew slightly from some charitable engagements, and with a single woman, Kristy Lou Puckett, who'd been occasionally seeing Juliette's brother for the past month. However, Kristy Lou soon turned her eyes away from Michael, focusing them on Shay with all the predatory skill of an experienced feline who was looking for a new menu item.

Juliette burned as she intercepted one of the platinum blonde's speculative looks. She wanted to race right over and yank her pale hair out by its darker roots and tell her to keep her looks to herself. She couldn't, though. Instead, she had to watch as the woman flowed up and over Shay, attaching herself to his side like a barnacle as her brother headed for the bar. The headache, which the blast of whiskey had subdued for a while, set up a drumroll. Her stomach lurched for a moment as a sour taste of alcohol rose into her throat. When had she last eaten? she wondered. Just in time, Beulah announced dinner.

Juliette took her place at the table, to find Shay seated next to her on one side and the blond bombshell far down the table, next to Michael.

A few minutes later, another man, middle-aged and squat, his manner agitated, walked into the room. "Stephen, I gotta talk to you about those guys in South—" He jerked to a stop, clearly appalled seeing all the people present. "Sorry, Beulah didn't tell me you—"

Stephen stiffened, then rose, ever the urbane host. "Gerald, please join us. No, no, I won't take no for an answer. There's always room for one more guest." He directed the maid to set another place at the table.

With another glance around, Gerald hesitated then said, "If I could just see you for a minute." The man's mind was obviously following one track only.

"I'm sure it can wait until later. You shouldn't let work consume you so much, old friend." Stephen waved him to the seat near Michael and turned to his other guests. "I'm not sure if y'all have met Gerald Raymond, who's with the Strategy Fund." Stephen continued to introduce everyone, leaving Shay until the end.

"And this is Shay Mallory. He and I are speaking about a possible transaction that could require your help."

"Delighted," Gerald muttered, taking a long gulp of water.

"You just got back from South America, you were saying?" Shay asked.

"What?" The man appeared startled, putting his water glass down so rapidly he almost spilled its contents. He glanced at Stephen. "I, uh, well—"

"No more business talk." Stephen smiled, lifting his wineglass. "It's Mardi Gras, time to celebrate. To new friends and old...and prosperity in all things."

They lifted their glasses and drank. Dinner went on, the conversation pleasant, animated and punctuated with laughter. Juliette tried to focus on her perfectly cooked fish and vegetables, but it was difficult. All she could see was Shay. She was aware of his every movement, his every breath, his every word as he chatted with others around the table. Juliette gave up trying to follow the conversation, only stepping in when someone addressed her directly or when her hostess training made her aware of a lag in the chatter. The rest of her time was occupied with trying to find a way out of her dilemma.

Her gaze drifted to Shay's hand as it wrapped around his wineglass—capable and strong, tanned and taut. She remembered how it had felt as he'd stroked her skin—his touch gentle, firm, or almost fierce at times. He was a complex man, she thought. One she didn't really know and didn't understand. How could he have turned her existence upside down in such a short time?

Under cover of the conversation, Shay said, "What are you thinking about?"

"You," she answered truthfully.

"Good thoughts?"

She slid a look his way. "Not all of them."

He chuckled. "That was honest."

"Are you?" she blurted. "Honest?"

Hesitating, he looked into her eyes. "Not always."

Juliette digested that, finally asking, "What do you want from me?"

"Honestly?"

"Yes."

Shay gave her a rueful smile. "That's a problem, because I don't know."

The moment was interrupted by the arrival of Beulah and a server with a magnificent flaming crème brûlée and an assortment of pastries. As the dessert was served and coffee poured, Kristy Lou asked, "Shay, darlin', how do you like our town?"

If Kristy Lou's drawl got any slower and thicker, Juliette thought, you could use it for maple syrup.

Shay didn't seem to mind as he glanced up at Kristy Lou. "I like it a lot. I just haven't seen much of it yet."

Kristy Lou arched her brows. "Why ever not?"

"I haven't had time to study the guidebook."

"Oh, my, no! Following a guidebook is no way to see New Orleans. Y'all should have a native show you around."

Juliette glanced at her brother to see how he was taking his girlfriend's obvious infatuation with Shay. Michael was ignoring her, but he seemed to be ignoring everything except his wineglass at the moment. A recent tendency Juliette was finding as disturbing as his secretive behavior.

"A native? Now there's a thought."

Juliette slid him a look from under her lashes, her attention caught by the dark undertone of laughter in his voice. He was staring at the oh-so-obvious Kristy Lou with open admiration. Juliette crumpled her napkin. *Men!* Always thinking with the wrong part of their anatomy.

Michael coughed as Kristy Lou cooed, "I'd be happy to—"

"We'd hate to put you out, Kristy Lou, when I'm sure you have a million and one other things to do," Stephen interjected, his voice smooth as silk. "Juliette is an expert on New Orleans and its history. She'd love to show you around, Shay. Wouldn't you, darling?"

Juliette jumped as Stephen addressed her. "Me?"

Shay grinned at Stephen, then snapped his fingers. "Just like that you're giving me your fiancée?"

Stephen bared his teeth in a grin. "Merely on a temporary

basis. It's the least I can do, since I might have to ask you to stay in town for a while in order to continue with our business."

Shay thought it over for a moment. "Well, I'd rather spend the time looking around your beautiful city than staring at four walls in a hotel room."

"But you don't live in—" Shay sent her a warning glance that made her practically swallow her tongue. Her breath quickened, but she strove to keep her tone steady and casually friendly. "Didn't you just tell me that you were staying with a friend?"

"You got me." Shay glanced around the table and chuckled. "I did tell her that. I only said the hotel room so you'd all take pity on me."

"I'll take pity on you," Kristy Lou said.

"Actually," Shay continued smoothly, as if he'd never been interrupted. "My friend's out of town. I'm staying in his apartment. However, it still has four walls to stare at in my spare time."

"We can't have that, can we, Juliette? Michael? Especially not during Mardi Gras."

"'Course not," Michael agreed, overenunciating his words. "There's so much going on this time of year."

Juliette met Stephen's eyes, then looked at her brother, who seemed a bit confused by the entire situation, but was obviously letting Stephen take the lead. Juliette felt she had no choice but to say, "I'll be happy to show you around town, Shay. Luckily, my schedule is rather light at the moment. When would you—"

Stephen smiled. "Why not tomorrow? That way you can see the Mummery Parade."

"Tomorrow?" Juliette could feel herself faltering a bit. She needed more time than that to reconcile spending an entire day in Shay's company so soon after she'd told him she never wanted to see him again.

"Perhaps I can even join you for a late lunch, darling. I'll check my schedule."

Michael muttered, his voice a bit thick and slurred, "I thought tomorrow—"

"Have another drink, Michael," Stephen interrupted, his expression cold and cutting.

Juliette's brother shut up as if he'd been pole-axed. He flushed and reached for the wine bottle as an uncomfortable silence settled over the table for a moment.

Stephen smiled at Michael, "I bought this wine especially for you. I know it's your favorite year."

The tension in the room was tangible. Automatically, graciously, Juliette rushed in to rescue the situation. "Of course we'd love to have you join us for lunch, Stephen. Have you any place special in mind?"

Gerald looked up from his food long enough to say, "There's a new place near the levee that's good. Me and Felipe were—"

Shay's head snapped around so fast, Juliette was amazed he didn't get a crick in his neck. Before he could say anything, Stephen once again stepped smoothly into the conversation.

"Good suggestion, Gerald. Darling, I'll call you tomorrow morning to confirm." He rose to his feet. "Please, everyone, let's adjourn to the veranda. There are some spectacular fireworks scheduled for tonight."

Smiling and chattering, the party moved from the dining room to gather outside in the back gardens. Juliette followed more slowly, having lingered in the dining room to ask that Beulah express her appreciation to the cook. After a few moments, she stepped into the hallway, blinking in the bright light of the chandelier there. *Lord, my head's pounding again. Will this evening ever end?*

Feet dragging, Juliette trailed down the long hall, then stopped in the powder room on the first floor, hoping to find some aspirin. All she wanted was to go home, crawl into a hole and never see anyone again. Emerging, she spotted a shadowy recess where red velvet curtains framed an archway near the French doors, and impulsively slipped inside. The spot brought back memories. She'd played hide and seek here when she was a child, with her brother and Stephen indulging her passion for the game. Such lovely, simple times. She sighed, wishing she were seven again. However, she was all grown up, and duty called.

As Juliette started to step into the hall, she was surprised to overhear Stephen saying, "You need to relax, Michael."

"Relax? How can I relax? You told me they won't pay until they get confirmation of delivery. You said it'd be tomorrow, and now you're gallivanting around the city with my sister and some Yankee."

Juliette shrank back, staying out of sight of the two men standing near the doors, but able to see them through a crack in the curtains. Luckily, Stephen and Michael were focused on watching the other guests, who were milling about in the garden.

"We've had a slight change that might delay things."

"But—"

Stephen grabbed Michael's arm. "Michael, cool off or you'll blow the whole thing."

"The more it's delayed, the more there's a risk my father might find out what's going on. I think—"

"Don't think. We both know you're not too good at it, under the circumstances. Do what I tell you and you'll be fine."

"Damn it, Stephen…"

"Find Gerald and tell him to meet me in the study after everyone leaves. And be subtle about it, will you?"

"I'm not hired help, Stephen. You can't just order me around."

"Michael, Michael, take a deep breath."

"It's difficult when you keep changing things. And who's this Mallory?"

"Don't worry about it. I'll handle him, just as I'm handling everything else. Until I do, I want him where I can find him. All right?"

"I still don't like it."

Stephen's voice became soothing as Juliette heard the sound of the door opening. "Michael, you're my best friend, practically my brother. Trust me, I won't let..." Their voices faded away as they went down into the garden.

Juliette pressed her hand against her throat. What in the world was going on? What was that all about? A shipment? Shipment of what? It was obviously something her father wasn't meant to know about.

She stood still for a moment, wishing she could speak with Lucille after all, wondering if she should call her, then realized she'd better get into the garden before anyone noticed her absence.

She'd just stepped through the door when Stephen appeared in front of her. Giving her a sharp glance, he practically growled "Juliette, where have you been?"

Plastering a smile on her face, she wrapped her shawl a bit closer in the night air. "In the kitchen, complimenting Marcel on another outstanding meal. I declare, Stephen, I don't know how he does it." She chattered on, the look on his face alarming her so much that she made every effort to put him at ease. "Every time I dine here, the food is more delicious. I wish I could get him to Belle Rivière to give our cook some lessons."

Stephen seemed to relax. "After we're married you'll be able to do whatever you like with Marcel, darling."

Juliette hesitated, then plunged ahead. "We need to talk about our marriage, Stephen."

"And so we shall, darling, but right now is not the time."

"Everything all right?" Shay asked, as he walked toward them. "Not trying to get out of showing me around tomorrow, are you, Juliette?"

Stephen smiled. "Juliette's mind is already wrapped around planning our wedding, would you believe that?"

"Yeah." Shay's expression hardened and his stare bored into her, making Juliette wince. "My sister was just the same. From the minute the ring went on her finger that's all anyone heard about."

With a soft chuckle, Stephen smoothed Juliette's hair. "Is that what I have to look forward to, darling?"

"She won't be able to help herself, Stephen. If I were you, I'd run for cover."

Juliette balled her hand into a fist, wishing she could take a swing at Shay Mallory for baiting her, which was exactly what he was doing. She opened her mouth to put him in his place, when a huge burst of fireworks made any more conversation difficult. With two men politely grasping her elbows, she walked toward the rest of the guests, not sure which man she found more annoying at the moment—her lover or her fiancé. All she knew was that she had a violent headache and wanted to go home.

THE NEXT MORNING, Shay O'Malley stood in an alley, tucked in the shadows of a building, and watched Juliette Fortier as she stood on a veranda across the street. She'd said she had some business to attend to before showing him around the city and they'd agreed to meet at eleven at the Fortier Foundation.

The late start was fine by Shay, as he'd used the morning to stop by the station and fill Lucille in on his recent activities. He'd left her with the assignment of tracking down more information about their elusive South American, the funding groups associated with Stephen and Michael, and the incoming shipping schedules for the next week and a half. He refrained from telling her about his day with Juliette, preferring to keep the information to himself until he decided what type of involvement the princess might have.

The foundation offices occupied a charming turn-of-the-century building that looked more like a home than a business, which made a nice impression. Almost as nice as the woman standing in front of it. Shay smiled as she glanced at her watch, then looked longingly at the entrance door. She was probably praying he wouldn't show. *Not a chance, Red.*

He studied her face. Regardless of her title and circumstances, there was still an innocence about her, he thought, even as he told himself not to be a fool. Once again he wondered what she knew about her fiancé's affairs. Even though

Shay prayed she was ignorant, he wasn't positive she could be. Sure, she might be innocent of any wrongdoing, but he had a feeling she was smart as hell, which meant she had to have some suspicions. She'd already suggested as much to him with her concern about her brother. Following that reasoning, Shay decided she might know something and not even realize it. In which case, life could get very dangerous for her. The people Stephen served weren't the kind you played around with if you wanted to live a long and healthy life.

Juliette began to pace, then completely surprised him when she stopped and blew a big pink bubble before pacing again. He grinned. Somehow, he would never have expected Princess Juliette Fortier to chew bubble gum. He wondered what else she did that was completely out of character. But then, he already knew.

He sensed that Juliette's behavior had been completely out of character since he'd met her. When he touched her, it was as if he'd somehow uncorked a magic bottle and all the mystery and yearning and passion inside spilled free. The thought that another man might reap the treasure he'd brought to the surface made him want to kill. If there was one thing he knew, it was that Juliette belonged to him. Maybe not forever, but he'd put his mark on her. He'd challenge anyone who tried to erase it. An attitude that was completely unrealistic, not to mention insane.

Tapping her foot, Juliette looked up and down the street, then glanced at her watch again, blew another bubble. Shay stepped out onto the sidewalk and waved. He bit back a laugh as she caught sight of him and her bubble burst. He checked the traffic, then strolled across the street, never taking his eyes from hers.

"Hey there, Princess."

She scowled, removing the gum from her mouth with a self-conscious movement. She folded it neatly into its wrapper and slipped it into the pocket of her jacket. "I thought we agreed that I didn't like being called princess."

"No. I remember you said you didn't like it, but I don't remember agreeing to anything."

Her head bobbed emphatically as she nailed him with a look. "Well, I don't like it. It sounds pretentious."

"You can't run away from it. You are a princess."

She raised her brows, the simple haughty expression reinforcing her status. "Yes, I am, courtesy of a sexually irresponsible, long-ago ancestor whose bastard son married well enough to retain his title as a courtesy."

"That's good enough for me." Too good. How could a cop compete in such high-flying circles? He had to be nuts even to consider it. Shay tried to keep his thoughts from showing on his face, but must not have succeeded, for her eyes gentled along with her voice.

"I'm nothing special, you know, Shay. A title doesn't make me different from other people."

Shay reached out and fingered her hair for a moment, amazed at the silky texture, before replying. "Not true, Red. You'd be special if you were a garbage picker." He wanted to kiss her. He wanted to taste her pouting lips and lose himself in her body. He wanted to forget why he was here and what he needed to do.

Juliette caught her breath as she stared up at him. "You shouldn't say things like that."

"It's the truth."

"Truth is such a fragile thing."

"I know."

She shoved her hands in her pockets, seeming to look within. "For example, the things I've always believed in are no longer what I thought them to be. Isn't that sad?"

"Very." What was she talking about? His senses kicked into high alert and he shifted from would-be lover to cop before he was even aware of making the transition.

"It's the death of my innocence," she said with a small, sad smile.

Saying nothing, he stepped closer to her. For long moments they stared into each other's eyes, Shay looking for the truth,

Juliette looking for...what? Understanding, sympathy, help? He'd just opened his mouth to speak when she pulled her gaze away.

Smoothing her hands over her immaculate hair, she attempted to change the subject. "I sound like an idiot babbling on like this, don't I?"

"Listening to babbling is my favorite thing."

Juliette gave a tiny laugh and shook her head. "So what do you have in mind for your tour of New Orleans?"

"I don't want a tour. I only said that to get everyone off my back."

"Too bad. If we don't take a tour, I'll go back to work and you can explain yourself to Stephen. Then where will your business deal be?"

"I'm putty in your hands."

"That'll be the day," Juliette muttered.

"You have a better shot at handling me than most, sweetheart." Then he hunched his shoulders and looked away. *Jeesh, shut up, will ya? Do your job. This was an investigation, and somehow the woman was in it up to her delicious ears.*

"I'll keep that in mind." Juliette tried to change the subject. "Now, where should we—"

"Why do you think your fiancé was so eager to get me out of the way today?"

"Pardon?"

"Didn't you get that impression?" Shay had. So strongly that he'd told Lucille to arrange for a tail to follow St. James. He wanted to know every move the man made. Shay had had to do some fancy talking to arrange it, though, because Lucille still wasn't entirely convinced he was on the right track. At least she was starting to find enough inconsistencies and connections that she was eager to discover the truth, if for no other reason than to help Juliette. "I did."

Juliette thought for a moment. "Stephen loves New Orleans, and I suppose he wanted you to have some fun, especially if he's the one keeping you here."

Unable to stop himself, Shay touched her cheek. "He's not

the only one keeping me here." Ah hell, where had that come from? He couldn't afford to forget what she was mixed up in, and yet every time he saw her...

Juliette looked away for a moment before commenting, "Stephen can be very considerate that way."

Accepting her reluctance to follow a path that was dangerous to both of them, Shay rubbed his chin, saying sarcastically, "Oh, yeah, I've seen how considerate he can be. Didn't he forget to consider whether or not you wanted to announce your engagement, or even if there *was* one? Or so you said."

"It was the truth."

"You just said the truth was a fragile thing."

"Never mind what I said." Juliette glanced at her watch. "It's almost eleven-fifteen. We should get going."

"What time is your fiancé meeting us for lunch?"

"Will you stop calling him that?" she snapped.

Shay shrugged, watching her intently. "That's what he is. But if it bothers you..."

"Never mind. Call him whatever you want."

How about a criminal? Damn, Juliette, if I could only tell you what I suspect about your charming husband-to-be. Shay practically had to bite his lip to keep his thoughts from spilling out. With an effort he reminded her, "About lunch?"

"We'll meet later, probably around two. I hope you won't be too hungry."

"I'll survive." *But will you, sweet Juliette?* Hell, he looked at this woman and his mind turned to poetic mush.

"I thought we could take a streetcar and see some of the city that way."

"I'm familiar with the streetcar. It goes by not too far from my apartment." He sent her a small glance, trying to keep it light. "In case you've forgotten, that's in the Garden District."

Flushing scarlet, she looked down, clasping her hands together. "Oh yes, that's right. I...I suppose you could explore that area on your own, so maybe we should go the other direction. I'm sure you'll want to see more of the French Quarter."

"More than I saw the night we met?" The only thing he'd really seen that night was her.

Her white knuckles revealed how difficult she was finding the conversation but she kept going. "Then we can wander through some of the galleries and shops, see the cemetery, go to the riverfront. We could take the ferry across, or maybe you'd prefer the casino? Then we can—"

"We only have a day. One day," he emphasized. His gaze intense, he cupped her chin with his hand, tipping her face up to his.

She stared back at him for a long moment, open and revealing. "Then we'd better make the most of it, hadn't we?"

8

HE'D GIVE ANYTHING if he could have the power to stop time and pretend they were just casual tourists, new lovers enjoying the city and each other.

Even as the thought crossed his mind, Shay knew how ridiculous it was. He was here to work a case. However, since Juliette was sitting right smack in the middle of it, he was working his case whether anyone knew it or not, he told himself. The smart thing would be to use this day to pump Juliette Fortier for information, but everything decent in him rebelled at this necessary deception. How ironic that he, who had worked scores of undercover operations and gained the trust of dozens and dozens of people under suspicion, was now worried about deception. What was deception when lives could be at stake? And there *were* lives at stake in this situation—lives of people who had no one to watch out for them but the authorities. He had to keep remembering that.

He swallowed a sigh as he followed her trim, graceful body down the steps. Maybe he could combine the two tasks—enjoy his moments with this woman who'd somehow worked her way under his skin, and get more information at the same time.

Looking back over her shoulder, Juliette smiled. "Coming?"

Forcing a grin, Shay caught up with her as she walked to the street corner. Combine the two objectives? How dumb was that idea? There was no way he could serve two masters. He reached for her elbow, helping her onto the streetcar when the door opened. At the feel of her smooth skin beneath his fingers, he decided, despite his better judgment... *Maybe I can't, but I'm going to give it a try.*

They rode the streetcar, with Juliette playing the role of tour guide to perfection as she pointed out mansions and important houses, and provided little known facts about the places and historical landmarks they passed. For a while, Shay was able to relax—and pretend. He smiled, laughed, chatted, asking questions as if his life depended on it, more to see Juliette smile back than because he wanted to know about New Orleans.

"You love it here, don't you?"

Juliette nodded. "It's my home."

"Your father also lives in France, doesn't he? Isn't that home, too?"

"I have a great affection for our house and property there. Not the passion my father does, of course. His grandparents lived there, and we have family all over Europe, in addition to the United States, so it's very special to him. Plus, he's fervently committed to his vineyards. While I can appreciate that, for me it's not home. This—" she spread her arms wide "—this is home."

"So he can't tempt you to move to Europe?"

"I'm firmly rooted in American soil. My life is here, my work is here, my family and friends...almost everything I want is here."

"Almost everything?"

"Yes."

"What's missing?"

Juliette hesitated, then met his eyes, answering honestly, "Happily ever after, I suppose."

"True love, you mean?"

"Something like that."

"No prospects on the horizon...beyond your intended bridegroom, of course?" Ignoring her narrow-eyed glance at his comment, he held his breath, waiting for her answer—hoping, and fearing, she might really give him one.

"Finding the person you want to spend your life with is not

as easy as the books make it seem." She was silent for a moment, avoiding his gaze. They sat isolated in their thoughts, in the midst of the energetic sounds coming from the street, the clatter of the streetcar and the chatter of other passengers. Finally, Juliette said, "You build up an image in your imagination, and sometimes even convince yourself that it might be real. That it could be real if you wish hard enough. Then one day you bump into the real thing, and all your other ideas go out the window. Before you know it, everything is scrambled. It's all too complicated, and as a result, will probably come to nothing."

"And you've met this real thing?" *Come on, Red.* It was the man speaking, not the cop. *Let me inside.*

Eyes dark and disturbed, she glanced at him and just as quickly glanced away. "In other circumstances, perhaps."

What did he expect? That she'd come right out and say, "I love you, Shay"? And what would he do if she did? Say, "I love you back, now step aside while I throw your brother and his best friend in jail"? Why did he keep pushing her anyway? There wasn't any hope for him here. Even if she wasn't who she was, and he wasn't who he was, too many things stood in their way. Her deception, his deception, her family, his job... She was right. Right and realistic. In other circumstances, perhaps. "There are times when the planets are just plain out of alignment for some people, I think. At least that's what my sister would probably say," Shay murmured.

"You mentioned your sister last night."

"Yeah, but she's not married. I only said that because you looked so uncomfortable. Like something was going on between you and Stephen?"

Startled, she met his probing gaze and then looked away.

"Anything you want to get off your chest? I'm a good listener."

"I always wanted a sister. Is yours older or younger?"

Damn. "Younger. There are only the two of us, like you and Michael. I looked out for her, or at least I tried." Unlike Juliette, his sister was always sure about who she was and what she wanted to do. Which was one of the reasons she'd joined the police force straight out of college.

"You tried?"

He grinned. "Every time I tried to stand between my sister and some problem, she'd tell me to back off, she could handle it herself." Not Juliette's usual reaction to her brother, Shay was sure.

"And could she?"

"Most of the time. She's pretty independent." He laughed. "No, make that damn stubborn."

"She sounds like her brother. What does she do?"

Shay opened his mouth to tell her, then realized he couldn't say, "She's a cop, too," so promptly shut it again. Looking for inspiration, he smiled, feeling like a clown with a badly painted grin. "Uh, she's...resting at the moment." Which was true enough. Stress leave, they called it.

"Resting? You mean she's between jobs?"

"Yes. Between jobs." Time to change the subject before—

"What about your parents?"

Too late. "My parents?"

Juliette smiled. "You must have had parents, too."

"My father is a..." *cop* "...civil servant. Been working for the city all his life." Shay rushed on, anxious to avoid any probing. "My mother died in a car wreck when we were kids. Drunken driver."

"Oh, I'm so sorry."

"It was a long time ago."

"I'm sure that doesn't make it any less difficult. Losing a parent is hard."

"People get used to things. You did. Your parents divorced, but you seem to have it all together."

"Sure I do."

Shay chuckled. "Now that lacked sincerity."

"Really?" Juliette grinned back before fixing him with a curious look. "Do you know anyone who has it completely together?"

"Your fiancé—sorry, Stephen—seems to."

"Do you think so?"

"That's the impression he gives. Rich, smooth, classy..." *And as rotten as overripe fruit.*

"Yes, he does give that impression, doesn't he? So why do I keep—"

She stopped so abruptly that Shay turned sideways in his seat to look at her. "Keep?"

"Oh, wait, we have to get off here. We're entering the Vieux Carre." With an abrupt movement, Juliette stood up and moved to the front of the car, saying over her shoulder, "The French Quarter."

Damn, moment lost. Shay wanted to push, but was canny enough to know he had to back off. Never mind, he'd pick up the thread again. For now, it was important that Juliette relax. Relax and trust him. A small pain pierced his heart. *Trust me? You're a sleaze, O'Malley.*

He followed Juliette down the steps and off the streetcar into Jackson Square, which formed the heart of the French Quarter. He couldn't help admiring the way her tailored slacks fit her body, following the curves with just enough definition to whet his appetite, while still maintaining the impression of elegance. She glanced back at him, giving him a small smile, and his heart leaped before he acknowledged, *I'm going to hurt this woman, hurt her badly. How can I live with that?* The realization hit him with the impact of a Mack truck loaded with concrete.

For the first time in his life he wished he was in a profession that didn't involve digging under the surface for the truth, a process that generally uncovered more dirt than he wanted to deal with. Shay didn't relish putting himself in that position, not with this woman. He wondered if he'd become too cynical and jaded to believe that things were actually as they seemed, that Juliette really was as lost as a child in a dark scary forest of lies and deceit.

She stopped and began pointing in different directions like a traffic cop. "This is the heart of the French Quarter. The old settlers put everything they needed in one place—government buildings, shops, places to live and..." she hesitated, giving him an uncomfortable glance, obviously remembering their previous encounter at St. Louis Cathedral "...a place of worship."

He gave her a wry look. "I remember the place of worship."

She flushed and hurried on. "Of course, most of these government and residence buildings are museums now."

He returned to the subject like a starving dog gnawing on a bone. "I remember that church over there being the place where you told me you didn't want to see me again, and we've seen each other every day since." He had no reason to remind her, beyond the fact that she looked so lovely when she blushed and lost her customary self-possession. It wasn't that he'd been hurt when he'd realized she could throw him out of her life without a second thought. No, that wasn't it. As a cop it was his job to probe, to see what might slip out when the suspect wasn't thinking. And for better or worse, a cop's blood still raced through Shay's body, even though this woman heated it to fever pitch.

"And I still don't want to see you," she snapped.

He smiled, taking her elbow to steer her out of the way of other pedestrians. "Life's funny that way, isn't it? There you are, walking a straight path, and a big old foot kicks out and trips you. One day I'm seeing Stephen on a business matter, and the next thing you know, here we are."

Juliette stared at him, her eyes warring between revealing and concealing her innermost thoughts. "Yes, here we are. Should I see when the tours start? We have time, since the Mummery Parade doesn't begin until later."

"I told you before that I'm not here for a tour, or parades, either."

"Why *are* you here?" Her question was a bit breathless.

Buying time, he purchased a bag of popcorn from a vendor, then steered her to a seat on a nearby park bench. After pouring some popcorn into her hands, he said, "I already told you, Stephen didn't give me any choice." He regretted his answer as he saw her eyes fill with emotion, but forced himself back to the issue. "From what I've seen that's the way he generally operates."

Juliette was silent for a moment. "You could be right."

"Does he always do business like that?"

"I don't know how he does business."

"I thought his family and yours were partners."

"In certain enterprises, I think. But I'm not sure what."

"The shipping line."

She shrugged her shoulders. "Perhaps."

"You said you were a businesswoman, yet you don't know anything about the family business?"

Flushing, Juliette turned to face him. "The Fortiers are involved in a lot of businesses. It's what comes from having a large, well-connected family. Besides, my father and brother have always handled the transportation operations. It wasn't in my scope of interest."

"So you're just here to look decorative and spend the money, right?" Although he'd meant to say it in a joking manner, it didn't come out that way. Partly because of his frustration over a relationship he had no hope of continuing, partly because her ambiguity made him wonder if she knew nothing or knew everything and was very cleverly keeping him guessing.

"I just spend the money?" Her brows lifted. "Is that what you think of me?"

"Let's face it, Princess, you're very social, well connected—one expensive piece of work, inside and out, I'd say. That little outfit you're wearing today, for example, would cost most women a year's salary."

She gave him an aristocratic look that Shay was positive she didn't even realize she possessed. "You think so, do you?"

"Absolutely."

"Would you care to make a small wager on that?"

"A wager? You like to gamble?" He'd already found out about Michael's past problems, but now prayed Juliette didn't share her brother's vices. From what Shay had seen so far, he doubted it, but decided to check just the same.

"Why wouldn't I? Gambling is the sport of kings."

"I thought that was horse racing."

"That is, too. Big of us royals to let the masses in on those type of pleasures over the years, wasn't it?"

Shay lifted his hand, surrendering to her sarcasm. He'd asked for it. "Okay, I'm up for it. What kind of wager?"

"If I prove you're wrong about the cost of my outfit, you'll kneel at my feet and apologize."

"And if I win?"

"You won't win."

He grabbed her arm, preventing her from moving. "If I do?"

"You can have anything within my power to give. There. Royal enough for you?" She rose to her feet, throwing the popcorn in her hand onto the ground, scarcely noticing as a flock of pigeons waddled over. "Follow me."

Standing up, he lobbed the popcorn bag into a trash can. "Where are we going?"

"I'm going to show you a part of the Fortier family business that I *do* know something about."

Shay followed her as she marched to the intersection, turned right and started down the sidewalk. They walked for fifteen minutes, the neighborhood changing from well-kept and renovated to seedy. Shay kept his wits about him, amazed that Juliette could walk here so confidently, waving and smiling to people on the streets and in the doorways of the small shops. Without hesitation she turned to walk down an alley.

He grabbed her arm. "Wait a minute. Where the hell are you going? I don't like the looks of this place."

"Scared?"

"I don't know what you're trying to prove, but you don't belong here, Juliette."

"We'll see," Juliette said as she stopped in front of a run-down building, the first floor of which boasted a bright, newly painted door and clean windows. She pulled open the door, looking over her shoulder at Shay. "Are you coming?"

Shay considered pulling out his weapon before he let Juliette go any deeper into the interior of the building, but then he heard a man's voice.

"Ah, welcome, welcome, Princess Juliette."

Shay rushed to her side just as a small man grabbed her hand and bowed over it with shy grace.

"Julio, I've told you not to call me Princess. It's Juliette, or *señorita* if you prefer."

"Señorita Fortier."

"Señorita Juliette." Juliette smiled. "And this is my friend, Mr. Mallory, come to see your shop."

The man shifted his attention and before Shay knew it had grabbed his hand and was pumping it up and down. "Please come in." He backed up and reached behind him for another door, pushing it wide to reveal a large room full of long tables, a few sewing machines, chattering women and a few men. "Welcome to Freedom."

"Freedom?"

"It is the name of the business, Princess—I mean, Señorita Juliette—helped my family start. She is our angel."

"Not me personally," Juliette said, looking at Shay. "The Fortier Foundation was the angel."

Shay thought she might as well have saved her breath. The man in front of him, and everyone else in the room, was regarding Juliette as if she'd appeared wearing wings and a halo. "This is the part of the family business you know something about?"

"It's the Foundation's first venture into this type of activity, and it's working splendidly." She beamed at Julio, then indicated the shop. "Julio's people make such beautiful clothes that I'm doing what I can to get them into the marketplace."

"*Sí,* that is so, *señor.* We send some of our things to a big department store one of the *señorita*'s friends owns—"

"Not an expensive designer shop, but a *moderately* priced store, because the more affordable their merchandise, the faster they'll build their business. That department store is where," Juliette said, with an arch look at Shay as she indicated her pants and top, "I bought this custom-designed outfit for a total cost of $150. Now what do you say?"

"I should start kneeling?"

"Yes. Then you'd better pray I let you off the hook before you get sore knees."

Julio smiled and nodded as he watched them. "We are happy to give some to the benevolent fathers, too."

"For a lower income parish store, he means."

"Okay, okay, you've made your point."

"Ah, *señorita*," the man said, as a woman waving from a corner of the room caught his eyes. "Please, my daughter Consuelo has designed a new dress she wants to show you. You'll look at it?"

"Of course."

"Wait here, if you please." He bustled away.

"These people are immigrants." *Illegal ones?* Was this one way Stephen was hiding people? If so, did Juliette know? "This is a sweatshop?"

"It is not," she retorted, bristling. "And they aren't immigrants, either. Not anymore. Julio and his family—" she indicated everyone in the room "—have been taking English and citizenship classes practically since they arrived. They will officially become U.S. citizens in two weeks."

"How'd these people get to you? They didn't just fill out an application?"

"No, they had a sponsor."

"Stephen, or your brother?"

"No."

"Felipe, perhaps?"

Looking at Shay curiously, she shook her head. "I don't know anyone named Felipe. Their sponsors were a husband and wife."

"An American couple?"

"Why do you ask?"

"No reason, except I've been surprised to discover what a melting pot of nationalities New Orleans is."

"Well, you're right—this city is very diverse, as much because of location as the cosmopolitan atmosphere, I'd say. My French cousins love to come and visit. But this couple was from Colombia originally, I believe."

"How'd you meet them?"

"I'm not sure. I think Stephen might have introduced them to me at a party, but I don't remember. The important thing was they were interested in donating a large sum of money to our foundation, for use as a special fund for immigrants who've come to America to make a new life for themselves." She looked out at the group of people working industriously and smiled, before glancing back at Shay. "We were lucky to find Señor and Señora Hilmaga de la Salavardas. They've even arranged to sponsor another family."

"Recently?"

She nodded. "As a matter of fact, they were part of the business dinner party that I walked out on the night we met."

"No kidding."

Smiling, she shook her head. "My brother had invited them to meet some other associates, after I'd introduced them a few days before at the foundation offices."

Shay whistled. "And they still gave you money?"

"Why wouldn't they? Our foundation is perfect for their needs."

"I'm sure it is." Shay had a sinking feeling that she didn't know how perfect it might be. Unless he missed his guess, what Juliette was saying indicated Stephen was using the Fortier Foundation so business associates could donate big sums of illegal money in order to eventually launder it. Which was one more big reason for St. James to tie the Fortiers to him by marriage. As Shay looked at Julio and his family, he wondered how many other so-called legitimate, and not so legitimate, businesses were harboring illegal immigrants supplied by the St. James organization.

"The Hilmagas haven't given us their next check yet, but

they will." She chuckled. "I was very polite when I excused myself from the party. I'm always polite. The only time I'm rude is when I'm with you."

"So I bring out the worst?"

"Let's say when I'm with you I react in ways I never have before." Her diplomatic expression was belied by the sudden mischief in her eyes.

"Good."

Their conversation stopped as they were surrounded by Julio's family and given an impromptu fashion show. Then, after a few moments more chitchat with Julio, Consuelo and the rest of the family, Juliette and Shay took their leave.

"Be blessed and enjoy the day, young lovers," Julio called as they reached the door.

Startled, Juliette whirled around. "Julio, you have the wrong idea. We aren't lovers."

Julio looked wise as he agreed. "Ah, no."

"We aren't," Juliette insisted. "We aren't even friends."

"Would you agree, *señor*? I've seen the way you look at her. The way she looks at you."

Shay almost swallowed his tongue before he came up with a response. "Are lovers ever friends?"

Chuckling, Julio reached out and squeezed his plump little wife, who giggled. "Love is all and everything. You'll see."

Juliette avoided Shay's gaze as she muttered goodbye, yanked open the door and charged through. Shay caught up with her in the alley. "Hey there, hold on."

"I can't believe Julio thought that we were lovers."

Shay chuckled. "My admiration for Julio's skill grows every minute."

"I'll have to set him straight the next time I see him."

"Good luck."

"What do you mean by that?" she demanded.

"Our relationship doesn't lend itself to an easy explanation."

"We don't have a relationship."

He pulled her to a stop and turned her to face him. "No,

Red, we don't want to have a relationship. But that doesn't seem to be stopping us."

"I know."

"The big question is, what are we going to do about it?"

Eyes huge, Juliette stared up at him. "I...tried to tell Stephen I didn't want to marry him last night."

"Is that what I interrupted?"

"Part of it."

"What was the other part?" She was silent for so long that he pressed, "Juliette, what else was going on?" All thoughts of love were swept aside as he focused on his job.

"I'm not sure. I didn't understand it."

"Tell me, maybe I can help." Could she have overheard something, something he'd missed last night?

"No. I can't. I have to think about it. I might have been mistaken."

Shay knew he would get nothing more from her at the moment, so he didn't try. Instead he came at the subject from a different angle. "Thanks for taking me to see Julio and his family. I liked them."

"Were you surprised?" Juliette asked, as they emerged onto the street.

"By seeing what you've done there? Or by your compassion?"

Juliette bit her lip. "Both, damn you."

He stopped and cupped her chin in his hand. "Yes to the first and no to the last. I didn't think you were only around to look good, although it'd be easier for me if that was the truth. I guess all along I was hoping there was more to you than that."

Her lips twisted. "How big of you to admit it."

"That comment came out wrong. You throw me off balance, Juliette. You always do."

"You do the same to me." She said it slowly, reluctantly.

As they walked back toward the French Quarter, Shay said, "I have to admit, Julio's shop wasn't what I was expecting to see when I got into that area."

"What were you expecting? A crack house? Or something worse?"

How like her to hit the nail smack on the head, Shay thought. He chuckled. "The neighborhood was right for it."

"There was only so much they could afford, even with our help. The Mendozas are committed to working to make the neighborhood better." She laughed. "You watch, in a couple of years that block will be prime real estate. A smart man would start investing now."

"Spoken like a true businesswoman."

Juliette smiled, acknowledging his subtle apology. "Thank you."

"You're welcome." Shay tucked a flyaway wisp of hair behind her ear. It felt like warm silk. "I guess I figured your foundation would mostly deal with high-toned cultural things, like historic renovation or esoteric art or..."

"I hate to spoil your most recent image, but we do that, too. As a matter of fact, we have a new artist showing her work tomorrow night. Would you like to come?"

"See each other again, you mean?"

"Only in the interest of education. You have a bad habit of labelling people. I think you should open yourself up more."

Shay wanted to deny it, but he couldn't. It was the truth. Cops often thought in basic stereotypes. It was faster that way, and when you were on the street, every moment counted. Shay didn't consider himself biased. The simple fact was a cop needed every edge he could get today if he wanted to stay alive.

He stepped closer. "Do you want me to come?"

Before she could answer him, a cell phone rang. Automatically they both checked to see whose it was. Juliette clicked on her phone, smiling to excuse herself before turning away to speak. Shay tried to overhear without being obvious.

"Hello? What? Oh, all right. Yes, yes I will." She ended the call, putting the phone back into her shoulder bag. "Stephen won't be able to make it today, after all. Something's come up. So I guess that just leaves you and me."

"Nothing wrong, I hope?"

"No. He said it was business, regrettable but—I didn't get all of it, my phone was cutting in and out. Maybe something about a time change..." She shrugged.

A time change? Shay looked around, trying to figure out how he could get away to make a quick call to Lucille. He saw a sidewalk café. "Whaddya say we get a cool drink while we decide what we're going to do next?"

At her agreement, he steered her to a table and excused himself for a moment. Dashing back toward the rest room, he pulled out his phone and rang his partner, telling her about the call from St. James and suggesting she keep her eyes open. He promised to check in later, then he strolled back to Juliette and sat down opposite her. Sipping his drink, he admired the way the sunlight touched her hair, the warmth of her smile and the way her eyes glowed as she watched the people go by. He wished they could be what they had seemed to Julio— a couple falling deeply in love.

He toyed with her fingers. "Juliette, back there, with Julio's family, you seemed...different."

"Different how?"

"I don't know, less remote maybe. More approachable."

"I don't like to think of myself as remote. I haven't been with you." Blushing, she looked away, gathering her wits for a moment before saying in a soft voice, "The fact is, I'm shy."

"How can someone who looks like you and possesses everything most people want be shy?"

"It doesn't have anything to do with what you look like, or what you have. It has to do with who you think you are."

That explained the vulnerability he'd recognized when he first saw her in the park. "You know who you are."

"Do I?"

"You're a princess."

"In an age where that doesn't mean much."

"Still, you're a legitimate blue blood." He grinned. "With better credentials than most show dogs."

She laughed. "Ah, now that is something to remember when my spirit's low."

He took another sip of his drink. "So who do you want to be?"

"It's who do I want to become that I'm concerned about." She took a deep breath. "I've been privileged all my life, as far as having material things. That's why I was so excited when I got the idea for establishing this foundation, about creating an opportunity to do something valuable for society. It was a chance to give back to those who didn't have my advantages."

Shay smiled. "Maybe you're the one who should be going into politics instead of your brother."

She sent him a curious look. "How did you know about my brother? He hasn't announced his candidacy yet. He's still deciding."

"I think I heard about it at the ball. Or maybe your fiancé mentioned it."

"It would be a good thing for Michael."

"I thought the objective was to be good for other people, not for the politician."

A blush rushed up her neck and spread over her cheeks. "Of course it is. That's what I meant."

Shay stared at her for a moment, thinking, *I could love this woman.* He would give anything he possessed to be able to stand in front of her and say, "I love you." Which made his current position so untenable. "That's why I think you might make a bigger impact."

"It's not what I want to do. I want to run my foundation, then someday marry and raise children. Children I can bring up with love and respect. Who will know both of their parents are committed to them. That's how I want to make an impact."

His longing increased until he was amazed he didn't throw her over his shoulder, look for a white horse and ride off with her into the sunset. Unable to say what he was thinking, he summoned a smile instead. "That's probably the best way I can think of to make a difference in this world, Red." As he stared into her eyes, he wanted to level with her, tell her who he was and why he was here.

When his phone rang, it startled the hell out of him. Automatically, he reached into his pocket, fumbled around for a second before he found the phone and flipped it open. Turning slightly away, he muttered, "Yeah? When? Okay, give me directions and I'll see you there." He hung up, then looked over at Juliette. "Sorry, I have to go."

"Go where?"

"It's business. You know how that is."

"I thought you told me I know nothing about business."

"I changed my mind, remember? Besides, I'm beginning to think the one who knows nothing is me." He stood up, threw some money on the table and asked, "Can you get home from here without any problem?"

"Of course I can. I'm a big girl."

He hesitated, then blurted, "Juliette, today was the most..." He came to his senses before he said anything else.

She waited for him to continue. When he didn't, she prompted, "The most what?"

"The most I've seen of New Orleans since I got here."

Her face fell but she recovered to say in a light tone, "I thought you didn't care about seeing the city."

"Now that I've seen it with you, I care. Believe me, I care. I can't tell you how much." He leaned over and with one finger tilted her chin up to drop a gentle kiss onto her lips.

"Goodbye, Princess," he said, resisting the urge to linger. With that he turned on his heel and left, intending to arrest her fiancé, and possibly her brother.

Dusk was dropping its veil of darkness over the bayou as Shay looked his partner straight in the eye and let loose. "What the hell is going on, Lucille? Where are they? I come racing out here and—nothing!"

Lucille shrugged, obviously used to male cops venting

their emotions. "It seems we've been sent on a wild-goose chase."

"You said you got a tip from a good source. You said that shipment we've been chasing would be delivered tonight. Right here. Tonight."

She propped her fists on her hips and yelled right back at him. "Well, hell's bells, Detective, I guess my 'good source' got it wrong. So sue me!"

"Son of a— He's playing with us. St. James is just toying with us, playing cat-and-mouse games, getting the word out on the street, then jerking us around. First he invites me to dinner to look me over, gives me half promises, then sets me up to spend the day with his fiancée to get me out of the way. Then he—"

Lucille grabbed his arm, jerking him around. "Slow down there, Yankee. His fiancée? You've just spent the day with Juliette Fortier? Is that where you've been?"

Shay stopped his ranting and stared down into his partner's disapproving gaze. "Uh, yeah."

"Doing what?"

"What do you think I've been doing?"

Her eyes narrowed. "I don't know, but I hope it was your job."

He could feel his ears turn red at her pointed tone. "Why would it be anything else?"

"I don't know. All I know is, you show up down here and turn everything topsy-turvy. And now I hear you could be involved with a suspect? A suspect who's my friend, I might add." She folded her arms, staring at him like a judge passing sentence. "*Now* who's too close to the situation?"

"I'm not involved. I didn't say I was involved." He prayed her woman's intuition wasn't working, or she'd see right through him. He didn't want to lie to her, but he didn't see any reason to tell her the truth, either. For Juliette's sake if not for his own.

"You aren't, eh?"

"I told you, St. James wanted me out of the way, so he arranged for me to meet Juliette. He said he'd join us, but he didn't show. That's it. End of story."

"Hmm...okay, but there's something I can't put my finger on here." Lucille was still regarding him suspiciously. "Juliette was very interested in you at the ball. If it had been anyone else I might think..."

"Think what?" He had to work to keep his feet on the ground after her comment. Juliette had asked about him. Ridiculous to feel pleased, but he was.

"I'd think there was something more here than a cop trying to shut down Stephen St. James's bad-ass smuggling operation."

Shay leaped at the chance to change the subject. "So now you agree St. James is a possible culprit. The circumstantial evidence is convincing you? Come on, Lucille, you can admit it. I won't rub your face in it."

"All right, I agree with you, and then some." Lucille glared at him, her expression fierce as she spat out the words. "Even worse, when we nail him he's going to tangle up in his scandal a family I love and respect. And we will nail him. If I have to personally arrest him at the altar while I'm wearing a bridesmaid dress, we will get the bastard."

Shay grinned. "I almost hope it works out that way just so I can see you hike up your petticoats and grab your gun."

Lucille grinned back before sobering. "God knows what it will do to Juliette."

"I think Juliette Fortier is a lot stronger than anyone gives her credit for being."

"I hope so, Shay. She's going to need to be. Because somehow Michael is mixed up in this, too. I just know he is."

"We don't have hard facts yet, but my gut tells me he is, just like yours does."

Lucille shook her head. "Juliette has always put her family first. I don't think she can do that this time. It's not a question of the Fortier family throwing their money and influence around to hush up a scandal, as they've done before. This time someone is going to pay a big price."

"You're on target there, Luce." *I'm the one who'll do the paying.* It's what always happened when an ordinary mortal man got mixed up with a goddess.

Shay pulled his gaze from his partner's, looking out to the west as the setting sun spilled its last rays over the water. The sooner he could wrap up this case, the better it would be for all of them. "Come on, let's get out of here. I'll clue you in on what I found out today."

"Right. I've got some information for you, too."

He sent another long look at the water. "I'll tell you what, though—from this point on either you or I are going to stick to St. James like glue. The minute we think he's making a move, no matter what it is, no matter what time, we'll track each other down. Got it?"

Lucille nodded. "You got it, partner."

THE NEXT EVENING at the artist's exhibition her foundation was sponsoring, Juliette found herself watching for Shay Mallory. After the way he'd left her the day before she didn't really expect him to come, but she kept hoping anyway. His goodbye had sounded so final that she wondered if she'd ever see him again. She glanced around the glittering crowd—this was the milieu he obviously expected her to prefer. She prayed for an opportunity to set him straight.

She'd done a lot of thinking about him last night and had come to several conclusions. Shay brought her to life. He teased her, provoked her, made her mad as fire, then turned around and stunned her with his sweetness. He was out of the ordinary; he brought her out of the ordinary. With him, she felt she could be more than she'd ever imagined. But first she had to settle things with Stephen, then with her brother.

She looked around at the crowd again and was stunned to see Stephen coming toward her with Shay in tow.

"Juliette, darling, look who I found."

She recovered in time to extend her hand graciously, but then Shay stunned her by bending over and kissing her fingers. She pulled back, hoping Stephen hadn't noticed. "I see you decided to come." At a curious glance from Stephen, she said, "I mentioned this event yesterday."

Stephen nodded, sending Shay a small smile. "I didn't know you were an art lover, Shay. Somehow it doesn't seem like your thing."

Juliette was surprised at the slight sneer in Stephen's voice, not that she should have been. He'd often demonstrated a superiority she found insulting, now that she thought about it. She supposed she was used to him and hadn't paid much attention until now. Until he'd directed it against Shay.

"I like art, Stephen, but I'm picky about what kind. Which is probably why your fiancée invited me to come. I said something a bit insulting yesterday and she decided to put me in my place."

Stephen traced a lazy finger down Juliette's cheek. "Juliette would never be so rude. She's known for being polite in all situations. She'd probably thank the hangman for tying a perfect knot."

"That doesn't seem polite to me." Shay grinned. "That sounds practical."

Stephen laughed. "Good point."

"Yes, it is," Juliette agreed. She hated it when people talked about her as if she were invisible.

"Shay." Stephen clasped his shoulder in a friendly gesture. "I wonder if you could do me a favor?"

"Sure. Name it."

"I have to leave." He glanced at Juliette. "Sorry, darling, I was looking forward to spending the evening with you, but I have to rescue my mother."

Surprised, Juliette looked at Stephen as Shay said, "Nothing wrong, I hope?"

"No, not really." Stephen smiled. "It seems her gentleman friend has bowed out at the last minute and I must escort her to an old friend's Mardi Gras party this evening. Would you make sure Juliette gets home safely?"

"Really, Stephen, it's not necessary to foist me off on Shay."

"Darling, I couldn't possibly leave you alone. You look far

too beautiful in that little evening suit. Don't you agree, Shay?"

"Absolutely."

"If you wouldn't mind seeing her home, I'd appreciate it."

"No big deal. Happy to do it."

"So kind." Stephen leaned over and kissed Juliette's cheek. "I'll call you tomorrow, darling. Good luck with the exhibit. Everyone seems very impressed."

"Thank you, Stephen. My best to your mother."

Juliette watched as he left, uncertain what to do next.

"Damn," she thought she heard Shay say under his breath.

"Is something wrong?"

"Excuse me. I have to make a phone call."

"Shay, this is ridiculous. There's no need to stay with me."

"No, no, I want to stay, I just have to rearrange a few things, that's all. I'll be right back."

Wondering at his suddenly tense demeanor, Juliette watched him head toward the entrance. Her attention was distracted by one of the guests, and for the next fifteen minutes she played her social role, smiling and chatting, introducing potential patrons to Erika Lee, the painter and performance artist the foundation was sponsoring. All the while, she stayed alert for Shay's return. She was standing alone in front of one of Erika's most striking pieces when she sensed him. He came up behind her. It was amazing how attuned she'd become to this man in such a short space of time.

"What do you think of the art?" Juliette asked, turning to smile at Shay over her shoulder.

Shay snorted.

"Was that a professional opinion or merely a snort?"

"That was my professional opinion."

"You don't favor avant-garde artists?"

"Not on my walls. I like things that put me in a mellow frame of mind, not something that makes me want to lose my lunch when I look at it."

Juliette smiled as she pointed to the painting in question.

"You're right, I wouldn't call this mellow. She's portraying violence, the violence inherent in today's society."

"That's not what violence looks like." His eyes clouded. "Violence is the face of a little kid whose crack-head mother just shot her boyfriend. It's a twist of metal, crumbling bricks, black despair, red pain, suffocating grayness, not a jarring swirl of color. It's innocents caught up in something they can't control. It's—"

Shocked, Juliette placed her fingers over his mouth. "Shay. Shay, what are you talking about?"

He rubbed his forehead. "Hell. I'm sorry, I don't know what came over me."

Juliette took his hand. "Would you like to take a walk?"

"Don't you have to stay?"

"My assistant is here this evening. She can do the honors, and we can leave. Unless you want to stay for the performance-art presentation."

"Performance art?"

"Erika Lee is going to roll around in paint and then, by applying her body to canvas, create a living, breathing testament to the reality of women in today's world."

"Wouldn't she be better off just living it?"

Juliette chuckled. "Now that I hear myself say it aloud it does sound absurd."

"You said that, I didn't."

"You're right, I did. Although I must say Erika is a young, vibrant, multitalented up-and-coming artist."

"Uh-huh."

Juliette peeked at Shay, surprised to see he was keeping a straight face, which made her want to smile at his superb control. She yearned to touch her lips to his to see if she could break his concentration. Tempting, very tempting.

"Now, if we were talking about a woman rolling around in paint while some great jazz was playing, that might be another story."

"Great jazz?" Juliette slipped her hand into his. "Let's get out of here. I think I can safely leave now without offending anyone, and I know a place you'll like better."

9

THE AIR WAS GETTING COOL and the night shadows were deepening as Shay wound his way up Bourbon Street with Juliette in search of the hottest jazz in the city. In the midst of the Mardi Gras crowds they clung together, trying not to get separated. Shay pulled Juliette under his arm, clamping her to his side, leaning down to press his lips against her ear.

"Where's this club you mentioned?"

Juliette turned her face up to him, a sudden bump from a person behind her practically putting her lips against his chin. "Right up the street."

Shay looked at her, taking in the lovely face with its soft, luscious lips and bewitching eyes. With an automatic gesture, he slipped his other arm around her, folding her closer. "Right up the street," he repeated, smoothing his hand over her back.

"Yes..." Her voice was breathless. "Half a block."

"It's pretty crowded tonight. Are you sure it's worth it?"

She smiled. "Only if you like hot, smoky jazz that sets every nerve in your body on fire."

The thought of her and hot music set his mind whirling into realms best not explored. Holding her like this, he didn't need any help to fire up his nerves. "Sounds promising."

"Wait till you hear it. Jazz isn't jazz until you hear it in New Orleans."

He leaned a bit closer, wanting nothing more than to kiss her senseless, here in the middle of this crowd, many of whom were doing the same thing. Lucille had told him that sin and Mardi Gras went together like red beans and rice. From the way his pulse was drumming in his ears, he believed it. Instead of kissing her, his lips stopped an inch from hers, whispering instead. "I can't wait." By Juliette's shiver she'd obviously realized he wasn't talking about the music, but she pretended to misunderstand.

"Then we'd better go before it's so crowded we can't get in the door."

Reluctantly, he released her so they could squeeze their way up the street to their destination. The owner of the club recognized Juliette and moved everyone aside to usher them in and seat them at an intimate table not far from the stage, even delivering their drinks personally.

Shay pulled out his wallet, only to have his money waved away. He glanced at Juliette. "My, my, how nice to be with a person of influence."

"I did a little favor for Tony's family awhile ago. He likes to pay his debts."

Shay tensed. "What kind of favor?"

"It was a personal thing. I helped his daughter when she got into a bit of trouble, that's all."

Shay stared across the table at Juliette. She looked uncomfortable, as if she wished he'd change the subject. He met her eyes, eyes that could be cool, guarded and haughty, but which were always clear and honest. Against his better judgment, against all of his training, he decided she couldn't be involved with what was going on here. How could he get her out of it without any of the dirt sticking to her when it went down? It was a question for which he had no answer. Instead, he reached over and took her hand, folding it in his palm, brushing his thumb over her knuckles.

"Ah, Juliette," he murmured, feeling helpless as the torrid sounds of a sax filled the air, further igniting the flames already flickering in his blood, "what in holy hell am I going to do with you? Tell me, what?"

She was silent for a moment. So silent that Shay thought she hadn't heard him. Then she whispered, "What do you want to do with me?"

He looked up, knowing both desire and frustration were apparent in his gaze. "Everything I can think of."

She licked her lips. "Such as?"

The shudder that rolled through him was so intense it almost knocked him off his seat. He cleared his throat, trying to talk though his mouth was dry with desire. "Juliette..." His voice sounded raspy to his ears. "You're playing with dynamite here."

"I know," Juliette sighed. "The only problem is, I can't help myself."

"I know." Desperate, Shay reached for his drink and chugged it, feeling the whiskey burn all the way down his throat, adding to the fire already raging.

"I've been telling and telling myself that this is wrong, that you're wrong," she murmured, "but I still can't... I don't understand myself when I'm with you. Nothing makes any sense, only this—this feeling between us."

He pressed his hand against her mouth, his thumb parting her lips to caress the smooth inside. "Red, I swear, one more word and I'll take you on the table right here and now, and anybody who's watching be damned."

She looked back at him, her eyes wide and almost navy with desire. "I wouldn't care."

Shay forced a laugh. "Good. 'Cause you're this far—" he spread his thumb and index finger an inch apart "—from it happening." If she knew how much effort he was exerting to keep himself under control, she'd have had to give him a medal. He grabbed a waiter and ordered two more drinks. "Let's just..." He couldn't finish the sentence, so tempted was he to say, "...get out of here." He let go of her hand, leaned back in his chair and focused on the entertainment, trying to cool his engine. He was aware of her trying to do the same.

About a half hour passed while he tried to pretend that the feelings of desire weren't still raging. He tried to concentrate on business, excusing himself to call Lucille, and finding out that Stephen St. James was with his mother, safely in sight of the police at a party, instead of knee-deep in criminal activity on the waterfront. Given that news, Shay tried to relax and enjoy himself. And he succeeded far too well.

The music, the atmosphere and his uncontrollable response to the woman by his side seduced him totally. He met her gaze and that was that. He stood up, tossed some bills on the table and grabbed her hand, practically jerking her to her feet.

"Come on, let's get out of here."

"Where are we going?"

"Anywhere. Anywhere I can cool off. Maybe even get a cup of coffee so I can think straight."

"Coffee would be good. The drinks were pretty strong."

She was grasping at straws and he knew it. He couldn't help but grin, and had a feeling he was coming across like the Big Bad Wolf poised to nibble on Red Riding Hood. "I wish it was the drinks, Red. It'd be the answer to my prayers."

"I know," she whispered. "What are we going to do?"

He hesitated, staring at her for a long moment, knowing his heart was in his eyes and not knowing any way to shut off his emotions. He was head over heels in love with this woman. He wasn't looking for it, but it had happened, anyway. He had to tell her the truth. "I know a place we can get good coffee and talk about it."

"Where?"

He shook his head. *For God's sake, think. Think what you're doing.*

She put her hand on his arm, stepping closer to him. "Shay?"

He stared down at her, feeling about ready to snap like a taut string. "Ah, the hell with it." He pulled her along behind him and sailed up the street, deftly avoiding the people spilling out of clubs. Two streets over, he found a cruising taxi and stuck out his hand. He'd scarcely lunged into the car and given his address when he turned to take Juliette in his arms.

Before he knew it, he had her in his apartment. They'd scarcely broken contact for a moment. "This isn't right," he muttered, even as he caressed her.

"I know," she said, her hands as busy as his. "I'm afraid,

Shay, afraid of this feeling, of what's going to happen, but I don't care anymore. Do you?"

"I should, but I don't. The only thing I care about is you. I won't let anything hurt you, I promise."

They careened up the hallway, frantically shedding jackets and shoes, attacking buttons, until they reached the living room. Shay pulled the pillows off the sofa and threw them onto the rug, pulling her down beside him.

"Touch me," she said, as she came to him, tearing off her jacket and unbuttoning her silk blouse. "No one has ever touched me like you do."

He stroked his hand down her throat, his fingers sliding into the valley of her breasts. "I want to touch you so bad, I'm afraid I'll break you."

"You can't break me." She slipped his hand into her bra, tensing as his fingers closed over her nipple. "Oh, Shay..."

"Does that feel good?" he whispered.

Her tiny chuckle was practically a sob. "Oh, yes."

He smiled and unhooked her bra, cupping her other breast, his fingers stroking the crest. "How about this?"

"You have no idea."

He licked her, reveling in the taste of her skin, smelling the ripe scent of her desire. "And this?"

She arched, presenting her breasts to him. "More. I want more."

He obliged, feasting on her until finally his tongue traced a path down to the waistband of her slacks. He let his gaze move over her with lazy satisfaction. Her breasts were high and taut, the peaks full and pouting as they begged again for the pull of his mouth. He couldn't resist. Just one more time and then it was on to other delights. He slid her zipper down, working her silk evening slacks off her legs until finally she lay there with only a strip of lace covering her innermost secrets, secrets she wanted to share with him. He unwrapped her then, like a kid with a huge chocolate truffle, throwing her covering aside while he worked to get at the soft luscious center waiting for him within.

He tasted her, the hot honey of her melting onto his lips, the tip of his tongue flicking forward to find the sweetness inside. Greedily he parted her, until finally he had no choice but to feast as she responded to his intimate caress. She wrapped her legs around him, her body arching up to him until she seemed ready to break in two. The need was there and so was the tenderness. He'd never felt this way with another woman, doubted he ever would. For him, there was only the moment. This moment, only this, when he could play Juliette's body like a finely tuned instrument until it sang with the sweetest sounds he'd ever heard.

But sweetness wasn't all he wanted. He wanted heat, too. As Juliette's hands tore at his trousers, he realized she wanted the same. After she'd helped rip away his briefs, then had held him, hard, heavy and throbbing, in her hands, he gave her what they both wanted. With the triumph of a conquering leader, he took her—fast and hard and urgently. Together they climbed, only to pause at the summit before climbing again, peaking where the air grew thin and the emotions hot, erupting with all the power nature could give a mere man and woman.

Afterward, he dropped his forehead onto hers, waiting until his heartbeat slowed beyond alarm status before he tried to speak. Finally, he muttered, "Juliette?"

"Shh, don't move. Don't say anything. Just be with me."

He shut his mouth. *Just be with me.* He wanted that more than anything else in the world, but he knew how fragile their moment was. He needed to tell her everything, praying she wouldn't draw away in disgust. But he wasn't sure how to start.

"Juliette, I need—"

Her fingers stilled his lips. "I need, too. I need to pretend this is forever."

"Forever? That's what you want?"

She smiled. "It makes no sense, does it? We don't even know each other. I'm involved in a situation that could get sticky, but still...there it is."

He met her gaze, wincing at the open tenderness in her eyes. Nothing could make a man feel like a slug faster than a trusting woman. "Look, there's something I have to tell you." *Don't let her hate me.*

She smiled again, moving against him, pulling his face down to hers. "Tell me later. Let's enjoy the now."

"But—"

"But you don't find this enjoyable?" she teased.

"Did your brain cells die? Of course I do." Shay wasn't sure what part of his body was more desperate, his intellect or his libido, which was fast arising to assert its dominance. "Look, we have to—"

"Oh, I agree. We do have to." Juliette ended the argument by pushing him onto his back and throwing a leg over him. Kneeling, she raised her arms up to embrace the sky like a pagan goddess, then arched forward wantonly, rocking against his hips.

"I've been dreaming about this," she said, as he filled her. He was so big, so hard—so hot. Her muscles clenched in response as he thrust upward. Almost helpless before his fierce, sudden desire, she looked down at him, taking in his strong features, now etched in passion. *Shay.* It had happened too fast, and too unexpectedly, but that didn't matter. It had happened.

She was definitely, totally, completely in love with this man, with this stranger who'd stormed into her life and now filled all of the empty spaces. She would never marry Stephen. She refused to pretend anymore, not for her brother's sake and not for her family's. Surely Michael wasn't in so much trouble that their father couldn't get him out of it, as he usually did.

Shay grasped her hips with his big hands and pulled her closer. She forgot about Michael, forgot about Stephen, forgot everything but Shay. Shay and the need to move harder, faster...focusing only on her own needs.

I want this man. And by God, I'm going to have him!

JULIETTE OPENED HER EYES to see the hard shadows cast by the light in the entrance hall as it bounced against shapes in the living room. The harsh shadows made the space seem primitive, as if she was the first woman on earth and had just been discovered by the first man. Her skin glistened, exuding sweat and the tangy scent of sex. She stretched out against him, all seventy-four carved inches of him, and sighed. "I could get used to this."

She was rewarded by Shay's chuckle. "You could, huh?"

Tracing a finger down his damp chest, she followed it with her tongue, tasting the salt and heat that blanketed his body. "I think so. How about you?"

"Oh yeah."

Juliette chuckled at his heartfelt reply. "You sound pretty enthusiastic. What happened to the reluctance you were showing a few minutes ago?"

"You did one hell of a job convincing me, Red."

Juliette gave him a smug smile. "We aim to please."

"And you do, Princess, you really do."

His use of her title reminded Juliette of the gulf between them, or the supposed gulf. His background might not be what her father and brother had in mind for the only Fortier daughter, but that was all right. Eventually she'd bring them around. All that really mattered was the feelings they had for each other. She'd have to speak with Michael immediately, she decided. She wasn't going to let Shay Mallory run around loose, not when there were so many man-hungry women out there. She'd make sure he was good and committed before she let him run tame around her friends. For a moment she disappeared into a little daydream of her own making—she and Shay sitting in their own home, laughing and loving, while children shouted and played in the yard. Her dream possessed a normalcy she'd never experienced, one she was eager to embrace.

Shay stroked his finger over her brow. "What are you thinking about?"

"Hmm?"

"You're smiling. I just wondered why you're smiling."

Juliette let her smile expand until she was positive it could have lit the entire city. "I was thinking about you."

"Good thoughts?"

She remembered him asking the same thing at dinner a few nights before, but this time she could answer him with her heart. Her smile deepened and she stretched like a cat enjoying the sunshine. "Very good thoughts."

Shay watched her silently for a moment. "Juliette, we have to talk."

"Yes, we do."

"There's so much to say, I don't know where to begin, but I have to tell you the truth. I came to New Orleans because—" Whatever else he was going to say was lost as a loud thumping on the door interrupted him.

Juliette jumped at the noise, and Shay levered himself off the floor. "What the hell?"

"Shay?" a woman yelled, knocking and pressing the buzzer. "Shay, are you in there?" The doorknob jiggled. "Shay, I'm coming in."

Shay reached for a throw rug, wrapping it around him like a sarong as he strode to the hallway. "Knock it off, will ya, Lucille?"

Lucille? That did sound like Lucille. Juliette's thoughts scattered as she tried to understand why her friend was at Shay's door. She began looking for her clothing but only managed to slip into her jacket and grab a few sofa pillows before Lucille burst through the door, still holding the credit card she'd used to jimmy the lock. She landed in the hallway like a rocket, her customary drawl faster than usual. "Shay, you told me to find you, no matter what, the minute I knew it was going down."

"Damn. We'd better—" He reached for the doorknob.

Lucille yanked him back. "Wait a minute, O'Malley, put your pants on first. And get your badge and gun."

"O'Malley?" Juliette rose to her feet, clutching the pillows in strategic places. "I thought your name was Mallory. Shay Mallory."

Lucille's head snapped around and she automatically reached for her weapon, then stepped out of the light to peer into the living room. "Juliette?! Oh, sh—" She slid Shay a withering glance, holstering her gun. "So there's nothing going on between you, is there? Isn't that what you said? God-damn it, why couldn't you stick to romancin' little ole Northern girls? Why did you have to pick on Juliette?"

Shay glared. "Shut up, Lucille, you don't understand."

"You're right." Lucille sent them each a hard glance, then began backing toward the door. "Look, I'm a third wheel here, so I'll just wait for you down—"

"It's not what you think."

Wearily, Lucille rolled her eyes. "It never is, Shay. That's the bitch of it."

Still disoriented by the sudden appearance of her child-hood friend, Juliette stepped forward, knowing her total confusion must be evident on her face as she stared at the two of them standing by the door. "What did you mean, 'get your badge and gun'?" She knew about the gun, but where did the badge come in? She held her breath, knowing the answer was one she wouldn't like.

With a studied shrug, Lucille looked to Shay. "Uh-oh, over to you. I'll just—"

"Oh no, you don't, Ace. Y'all got yourself into this." The sarcasm practically dripped as Shay grabbed her by the elbow to keep her from leaving. "Y'all can get yourself out."

"Me? It looks like you're the one standing knee-deep in horse manure, Yankee."

"You don't know the half of it," he muttered.

"I do know that if the half of it is any less dressed than the two of you, I'd arrest it for indecent exposure."

Shay thrust a hand through his hair. "Damn it, Lucille..."

She turned to Juliette, her expression both apologetic and sympathetic. "Sorry, I didn't mean to interrupt...not that I knew there was anything to interrupt, of course, but still..."

She frowned and turned back to Shay. "Anyway, we gotta go. It's going down tonight."

"The hell you say? No more false alarms?"

"This is the real deal. We got lucky."

"When? Where?"

"Scheduled to move about an hour from now, down at the old town docks. Avenue G warehouses."

"Don't move," he commanded Lucille, as he raced over to retrieve his pants from halfway under the sofa. He dropped his sarong, stepped into his briefs and thrust his legs into his trousers. Throwing on his shirt, he said, "Gotta go, Red. I'll explain later."

Juliette moved over to him, grabbing his elbow to make him face her. "You'll explain now."

Shay gently shook her off, buttoning his shirt. "No time." He looked around for his shoes. "We have to leave."

Juliette threw on her clothes in record time. "You can tell me all about it on the way."

Shay tried to prevent her from moving. "Juliette, for God's sake."

Slipping her feet into her high-heeled pumps, Juliette ignored him.

"Stay here. I'll be back as soon as I can and then we'll—"

"No." She sailed to the door with all the majesty of a royal yacht. She glanced back at Shay, to find him still standing in the middle of the room, wearing a baffled expression.

If the situation hadn't been so pregnant with tension since Lucille's surprise arrival, Juliette might have laughed. As it was, she wanted answers.

"Shay, it's time to rock 'n' roll," Lucille said, giving Juliette a wary glance. "Get your stuff and let's go."

Quietly, Shay swore profane and colorful words. Then he dashed toward the bedroom, leaving Juliette alone with her oldest friend.

LUCILLE LOOKED MORE uncomfortable than Juliette had ever seen her. Finally the blonde cleared her throat. "I suppose you're the mystery woman Shay was tearing New Orleans apart looking for last week?"

"He tore the town apart?" That made her feel a lot better.

Lucille grinned. "You would have thought the Pope had disappeared, the way he was carrying on."

Even given the tenseness of the situation, Juliette couldn't help but give her friend a tiny grin in return. "He was that distressed?"

"The man was frantic." Then, with an unexpected move, Lucille reached over and hugged Juliette tightly. "I'm sorry. I just want you to know that I'm sorry. I'd give anything to change things, but I can't." Lucille let her go and, to Juliette's amazement, a cold, professional look dropped into place over the features of her childhood playmate. Suddenly, there was a cop standing in front of her.

Before Juliette could respond, Shay emerged from the bedroom, slipping something into the pocket of his leather jacket. His face was grim, his walk determined, which only added to his aura of overwhelming masculinity. The man practically took her breath away.

Shay strode over and opened the door, stepping ahead of them both, seeming anxious to escape. "Let's roll, Lucille."

Lucille followed him. "Right."

"Right," Juliette echoed as she followed her friend into the hallway.

Shay stopped at the doorway that led to the service stairs. "Civilians can't tag along."

"Civilians?"

Shay took a deep breath. "People who aren't cops."

"I can't come because I'm a *civilian?*"

"Yes. Even if you weren't, under the circumstances—"

Juliette's eyes narrowed as she interrupted. "And what about you, Mr....*Freelancer*, was it? Why can you go? Oh, please..." The sarcasm dripped from her tongue until she could taste it. "Let me guess. You're Lucille's driver?"

Shay shifted his weight. He opened his mouth, but nothing came out. Juliette waited.

"You know damn well I'm not Lucille's driver. I'm a cop."

"A cop. You're a cop." He was right. She did know. She'd known it for sure since Lucille came in the door, had sensed it a lot longer, letting it hide under the edge of her consciousness. "Aren't you also the same man who lied so convincingly when he told me he wasn't a cop?"

"Guilty." He reached in his jacket and produced his ID. "Detective Shay O'Malley, Cincinnati Police Department."

"O'Malley. Thanks." Her voice dripped with disdain. "It's nice to know who I'm talking to." *And making love to... No...falling in love with.*

Shay flushed, then yanked on the doorknob, throwing open the door to the staircase. Instead of going through, he stopped and waved his hand. "Lucille, go on. I'll meet you in the car."

"All right, but don't be..." She gave them each a sympathetic glance. "Never mind."

As Lucille left, Shay took Juliette's arm and led her back inside the apartment. "Look, call a cab, go home. I'll get to you later. We'll talk then."

Juliette jerked her arm free as an uneasy feeling washed over her. "What did 'under the circumstances' mean?"

He clamped his hands on her shoulders. "Goddam it, you're too close to it."

"What?" She wasn't sure if he was trying to relieve his own frustration or give her a type of rough comfort. Her stomach clenched.

"Someone close to you is involved and I can't have you—"

"Someone..." She was silent for a few moments, not sure what else to say. If she finished the question, she was afraid he'd tell her—afraid she'd hear her brother's name. Screwing up her courage, she took a step backward, freed herself from him and cleared her throat. "What did you mean, someone close to me is involved?"

"Juliette...are you sure you want to know?"

"For God's sake, don't tease me."

"I was going to tell you before, but..." He swore under his breath. "I need time to explain, and I haven't got it."

"Tell me."

He glanced toward the door, then started talking fast. "I came to New Orleans because I've been working on a case for the last eight months that involves..." He sent her a quick look.

Juliette squeezed her fingers into fists, practically cutting off her circulation. "Involves?" *Not Michael, please God, not my brother.*

"Someone very prominent in the city here."

"Just spit it out, all right?" Did her voice really sound as strained as she thought?

He didn't look at her as he said, "Stephen St. James."

Not Michael. She slumped back against the door. *Thank God, not Michael.*

Shay stepped forward, his face harsh, yet concerned. "Juliette? Did you hear me?"

Licking her lips, she said, "Yes, yes I heard you."

"We think Stephen St. James is the key to a smuggling operation that originates in South America and moves up some U.S. rivers to specific destinations. He's been using his company as a front for years, but now he's getting bolder, moving the merchandise in by Fortier ships. I don't have time to tell you more." Shay physically moved her aside, opened the door and stepped into the hall, heading for the stairs.

Juliette was right behind him, the shock receding enough to allow her to concentrate on the matter at hand—getting more information to make sure her brother wasn't under suspicion too. "What made you really suspect him now?"

"Someone made a mistake," Shay said simply, yanking open the door to the emergency stairwell and starting down the steps. "An associate got greedy and dropped off an...'unacceptable' shipment in Cincinnati. That set the ball in motion."

"What type of shipment?" The conversation she'd overheard a few nights before between Stephen and Michael echo oed in her mind. Still, she found it hard to believe a man she had known since she was a child could have any involvement with anything more than a casual bending of the law. After all, that's what a lot of businessmen did, didn't they?

Who'd told her that? she wondered. Stephen, her father, her brother? She couldn't remember. *And Michael. Where does Michael fit into all of this?*

"I can't go into that." Shay's voice was clipped, warning her the topic was off-limits. "But I'll tell you this much. In the end, crooks are only loyal to themselves. Everyone else is expendable." Shay reached the bottom of the stairs and turned to look at her, his gaze penetrating into her soul. "Everyone."

"Even me." For the first time she realized what her role was in all of this. Not only was she Juliette Fortier, of the Fortier shipping family, but she was engaged to Stephen St. James. The thought chilled her even as it shamed her.

"Even you." Shay's voice was rough, his expression like granite. "So if you know anything, come clean now before it's too late."

"Are you accusing me of—"

"I'm not accusing you of anything. I'm giving you the facts." His expression was remote, professional. It chilled Juliette to the bone.

"I don't know anything about this. I'm not involved in Stephen's business." Then it hit Juliette with the force of a speeding train. "Is that why you've been seeing me? To find out what I know?"

Shay flushed. "No. It wasn't just that."

"Just that." Her heart cracked. So much for true love.

"Don't say that. It didn't start like that. You know how it started."

"I think you knew who I was from the first minute you saw me."

"I didn't. I didn't know until—"

She shook her head. "Don't waste your breath, Detective. It's perfectly clear now." She could hardly get the words out through her raw throat. She pushed her way past him, opened the door and stepped out onto the walk alongside Shay's apartment building.

"Juliette, damn it, that's not what's going on here."

She walked to the front, wanting only to escape from the man behind her. "Every moment we've spent together has been a lie."

He grabbed her arms and whirled him to face her. "That's not true." Lucille honked the horn. "We'll settle this later."

"It's already settled as far as I'm concerned." Juliette was glad to have the last word, even as her eyes were beginning to ache with the hot tears of anger and betrayal. "You'd better get going. You wouldn't want to lose your opportunity to blow my family apart, would you?"

Another honk from Lucille stopped whatever he was going to say. He shook his head, turned and ran to the car, barely getting in and closing the door before Lucille peeled away from the curb.

Juliette stared after him. Who was this man? This hard-eyed stranger who'd just made love to her? She didn't know. For the first time, she emerged from her daydreams and acknowledged the enormous gulf between them. Not because of her royal ancestry and their differences in lifestyle, but because of the vastly disparate experiences. Because of the way she looked at life, and the way she was beginning to suspect Shay viewed it.

But she couldn't think about that now. Later she'd let the pain come, but not now.

Juliette reached into her bag, found her cell phone and called a taxi. Then she dialed home, asking to speak with her brother, only to be told he was spending the night at the apartment in town. When the taxi arrived a few minutes later, she climbed inside, giving the driver the address of the Fortier Building. Ten minutes later she was standing in a private elevator pushing a button for the penthouse that topped Fortier Shipping Operations and was available to members of the family, their friends and business associates.

She emerged into a thickly carpeted hallway and looked

around, calling, "Michael? Michael, where are you?" She went through a doorway into the living room. Telephone in hand, Michael was pacing in front of the fireplace, completely oblivious to her presence.

"But I don't understand. Why do you want me to— All right, all right. Where? Avenue G warehouses? What are you doing there? I thought it was scheduled for— All right, I've got it. I'm coming."

Juliette froze. Avenue G warehouses? The same ones Lucille had mentioned. Her heart hit her shoes and stayed there as she stared at her brother. He'd be walking right into a trap. She stepped forward.

"Michael."

He whirled around, grabbing his chest as he stared at her. "Good God, Juliette. You scared the hell out of me. What are you doing here?"

"Who were you talking to?"

"Just, uh..." He replaced the phone in its cradle. "We'll, um, look, I have to...uh, go...uh, to check on something."

"What?"

"Nothing to worry about. Just a little bit of business to tie up, that's all."

"Your business or Stephen's?"

He chuckled, but Juliette could hear the strain behind it. "Since he's going to be my brother-in-law, Stephen's business is my business, in a manner of speaking."

"He'll never be your brother-in-law."

Michael sighed. "Not this again."

"I know what's going on." *Not the details, perhaps, but enough to scare you into talking.* "I overheard you at Stephen's house the other night."

"Oh, hell."

She stepped closer. "How involved are you?"

"Juliette, there's nothing to be concerned about. Stephen and I just have some business to wrap up and then I'm free and—"

She walked across the room to confront him. "You're an idiot, Michael. The police know, too."

"Know what?"

"About Stephen's business activities. They've been watching him for months."

His fingers quick and nervous, Michael rubbed his forehead. "No. You're just looking for an excuse not to—"

Juliette grabbed him by his arms, shaking him as hard as she could. "Listen to me. The police are onto this. Now, tell me the truth."

Michael stared at her for a long moment, then sighed. "All right. Let go. You'll wrinkle my suit."

To Juliette, Michael looked like a sorry little spaniel as he gazed down at the ground, trying to get up the courage to tell her the truth. For once his contrite look didn't work; she had no patience with him. How dare he expose her family to disaster?

"Does Father know what you've been doing?"

"No! Hell no—not the details. What do you think I am, the village idiot?"

"I wouldn't ask that question if I were you."

He stared at her sulkily. "You don't have to rub it in. It wasn't my fault...exactly."

"Michael," Juliette snapped, "for once in your life be a man."

Straightening, he said in a quiet voice, "I was out one night with Stephen at the casino. He was playing and I wasn't. Then he said, 'Take over my hand, there's a guy over there I need to see.' So, I did." Michael shrugged lamely. "I mean, I had to."

"You had to." Her heart sank. She'd allowed him to delude her when she'd asked before; it was easier that way. But now she was kicking herself for not pushing harder.

"If I didn't the game would have stopped, and that wouldn't have been good."

Juliette's mouth twisted as the sarcasm poured from her lips. "Of course not. What a disaster."

Michael hunched his shoulders. "I picked up the cards and I started to bet. At first I was winning, and oh, Juliette, you should have seen it." His face lit up like Christmas. "I had a string of luck going like I've never had before. So I started signing my own vouchers. When Stephen came back and saw how well I was doing, he laughed and told me to keep on 'cause I was on a roll. Then I started losing. I didn't pay too much attention to that, though. I knew I could turn it around. So I signed more vouchers. But—"

"How much did you lose, Michael?"

"Around 250,000, give or take."

"You lost a quarter of a million dollars?"

He rubbed his foot across the carpet—a small boy who'd been reprimanded for stealing candy from the dish. "Yes, I didn't have the money to cover it. My trust was temporarily tapped out. And I didn't dare ask Father."

"That's the first smart thing I've heard you say tonight."

Flushing, Michael muttered, "He said he'd cut me off if he found me gambling again. If he'd just let go of some of the purse strings and give me more control I wouldn't need to gamble."

"You gamble because you're addicted to it. It's a sickness, like alcoholism or drugs." She tried to keep her voice matter-of-fact, not allowing the compassion to show, but it was difficult. This was her brother.

"It's not that bad."

"I call losing a quarter-million dollars very bad. How'd you pay the debt, since you couldn't call Father?"

"Stephen helped me."

"Stephen just happened to have that much money lying around?"

"Not exactly. Look, Juliette, Stephen was only trying to help me."

"Stephen the munificent. Except I don't believe it. What did he really want?"

"Nothing, except he said he wanted to integrate our companies more closely. Then he started telling me he was determined to marry you. So I figured it wouldn't hurt to let him take over some of the day-to-day stuff. After all, he'd spoken with Father about it, and he'd agreed, given his blessing, both to the business plans and to the engagement."

"Did you speak to Father about it? Did he confirm that?"

"Not in so many words," Michael said, shifting his weight, clearly uncomfortable. "I've been trying to avoid him until I can get out of trouble. You know how he can be."

Juliette looked at her brother, her charming, weak brother. The man who'd never really grown beyond the boy who always wanted everything without having to work very hard for it. The kicker was that with his good looks, great personality and charm, he generally managed to convince everyone to do his bidding, always had. It was only now, as she really looked at him, that she saw him for the spoiled child he was. For the first time in her life, Juliette felt years older than Michael.

"So you've turned over operations of the company to Stephen."

"What there was to turn over, from my point of view. I told you, Father turned over the rest. I saw the document. Hell, I even co-signed it." He shrugged. "Besides, turning over the company to Stephen wasn't a big deal, because the local party was talking to me about entering politics."

"Under the circumstances, you decided to expose yourself to the media and a political campaign?"

"Juliette, gambling, like drinking and chasing women, is just something men do. Hell, I can tell you of any number of politicians who do all three."

"The only problem is they know when to stop."

"Not all of them." He glanced at the clock on the fireplace mantel. "I have to meet Stephen."

"That's who called?"

Nodding, he walked past her, headed to the hallway. "Yes. He has something he wants to show me. Something to do with this shipment he's arranged." He grabbed his keys from a bowl on the antique Louis XIV table. "I'll be back."

She marched over to the door. "You're not going anywhere without me."

"Don't be ridic—"

"Listen to me." She tapped his chest with her fingertip to emphasize her point. "I am not about to let you and Stephen destroy everything the Fortier family has accomplished over the years."

"I...I'm trying not to...." His face crumpled. "I don't know what to do."

"I'll tell you what we're going to do. We're going to walk into those warehouses tonight and put a stop to anything Stephen is doing. Then we're going to talk to the police and explain the situation. It'll look good if you tell them what's going on and how you got involved. Then we're going to call Father and tell him the entire story."

"No, no, I can't do that. Nothing's going to happen to Stephen. He's a survivor. Besides, what's the big deal about a shipment? We ship things all the time. We're a shipping company."

Juliette lost the last shreds of her temper. "He's smuggling, you dumb ass, and you damn well know it! Now give me your keys."

With that, she yanked open the door and stalked to the elevator. She didn't care if her brother was behind her or not. She was Princess Juliette Liane Fortier, and she wasn't going down without a fight.

10

SHAY O'MALLEY STEPPED into a dark hallway at the Avenue G warehouses, moving carefully down the long corridor, checking to be certain Lucille was behind him. He turned and put his lips to his partner's ear. "Any idea of the layout here?"

Lucille answered the same way. "I'm not sure, but I think this leads to the main loading area. Then right out onto the wharf."

Shay nodded and continued moving forward, his footsteps cautious and quiet. He could see a glow of light through the frosted glass of a door at the end of the hall. He unholstered his weapon and glanced at Lucille, who did the same. When he reached the door, he pressed his ear against the glass, hearing a faint murmur of voices. Taking a deep breath, he turned the knob, opening the door just a crack to get the lay of the land. He didn't see a lot of activity in the immediate vicinity, but stacked boxes were blocking most of his view. He opened the door wide enough to slip through, with Lucille close on his heels. Moving forward, they took cover behind some crates. Peering through a crack in the stack, Shay could see a flurry of activity in the main part of the warehouse as some dockhands hauled boxes out through the shipping doors. He recognized Gerald, but had no idea who the man was talking to, although his companion looked like another sailor. Perhaps the captain?

"Any idea where the cargo is?" Lucille asked.

"No sign, just a lot of boxes on some skids."

"Boxes of what?"

"Could be anything. St. James isn't too fussy about what he takes as a consignment, I hear."

"Since he's basically an errand boy, he can't say no, right?"

Shay glanced at Lucille. "He's got a lot more power than that. At least he does with the Fortier ships behind him. His own money laundering businesses were important, but having absolute control of transportation makes him a real player." Crouching low, Shay moved behind the crates, taking care to keep close to the wall as he made his way around the perimeter. "Let's get a better look."

Shay inched toward the center of the warehouse. Luckily, the place wasn't too tidy. No neat stacked rows, just piles of crates here and there. He wondered if this warehouse was used for the regular operations of the Fortier company. From the abandoned look of the place, he was inclined to think not.

Creeping closer, Lucille on his heels, Shay looked around for signs of St. James's live cargo, the cargo expected to bring over five million dollars in fees, if Henry Sabin had been telling the truth. Shay did some quick calculations. That, plus the other freight of the smuggling operation—after all, why let any extra space go to waste?—made the shipment worth about seven to ten million, easy. Of course, St. James could make that many times over if he was running drugs, but so far he'd resisted the temptation. The last remnants of a Southern gentleman, Shay supposed.

A slight movement caught his attention. He glanced up to the loft area, just in time to see a figure draw back into the shadows. "Do we have a team in here already?" he whispered.

Lucille followed his glance. "They should all be outside, but we do have some eager beavers on the force who don't want the big bad detective from Cincinnati to get all the glory."

"Ah hell, just what we need—hot dogs on the job."

Lucille grinned. "Don't worry, Yankee. I think you can out hot dog them anyday."

Shay got ready to tell her what she could do with her compliments when Stephen stalked into the center of the warehouse.

"Gerald, what the hell's going on here? You're supposed to be half loaded by now."

Gerald turned around. "We're a bit behind schedule boss."

"And why is that?" Stephen said, in a smooth, creamier than-caramel voice.

Inclining his head toward the man by his side, Gerald replied, "The skipper here doesn't think he's getting paid enough."

"No?" Stephen's voice got even smoother. "How shocking. Well, we can't have that, now can we?" Smiling all the way, hand in his pocket, the very picture of casual elegance, Stephen strolled over to the rough-featured man and casually draped an arm around his shoulders. "I'm sure we can remove you and make other arrangements, if you prefer, Captain."

Watching St. James in action was like watching a snake charm a rat. Shay glanced at Lucille, then back at the scene unfolding before him.

"Your second mate might like an opportunity," Stephen continued. "Shall we see?"

"Uh, no, no, I think, um, I misspoke." The Captain gave a nervous chuckle.

Stephen smiled. "I'm sure you did. I love dealing with reasonable men, don't you, Gerald?" They both laughed as the burly sailor hurried away, but their laughter quieted when a voice came from the far side of the warehouse.

"Stephen, I have to talk to you."

Stephen turned. "Michael. We've been waiting for you."

Shay stiffened as Michael Fortier practically ran into the room. *Damn!* Shay hadn't expected to find him here, too. How was Juliette going to take it when she found out? And she'd have to find out, he acknowledged, much as he'd love to keep her in the dark about this part of it. Fortier was in too deep as it was.

"Hello, Stephen."

"Juliette?" Stephen called, for the first time seeming a bit shaken. He quickly recovered. "Well, isn't this a nice surprise."

Shay's heart leaped into his throat as a thrill of fear raced up his spine. Juliette. What the hell? She was supposed to go home. He started to rise, but felt Lucille give him a strong tug to pull him back. "Let go," he whispered, his voice low and menacing. He had to get to Juliette. "If that bastard touches her I'll—"

"Chill, Yankee. Let it play out."

Shay exhaled, a sharp short sound through his nostrils. "Yeah, right. You're right. We'll play it out." Feeling anguished, he watched and listened, looking for an opportunity to step in.

Juliette moved into the light, her face white, but her step determined. Her voice when she spoke seemed cool and composed. "Hello, Stephen. I hope you don't mind Michael bringing me along."

"Darling, of course not."

"He thought I'd find this interesting." Giving an airy wave that indicated the warehouse, Juliette smiled back at him. "I understand you've opened up a profitable new avenue of business for Fortier Shipping."

Thatta girl, keep him off balance, Shay thought as he watched her step forward.

"Well, darling, my aim has always been to make the most amount of money in the shortest amount of time."

"And you've tumbled onto the perfect way to do that?"

"I've not had much choice but to find one. It was a question of survival. My dear father had lineage and breeding, but a very bad head for business, regardless of what everyone thought. Poor man was up to his ears in debt when he died. Of course, Mama and I didn't know until it was too late."

Shay concentrated on what he could see of Stephen's face. His tone might have been light, but his look was murderous. Shay glanced at Lucille, who was staring up at the loft. He followed her gaze and made out a shadowy form lifting a rifle into prime shooting position. "Cops?" he mouthed.

"Not sure," Lucille answered. "I think so."

Shay looked back at the drama unfolding on the warehouse stage. *If anyone puts Juliette in danger, I'll kill him—fellow officer or not.*

"I—I didn't know...." Juliette seemed stunned for a moment. She pulled her gaze from Stephen and looked around the warehouse. Then she pointed at some boxes near the dock entrance. "Well, you seem to have come up with an admirable solution. What is all this?"

"Nothing that need concern you, darling. Just a little bit of this, a little bit of that. It amazes me what people will pay for these days."

"Oh? I hadn't realized that."

"Why would you? You've spent your whole life cloaked in cotton wool."

Shay could see Juliette flush even as her eyes flashed with temper. "Maybe so, but I'm out in the world now. And you know what, Stephen? I don't like everything I'm seeing."

Even as his blood ran cold at her foolhardiness, Shay smiled as he watched her stand up to Stephen. His gaze swept over her as she stood there, every inch a princess—feet firm, head held high, and as righteous as a goddess.

God, he'd never loved her more.

"When we're married, I'll have to make a big effort to change your view, won't I, darling?"

Juliette's brows lifted. "When we're married?"

"Uh, Stephen, Juliette is having some—some..."

"Some?" Stephen repeated, first giving Michael a hard stare, and then turning it on Juliette.

Shut up, Michael, Shay thought, his nerves suddenly on fire.

"Some...financial problems," Juliette stated.

Practically sneering, Stephen said, "That seems a common problem with you Fortiers lately."

Juliette looked down at the ground. "The, uh, the foundation is—"

Michael swiveled his head to look at her. "I didn't think

you knew. Look, Juliette, I'm going to replace all that money somehow."

Juliette snapped Michael a look. "What money?"

"From the foundation."

"You took money from the foundation? Oh Michael, how could you? How much?"

"How much?" Michael's eyes widened. "I thought...I mean the way you said that, I thought you'd already figured it out."

Bingo, Shay thought. Although it gave him no satisfaction to be right about the accessibility of the Fortier Foundation's fund to family members. Not when he had to watch Juliette lose even more of her illusions. He focused his attention back on Stephen.

St. James seemed relaxed as he watched the byplay between brother and sister, his head swiveling back and forth, as if he was in the first row at a tennis match. Finally he interrupted. "Don't worry, Juliette, soon we'll have more money than we need. So if you want to play the lady bountiful with your little foundation, then it won't be a problem."

Shay could see Juliette's temper begin to overflow. "Lady bountiful? I'll have you know—"

Before she could finish that statement all hell broke loose.

In the confusion, there was an instant when Shay wasn't sure what was happening. First there was a child's loud scream, then a man's anguished cry, then Gerald ran into the warehouse even as a child broke from someplace on the right and ran toward the dock door. A rough-looking thug was right behind him, and not far behind them was a man who could have been the child's father.

Instinctively, Shay and Lucille rose and started to move toward the scene just as the first shots rang out. Shay glanced up at the loft. Sure enough, two cops had gotten overeager and began to fire warning shots as they yelled, "Halt, police."

Terrified for Juliette, Shay still retained his cool as he dashed behind the boxes to get into a better position, with Lucille doing the same in the other direction. In that same moment, Juliette started to run for the child, who was now screaming at the top of his lungs. Stephen ran after her and managed to grab her before she reached the boy. Throwing his arm around her chest, he turned her around, using her as a shield as he backed toward the dock entrance, where Gerald was now subduing the child, even as the other man grabbed the boy's father and joined them near the doorway.

"Hold your fire," Shay yelled, as he saw a gun magically appear in Stephen's hand. Stephen's arm tightened around Juliette and he pointed the gun toward her in a threatening manner. Shay froze, yelling, "Hold your fire, damn it!" just as Michael rushed toward his sister.

The rifles fell silent, but still a gunshot rang out—one single shot that ended Michael's attempt to rescue Juliette.

"Michael," Juliette screamed as her brother clutched his arm and fell to the ground. "Michael!" Sudden silence followed her cry.

"Shut up. I just winged him," Stephen said, his voice all impatience as he subdued Juliette's struggles.

She glared up at him. "When I get my hands on you, I'll—" Stephen laughed. "You'll what?"

Shay stepped forward, gun at the ready. "She won't have to do anything, 'cause I will."

"Well, well, well, if it isn't our Mr. Mallory," Stephen said, his voice cool and controlled. "Perhaps y'all didn't understand, we're booked up this week."

Shay smiled, wanting to take a bite out of the man. "It's you who doesn't understand."

Lucille came around another stack of crates, her gun also ready for use as she kept it trained on the other men in the doorway. "Stephen's understanding was always moderate at best. He was just sneaky."

Stephen snapped her a look, snarling, "And the society cop, too. Quite a party."

Shay glanced at Juliette, confirming that she was all right. She was staring back at him, eyes huge but alert. *Keep your wits, Red. I won't let anyone hurt you,* he tried to tell her with his steady stare. To his relief, she seemed to understand.

He pulled his attention back to Stephen, and indicated the loft behind him. "You're done, St. James."

Stephen inched his revolver closer to Juliette. "I don't think so, Mallory. I have leverage."

"It's O'Malley, Detective O'Malley, and how far do you think you can get?"

"Far enough."

Shay moved forward in a slow, steady stroll that brought him near Michael. He glanced down and, seeing that Michael was sitting up, ignored him and focused his concentration on Stephen. "You're surrounded, pal." He indicated the docks. "We've got two other units out there." As he said that, he could hear more cops moving into position around the loading area.

Gerald glanced over his shoulder. "He's right, boss. That's what I was coming to tell you." The boy took advantage of his movement and pulled Gerald's hand away, once again starting to yell.

"Shut that kid up, now!"

Gerald got his hand back over the child's mouth, then yelled himself. "He bit me, the little son of a...!" He took his hands off the boy, who bolted, then butted the man holding his father. The boy's father started struggling, too.

Stephen took his eyes off Shay for a moment, glancing at Gerald and the resulting chaos. That half second was all Shay needed. As he rushed forward, Juliette also moved, catching Stephen in the ribs with her elbow and causing him to loosen his hold. She dashed toward Michael just as Shay hit Stephen low and hard, grunting as they both slammed onto the floor, struggling for control of Stephen's gun.

They were evenly matched. Stephen was tougher than he looked. The fight was vicious, both men desperate to gain the advantage. It didn't take long, but it seemed forever before Shay managed to get his hands on Stephen's wrist to lower the gun. He knocked Stephen's hand against the rough boards until he lost his grip on the weapon, then managed to drive his fist into his jaw. Stephen slumped backward, stunned enough so Shay could turn him over and get both hands behind his back, yanking them upward to keep him from moving. With his other hand, he reached into his pocket for handcuffs, only to discover he didn't have any.

"We Southern women always come prepared," Lucille said, as she slapped a pair of cuffs into Shay's hand.

Breathing heavily, he grinned. "And I thought that just meant extra lipstick."

Lucille laughed. "Oh, I have that, too."

Standing up, Shay hauled Stephen to his feet and turned him over to two cops who were waiting to take him into custody, along with the others. "Treat this one nice, boys. He's going to have a lot to say."

"I'm saying nothing," Stephen snarled over his shoulder.

Shay shrugged. "Suit yourself."

Stephen said something rude in return and the men started to take him away when Shay stopped them. "Wait a minute. Just out of curiosity, St. James, how'd you tumble to me? Where did I go wrong?"

Stephen turned around and stared at him. "Are you looking for a performance review?" he asked with a hint of his usual smooth, mocking manner.

"Why not? Sometimes it's better to get it from the source."

Stephen considered him for a moment longer before shrugging his shoulders. "Last week, some business associates heard a rumor about Henry Sabin being detained by the police."

Shay nodded. "I thought that might be it."

"It wasn't surprising to see a stranger show up with a big opportunity. You might have been legit, but—"

"But you decided to keep me busy and off balance, anyway."

"Spending time with my lovely fiancée couldn't have been that much of a hardship."

"It wasn't." Shay smiled, his expression making it clear

that if Stephen ever wanted to get near Juliette again, he'd have to go through him.

Stephen stared at him, then toward Juliette and her brother. "You won't make this stick, you know."

"You just keep believing that, St. James. It might make doing your time a little easier." Then Shay turned away from Stephen and looked for Juliette. He found her crouched over her brother, pressing a handkerchief against his wound. Shay walked over to them and squatted down. "How is he?"

Michael laughed. "Oh, I'm just fine. I've been shot and my life is in ruins."

Shay peeled the handkerchief away and looked at Michael's arm. "It's just a flesh wound."

"Perhaps," Michael sniffed, with a bit of his old aristocratic manner, "but it's my flesh."

Juliette giggled. "Sorry," she said, as Shay and her brother looked up at her. "I think it's stress. This isn't generally what I do every day...or every night, either."

Shay grinned at her, remembering one part of their night in great detail. To his delight, Juliette blushed, then pressed her lips into a stern line. "Yeah, I'd say today's been interesting," he murmured.

"It depends on your point of view," Michael stated, in a petulant manner.

Jerking his thumb toward the other people in the room, Shay gave him a disgusted look. "Your point of view isn't as bad as theirs."

Juliette followed Shay's gesture, her gaze falling on the father and his young son. "I don't understand. Where did they come from?"

Shay directed his stare at Michael. "Why don't you answer that?"

"Me? Why me?"

"You should know. Your business partner arranged it."

Michael looked puzzled. "What are you talking about?"

"Your special shipment."

"Our special shipment was cigars and cigarettes, the purest, sweetest-tasting tobacco you've ever put a match to."

Shay stared at him. "Where'd you hear that?"

"From Stephen and..."

"And?" Shay prompted, hoping another piece of the equation would fall into place.

"And from...there was this South American gentleman, Felipe, a friend of Stephen's or Gerald's—I don't remember. Anyway, he said it was a rush order. If we could get it there on time, he promised me an extra payment that I could use as a contribution to my political campaign."

"A foreign contribution? Isn't that illegal?" And handy, Shay thought. Not only could the South Americans and the crime associates move merchandise through Stephen, they could get their own politician in their back pocket.

Michael shifted, clearly uncomfortable as he tried to justify himself. "Political campaigns are expensive business. Stephen said all I had to do was look the other way while they brought this special cargo in on our ships, and that it was essential that we meet the deadline." He closed his eyes for a moment. "I mean, I had to do that. I didn't have any other choice."

"Why not?"

"Stephen gave me money when I first got into trouble at the casino." He licked his dry lips. "But I needed more, so I talked to him again, and that's when I found out that Stephen had borrowed the first batch of money from somewhere else to help me. At that point, we were both stuck for it, plus the daily interest. The lenders started pressing...then Stephen said we had to use the ships to run some extra cargo besides what we were doing for Felipe. I co-signed some agreements and looked the other way." Michael exhaled, then muttered, "Then came the other condition..."

"Like marriage to Juliette."

Michael looked at Shay, his expression ashamed. "Yes."

"And you had to agree to that, too?"

"He said he loved her, so I thought Stephen was..." He

glanced toward the door where St. James had exited. "It doesn't matter what I thought. Now I know differently."

"At least that's progress."

Michael gave Shay a flippant smile. "What's life if you don't keep learning?" Then he turned serious again. "It wasn't too long before I got the message that if I didn't set this thing up, Juliette would...would be..."

Lifting his brows, Shay looked first at Juliette, then back at Michael. "Hurt?"

Shoulders hunched, eyes lowered, Michael whispered, "Yes."

Shay swore under his breath. He'd expected as much, but he hated hearing it, hated knowing how easily he could have lost her now that he'd found her.

Juliette leaned over and kissed her brother's cheek. "Poor Michael."

Poor Michael indeed. Although Shay found it rather difficult to feel too sorry for him, there was no doubt the man had been hooked by an expert. "You were set up from the word *go*, Michael. First Stephen and his cronies got you in debt at the casino. Stephen provided the money to get you free of those same cronies, then pretended he needed more, so you skimmed it from the Fortier Foundation. The way it usually works is, to get you in deeper, Stephen would have forged legal documents to hold over your head as cosigner, so you'd look like a conspirator to fraud. He closed the deal tonight by getting you here."

Michael's eyes widened as he listened, his face flushed.

Shay whistled. "The man is good, I have to admit that. This operation was slick as a whistle. They just kept reeling you in like a tired trout until they flopped you onto the deck."

Michael glanced up at his sister, then over at the man and boy, who were now joined by a wailing, ragtag group of around twenty immigrants, whom the cops began to escort from the building. Pulling his gaze from them, Michael met Shay's hard stare straight on. "There...there never were any cigars, were there?"

Shay shrugged. "There might be somewhere in all those crates, but tobacco wasn't your primary cargo."

Staring at the group of men, women and children, Juliette whispered, "People were?"

"People. Illegal aliens, to be exact. People who were refused entrance into the U.S. for some reason, or who didn't want to wait for the immigration process to work. Some probably have relatives in the U.S. who paid for them, others paid their own way. If they didn't have the cash they sold themselves on the black market to the highest bidder. Anything to come to America."

"The land of dreams," Juliette murmured, her eyes sad.

"For some." Shay glanced at the group. "They come with all types of treasures they've collected, everything from works of art to stashes of gold and silver. Those who have nothing to bring..." He hated telling her this. This sordid tale and his real-life princess didn't belong together.

"Go on, Shay, let's hear it all," Juliette urged, still watching the people.

"Many end up enslaved to all types of illegitimate 'ventures.' If they live through their passage."

"I don't know if I can hear any more," Juliette whispered.

That was good, because Shay didn't want to tell her. It only reinforced the gulf between his world and hers. As much as he loved her, he wondered if they could ever cross it. If he should even try. His lips thinned as he pulled his attention back to Michael. At the moment Shay wanted to commit murder himself. "You knew nothing about this, Fortier?"

"No, God no. What do you take me for?"

"A weak fool who's dumb enough to get himself snagged in a classic blackmail setup."

Michael glared at Shay. "You don't waste words, do you?"

"No, I don't. Especially when your stupidity puts the woman I love at risk." Shay hadn't meant for those words to slip out.

"The woman you—" Michael turned to Juliette. "What the hell is he talking about?"

She glanced at her brother. "I..."

"You told me there was no one else, remember? When I asked you, you said there was no one else."

"I lied." Juliette shifted her gaze from her brother to meet Shay's stare head-on.

She wasn't going to make it easy for him, Shay could tell. He wanted to reach for her, to convince her of his feelings, but he was distracted by Lucille's arrival.

"Shay, we've got everyone rounded up—the crew from the boat, Stephen and Gerald what's-his-name, and we also have the other aliens in custody. We're getting ready to move them all downtown." She gave Michael a significant glance before returning her focus back to Shay. "Are we missing anyone?"

Shay slanted a look at Juliette, who was watching with worried eyes. Then he looked at Michael. He had no options, none at all. "Michael, we're going to get you to a hospital and have that wound taken care of, and then you'll have to come down to the station house and give us a statement."

"Am I under arrest?"

Lucille glanced at Shay.

Shay stepped closer. "Not yet, but you probably will be. At the very least you'll be detained until we can sort things out around the blackmail and the threats. See what we can come up with, if anything, to absolve you." Shay knew that any chance he had of convincing Juliette that he loved her was fading fast, because he was probably going to put her brother in jail. Not the most auspicious way to begin happily ever after, regardless of how determined he might be.

"I see," Michael said, with a surprising amount of dignity. He struggled to his feet, his sister helping him. He kissed her forehead. "I'm sorry, Juliette. I didn't mean to hurt anyone."

"I know, Michael."

"I...it just got out of control and I couldn't stop it, no matter how much I wanted to. I couldn't turn back the clock."

"I know," she said again.

"Tell Father..."

Juliette placed her hands on his cheeks and kissed first one and then the other. "We'll tell him together."

Shay stood up as some paramedics came in with a wheeled stretcher. Michael knocked their hands aside as they tried to convince him to get on.

"I'm not being taken out of here on one of those things. I'll walk."

Juliette slid her arm around Michael's waist. "I'll walk with you."

He hesitated, then said, "Thank you."

"No thanks required. You're my brother."

As they passed Shay, he placed his hand on her arm. "Juliette, I...can I help?"

"Thank you, Detective. Your help is no longer required. This is a family matter now."

"Everyone else stay clear, is that it?"

Her eyes filled with regret, then brightened to a feverish shine. "Good or bad, Fortiers stick together."

Resigned, Shay watched them go, then turned to his partner. "Go with them, Lucille. I'll finish up here and see you at the precinct."

TWO DAYS LATER, Shay walked into the squad house, nodded at the duty officer, then went right to his temporary desk. Sitting down, he began clearing up his files, packing them into a briefcase.

"What are you doing? Stealing the office supplies?"

Shay looked up at a smiling Lucille. "Nope. Getting ready to go back North."

"So soon?"

"We got the guy we were after, your department will clear up the rest. There's no need for me to stick around. I'll be back for the trial."

"I heard that my captain asked you to consider taking a permanent job here. You've got some special expertise we need."

"Yeah, well..."

"Well what?"

He glanced up at her as she perched on his desk. "I, uh, probably would have considered that, if things had worked out differently."

"What kind of things?"

"Drop it, Lucille."

"The kind of thing that has a title attached to her name?"

"Don't you ever listen? I said drop it."

"No. Not until I have my say. I spent last night with Juliette, listening to her, crying with her, drinking with her. She mentioned your name."

"I'll bet she did. I can imagine what she said, too."

"If you walk out on her now, Shay..."

"I'm not walking out on her. She called it quits, not me."

"So that's it? You're just going to cut and run like a yellow-bellied coward?"

Shay didn't say anything. He couldn't. All he could do was clench his fists and face the woman challenging him. Finally, he managed to say, "She doesn't want me near her. I put her brother in jail, remember?"

"How do you know what she wants if you don't ask her?"

"How am I going to ask her? She said she didn't want to see me again."

"And you believed her? Don't you Yankees have any staying power?"

Shay groaned. "Don't turn this into a North-South thing."

"Do you want her?" Lucille demanded.

"More than my life." Until that moment he'd suppressed his feelings, but Lucille's point-blank question jump-started them, the power of the words slamming into him.

Lucille hopped off the desk. "Then go get her."

"All right. I will."

"Men," Lucille muttered as he strode to the door. "Thank the Lord I've got Preston trained."

SHAY WAITED IMPATIENTLY as the housekeeper let him into the vestibule at La Belle Rivière des Fleurs.

"If y'all will wait here a minute, I'll tell Princess Juliette you're here," the stout maid instructed him.

"Excuse me," Shay said, smiling his most charming smile, "do you think you could just take me to her instead? I'd like to surprise her." He did his best to look lovelorn, which wasn't as much of a stretch as it might have been in different circumstances. He ached to see Juliette again.

"Well, I..." The older woman studied him for a minute.

"Please. It's really important to me." He produced a nosegay of sunny daffodils that he'd been hiding behind his back. He'd picked them on his way up the walk, but no one needed to know that.

The woman stared at the flowers and sighed, obviously a romantic at heart. "All right, I suppose it can't hurt. The princess is in the sunroom." Turning, she headed down the center hall, then jogged to the right and walked toward the rear of the house. When she got near the room, she stopped, glancing over her shoulder.

"In there?" Shay mouthed silently.

The housekeeper nodded, a wide smile on her face. She stopped him as he went past her and whispered, "Good luck."

He was going to need it, he thought. After giving himself a quick pep talk, he entered the room, pausing as his eyes adjusted to the light. There were floor-to-ceiling windows, and what solid walls existed were painted the color of sunshine. The wicker furniture was stained white and accented with yellow-and-blue-print material. The total effect was bright and happy, unlike the woman reclining on a chaise longue. Juliette's face was as long and sad as a puppy just torn from its mother.

Shay's heart broke as he realized he was responsible for much of that look. Not all of it, though, he told himself. Her ex-fiancé and her brother shared the blame, but he'd certainly added to it. He would give anything if he could make her happy again.

"Juliette," he whispered.

She turned her head, her eyes wide and unfocused for a second, staring at him as if he was something from a dream...or perhaps a nightmare.

"What are you doing here?"

"I...I just wanted to say—" He suddenly realized he had no idea how to proceed. He wanted to say what was in his heart, but wasn't entirely convinced she'd listen, in spite of Lucille's encouragement.

"Say what?" Juliette waved her hand. "Sorry it worked out like this?"

Shay stepped closer to her. "I *am* sorry. If I could have changed anything—*anything*—" he repeated, "I would have." *Except for making love with you. That I'd never want to change.*

After staring at him for a long moment, she pulled her gaze away to look out the window at the gardens. "I know."

"I'd give everything I own to make it different, to bring your smile back, but I can't. I can't erase what happened to your family, to you. Much as I'd like to, I can't. I...I wanted so much to protect you...to keep you safe. I didn't want my world to touch yours, but I couldn't—"

"How do you stand that world of yours? The violence and the betrayal? How does Lucille stand it?"

"You try not to think about it. You just do it."

"You just do it." She swung around to face him, studying him for a moment. "You can never really trust anyone, can you? Even the people you think you know. Everyone is there to be used, to give you an edge."

He stood there in an uncomfortable silence, then slowly responded. "Not everyone. It's just that sometimes..."

"You used me," Juliette accused, her voice harsh and hurting. "You used me to get to Stephen. To get to my brother."

"Yes, I did. And you used me. So we're even."

"I didn't try to get close to you and make you fall in love with me."

"Believe it or not, I didn't intend that, either. But at least I had a purpose beyond relieving my boredom."

"It wasn't boredom. I wasn't bored. It was more like frustration, desperation. That's how it started out. That's how met you. But even so, I didn't deceive you so I could arres someone. I only used you for an adventure."

"An adventure! Sure, why not? That makes it all okay right?"

Flushing, Juliette looked away from him. "No, of course i doesn't. It's not okay at all. It sounds spoiled, selfish and im mature."

"Look, Juliette, if we have any hope of a future together we'd better get this very clear. Just because you and I had incredible sex, and even though I'm so...so *obsessed* with you that I don't know what day it is, I didn't use you as a play-thing. I used you for justice."

"For justice."

"Yes. Can you forgive me for that?" He started praying as he waited for her answer, praying harder than he'd ever done in his life, knowing his future hung on her next words.

Juliette started to say yes, then caught herself. If she said yes, this would be her reality from here on, a reality that would be more demanding than she'd ever imagined. Much as she'd wanted a future with Shay, she wondered if she was really the right woman for him. Could she understand and accept what he did, the decisions he made, without judging him? She'd have to if she wanted a life with him. But even though she'd tried to tell herself she hated him after the scene in the warehouse, even as she tried to convince herself that she wanted nothing more to do with him, she had to admit she'd lain awake for the past few nights wanting him. Above and beyond the disaster to her family, she'd yearned for Shay. She wasn't sure how to tell him.

She glanced at him and saw from his tense expression how much her answer mattered. *Don't be an idiot. Just tell him.* Giving him a slow smile, putting all the love she felt in her heart into it, she said, "When you put it like that, and given what I saw at that warehouse, using me for justice sounds acceptable."

"Well, it's not. It's just that sometimes the end has to justify the means, even when you don't want it to." He stepped closer. "I heard you're appealing to immigration on behalf of those illegal aliens."

"It's the least I can do. Under the circumstances, I consider those people to be the Fortier family's responsibility. I'm trying to line up sponsors now. Hopefully, I'll convince the powers that be to consider their case."

"You've got a good lawyer?"

"One of my cousins, the same cousin who will represent Michael if his case goes to trial."

"Good, that's good." Shay looked as if he wanted to say more, but he didn't.

She watched him. Her body, which had been so cold and lonely for the past few days, was warming in his presence. Regardless of what she'd said to him a few nights before, he'd come. Now she wasn't sure what to do next.

He'd said he loved her at the warehouse. Had he meant it, or had he just said that in the heat of the moment? Was he here now because he loved her? Or was it really guilt that drove him here?

Even as she thought that, she rejected the idea. This wasn't a man motivated by guilt. He knew he was justified in the actions he took, and although he might regret some of them, she knew he was satisfied with the end result, even as he regretted the effect that had on her family. No. This man wasn't being driven by guilt.

She ached to hear him say "I love you" again, not "I'm obsessed with you." Not that she didn't enjoy the thought of being the most potent image in the man's mind, but she wanted more. Seeing him again made her realize she wanted it all, not just love, but commitment. She wanted to build a future with this man, have his babies, see his hair streaked with gray, his face lined with experience, his eyes alight with love and contentment. Was that what he wanted, too?

She peeked at him, both reassured and excited by his strong masculine presence. This was a man who'd go to the ends of the earth for the woman he loved. Would he do it for her? She wanted to ask outright, but now, when it was so very important, when her entire future was at stake, she hesitated. Instead she said simply, "What now?"

"Now?" His confused look was almost endearing.

"Yes. What do we do next?" *You take me into your arms, instead of standing there staring at me like a lump.* She bit her lip, amused at this tough male who suddenly seemed to forget everything he'd ever known.

"Oh." He looked around, obviously expecting inspiration to come creeping up from the corners of the room. "Next we, uh..."

At the rate he was going, they'd never get to it. Her nerves settled. Feeling in control for the first time, she smiled. "Are those flowers for me?"

Shay looked down, seeming surprised to see them in his hand. He extended them like a shy first grader handing an apple to his teacher. "Yeah, here."

Taking them, Juliette buried her face in the blooms. "I love daffodils. They always make me smile."

"Good. I wanted you to smile."

"Then you've succeeded." She placed them on the small table next to her seat and stood up. "For a while, I didn't think I ever would. I certainly didn't think I'd ever want to see you again. But sometimes what you think you want and what you really want are two different things. The trick is to reconcile the two. You shouldn't stop loving people just because they disappoint you, should you?"

"No, you should just be disappointed. Like you probably are in your brother."

"That's true. I am. He's disappointed a lot of people and he'll have to take the consequences. Our family can't protect him forever."

Shay smiled, his voice admiring. "You're turning into a hard-hearted woman, Red." His voice turned his words into a reaffirmation of strength.

"More strong-minded than hard-hearted, I hope. I'm going

to need to be, aren't I? That's the only way my family will get through this. Besides, it's time to be strong. It's taken me awhile to really stand up for myself." She wasn't just referring to her forced engagement, but thought back to the way she'd been conducting her life and realized that most of the time she'd just been going along, even as she'd convinced herself she'd been standing on her own two feet. It wasn't a mistake she'd ever make again.

"What do you think will happen to Michael, Shay?"

"I don't know, Red. With a good lawyer, and a recommendation for leniency, he ought to come out okay. After all, he was being blackmailed into going along, and he didn't know much of anything, or so he says."

"I believe him. Stephen wouldn't have trusted Michael with many details."

"I agree with that. But he'll still have to pay in some way."

"He should pay the price, whatever that is," Juliette agreed.

"Michael's hopes for a political career are probably history."

"Oh, I don't know." Juliette gave him a sassy little smile as she sashayed over to him. "You don't know Louisiana politics. There's nothing like a hint of scandal, especially when it sits on the shoulders of a good-looking prince. We take our scoundrels with a grain of salt, and a lot of pride."

Shay shook his head. "Oh, man, I don't think I'll ever understand Southerners."

"Sure you will. If you stick around long enough." *Will you?*

He grabbed her hands. "You want me to stick around?"

Judging by the look in his eyes, now was the time; he was clearly thinking the way she wanted him to think. So she could draw out the situation and enjoy it more, she teased, "I'm sure the NOPD would hate to lose you." Teasing Shay was very arousing, she'd discovered.

He laughed. "Well, Red, I have to tell you, I am finding New Orleans very appealing. It's hard to think of going back North for good. There are so many things I'd miss."

She shivered as his eyes touched her lips, the look as strong as a caress. "Such as?"

"Such as...real coffee, jazz and streetcars, the scent of flowers when the moon is full...stuff like that."

"That's very romantic."

"You think so?"

"Uh-huh," Juliette replied, licking her lips.

Groaning, Shay glanced around as if expecting a servant to walk in at any moment. "In a more appropriate place, I could show you exactly how romantic I consider this city."

Grinning, Juliette leaned forward, her lips tempting him. "An appropriate place has never been an issue before."

He grinned back, his fingertips stroking her cheek. "Sometimes you have to go where life takes you."

"I wish I could do that now. Under other circumstances I'd follow the man I love to the end of the earth without thinking twice about it. I'd even follow him into Yankee territory." She smiled, letting him read her heart. Still, although her heart had no limits, her duty did. "Given all that's happened, though, I have to stay here in New Orleans. I have no choice but to help put the foundation, and my family, back on its feet." There she'd said it. His turn.

Shay stared at her for a long long moment, then he smiled. "Well, luckily, I'm developing an appetite for all this spicy...food."

She lowered her lashes in a classic Southern-belle expression. "Nothing else?" All she needed was a fan to wave.

He moved closer, his breath tickling her ear as he whispered, "You. Only you. Every day, every night, every minute, every second."

"I thought you'd never say it."

Shay lifted her chin and looked into her eyes. "Juliette, you have to understand something. I've *never* found it so difficult to do my job. You know how important it was that we nail this operation, but every time I thought about using you, my heart practically stopped. On top of that, it was hard to believe you didn't know what was going on. I told myself you

lidn't, that you wouldn't condone something like that. But I
still had to—"

She kissed her fingers then placed them on his lips. "Shh...I
know. I understand. If you'd done anything else, you
wouldn't be the man I fell in love with. I do love you, you
know. I love you more than I'd ever thought possible."

He took her in his arms, folding her so tightly in his embrace that she could scarcely breathe. "God, Juliette, if you
knew how scared I've been that you'd turn away from me. I
wanted to tell you, but I couldn't."

She stroked his hair.

"Maybe I'm not the right guy for you."

She jerked away, putting her palm over his mouth. "Stop.
Don't even say anything like that again. It's not true."

He pulled her hand away so he could speak. "I'm not in the
same social—" She put it back.

"That doesn't matter. The only thing that matters is this."
She kissed him, seeking the thrill and the comfort that only he
could provide.

Shay was the only man for her, and his kiss told her she
was the only woman for him. All of her doubts vanished as,
tongues tangling, breath mingling, they explored the depth of
their feelings as everything around them disappeared. For
this moment, there was only a man and a woman in love. She
wrenched her mouth from his, slipping her hands into his
hair to hold him still as she looked deep into his eyes. "The
only thing I care about is how I feel about you, and how you
feel about me. Nothing else."

His eyes filled with emotion. "I love you."

"I love you." She adored saying that, and it thrilled her
even more because a little over a week ago she hadn't even
met him. Shay dipped his head again, but Juliette stopped
him before their lips met, prompting, "And?"

Shay frowned in confusion. "And what?"

"And what happens next?" she said, a hint of impatience
creeping into her voice as she waited for him to say the four
magic words that would commit them to life together.

"Oh," he teased, "you mean with us. Us, as in you and m● together?"

"Shay..." She gave him a warning glance.

"I thought about asking you to marry me...but that was b● fore I saw how impatient you are."

Her eyes narrowed. "Keep it up, Yankee. Keep it up."

He traced a finger over her lips. "No more innocent Re● Riding Hood scared by the Big Bad Wolf, huh?"

"Red Riding Hood has grown up and left the woods fo good."

"Good thing, because your naiveté scared me to death."

Juliette chuckled. "I didn't stay naïve for long. You saw t that."

"Are you sure you weren't a virgin?"

Giving him her most flirtatious look, she teased, "What d you think?"

"Well, if I look back on it and examine the physical aspect of the very exact moment, I'd have to—"

She grabbed his head and pulled him to her for a brief kiss effectively silencing him. Then she released him and said "Can we stop talking and get to the point, Shay?"

He chuckled. "Sorry. I'm Irish. We're born with the gift c gab."

"I guess I can deal with that—as long as you know when t● shut up."

"Do you want to deal with it permanently?" he asked.

Slanting him a glance, she pursed her lips, pretending t think hard for a moment. "I'm beginning to think I'm the onl one who can keep you in line."

"Then you'll marry me?"

She threw her arms around his neck. "My God, I though you'd never ask."

"What do you think I've been doing?"

"Making me wait to hear the words."

"You're hearing them now, Princess. Whaddaya say?"

"Ah, how romantic. Just what I've always dreamed of." She caressed his nape. "Yes, I'll marry you."

"You mean you'll walk away from all this luxury and marry a poor, shameless, Irish cop? What's the world coming to?"

"I don't know, but I think you've the tongue of the devil, Shay O'Malley. So why don't you put it to better use?"

Shay flashed that tilted, wicked grin she loved so much. He pulled her closer, "I think you're reading my mind. Where should I start? What do you think?"

She tangled her fingers in his hair and pulled him down to meet her waiting lips. "I *think* you talk too much."

BESTSELLING AUTHORS

Linda Lael Miller
Kasey Michaels
Barbara Delinsky &
Diana Palmer

Lead

TAKE5

Covering everything from tender love to
sizzling passion, there's a TAKE 5 volume for
every type of romance reader.

PLUS
With two proofs-of-purchase
from any two Take 5
volumes you can receive
THE ART OF ROMANCE
absolutely free!
(see inside a volume of
TAKE 5 for details)

AND
With $5.00 worth of coupons inside each volume,
this is one deal you shouldn't miss!

Look for it in March 2002.

HARLEQUIN®
Makes any time special ®

Visit us at www.eHarlequin.com   TAKE5POP

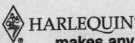

HARLEQUIN®
makes any time special—online...

eHARLEQUIN.com

your romantic
books

♥ Shop online! Visit Shop eHarlequin and discover a wide selection of new releases and classic favorites at great discounted prices.

♥ Read our daily and weekly Internet exclusive serials, and participate in our interactive novel in the reading room.

♥ Ever dreamed of being a writer? Enter your chapter for a chance to become a featured author in our Writing Round Robin novel.

your romantic
life

♥ Check out our feature articles on dating, flirting and other important romance topics and get your daily love dose with tips on how to keep the romance alive every day.

your
community

♥ Have a Heart-to-Heart with other members about the latest books and meet your favorite authors.

♥ Discuss your romantic dilemma in the Tales from the Heart message board.

your romantic
escapes

♥ Learn what the stars have in store for you with our daily Passionscopes and weekly Erotiscopes.

♥ Get the latest scoop on your favorite royals in Royal Romance.

All this and more available at
www.eHarlequin.com
on Women.com Networks

HINTA1R

This Mother's Day
Give Your Mom
 # A Royal Treat

Win a fabulous one-week vacation in Puerto Rico for you and your mother at the luxurious Inter-Continental San Juan Resort & Casino. The prize includes round trip airfare for two, breakfast daily and a mother and daughter day of beauty at the beachfront hotel's spa.

INTER·CONTINENTAL
San Juan
RESORT & CASINO

Here's all you have to do:

Tell us in 100 words or less how your mother helped with the romance in your life. It may be a story about your engagement, wedding or those boyfriends when you were a teenager or any other romantic advice from your mother. The entry will be judged based on its originality, emotionally compelling nature and sincerity. See official rules on following page.

Send your entry to:
Mother's Day Contest

In Canada
P.O. Box 637
Fort Erie, Ontario
L2A 5X3

In U.S.A.
P.O. Box 9076
3010 Walden Ave.
Buffalo, NY
14269-9076

Or enter online at www.eHarlequin.com

All entries must be postmarked by April 1, 2002.
Winner will be announced May 1, 2002. Contest open to Canadian and U.S. residents who are 18 years of age and older. No purchase necessary to enter. Void where prohibited.

PRROY

HARLEQUIN MOTHER'S DAY CONTEST 2216
OFFICIAL RULES
NO PURCHASE NECESSARY TO ENTER

Two ways to enter:

- **Via The Internet:** Log on to the Harlequin romance website (www.eHarlequin.com) anytime beginning 12:01 a.m. E.S.T., January 1, 2002 through 11:59 p.m. E.S.T., April 1, 2002 and follow the directions displayed on-line to enter your name, address (including zip code), e-mail address and in 100 words or fewer, describe how your mother helped with the romance in your life.

- **Via Mail:** Handprint (or type) on an 8 1/2" x 11" plain piece of paper, your name, address (including zip code) and e-mail address (if you have one), and in 100 words or fewer, describe how your mother helped with the romance in your life. Mail your entry via first-class mail to: Harlequin Mother's Day Contest 2216, (in the U.S.) P.O. Box 9076, Buffalo, NY 14269-9076; (in Canada) P.O. Box 637, Fort Erie, Ontario, Canada L2A 5X3.

For eligibility, entries must be submitted either through a completed Internet transmission or postmarked no later than 11:59 p.m. E.S.T., April 1, 2002 (mail-in entries must be received by April 9, 2002). Limit one entry per person, household address and e-mail address. On-line and/or mailed entries received from persons residing in geographic areas in which entry is not permissible will be disqualified.

Entries will be judged by a panel of judges, consisting of members of the Harlequin editorial, marketing and public relations staff using the following criteria:
- Originality - 50%
- Emotional Appeal - 25%
- Sincerity - 25%

In the event of a tie, duplicate prizes will be awarded. Decisions of the judges are final.

Prize: A 6-night/7-day stay for two at the Inter-Continental San Juan Resort & Casino, including round-trip coach air transportation from gateway airport nearest winner's home (approximate retail value: $4,000). Prize includes breakfast daily and a mother and daughter day of beauty at the beachfront hotel's spa. Prize consists of only those items listed as part of the prize. Prize is valued in U.S. currency.

All entries become the property of Torstar Corp. and will not be returned. No responsibility is assumed for lost, late, illegible, incomplete, inaccurate, non-delivered or misdirected mail or misdirected e-mail, for technical, hardware or software failures of any kind, lost or unavailable network connections, or failed, incomplete, garbled or delayed computer transmission or any human error which may occur in the receipt or processing of the entries in this Contest.

Contest open only to residents of the U.S. (except Colorado) and Canada, who are 18 years of age or older and is void wherever prohibited by law; all applicable laws and regulations apply. Any litigation within the Province of Quebec respecting the conduct or organization of a publicity contest may be submitted to the Régie des alcools, des courses et des jeux for a ruling. Any litigation respecting the awarding of a prize may be submitted to the Régie des alcools, des courses et des jeux only for the purpose of helping the parties reach a settlement. Employees and immediate family members of Torstar Corp. and D.L. Blair, Inc., their affiliates, subsidiaries and all other agencies, entities and persons connected with the use, marketing or conduct of this Contest are not eligible to enter. Taxes on prize are the sole responsibility of winner. Acceptance of any prize offered constitutes permission to use winner's name, photograph or other likeness for the purposes of advertising, trade and promotion on behalf of Torstar Corp., its affiliates and subsidiaries without further compensation to the winner, unless prohibited by law.

Winner will be determined no later than April 15, 2002 and be notified by mail. Winner will be required to sign and return an Affidavit of Eligibility form within 15 days after winner notification. Non-compliance within that time period may result in disqualification and an alternate winner may be selected. Winner of trip must execute a Release of Liability prior to ticketing and must possess required travel documents (e.g. Passport, photo ID) where applicable. Travel must be completed within 12 months of selection and is subject to traveling companion completing and returning a Release of Liability prior to travel; and hotel and flight accommodations availability. Certain restrictions and blackout dates may apply. No substitution of prize permitted by winner. Torstar Corp. and D.L. Blair, Inc., their parents, affiliates, and subsidiaries are not responsible for errors in printing or electronic presentation of Contest, or entries. In the event of printing or other errors which may result in unintended prize values or duplication of prizes, all affected entries shall be null and void. If for any reason the Internet portion of the Contest is not capable of running as planned, including infection by computer virus, bugs, tampering, unauthorized intervention, fraud, technical failures, or any other causes beyond the control of Torstar Corp. which corrupt or affect the administration, secrecy, fairness, integrity or proper conduct of the Contest, Torstar Corp. reserves the right, at its sole discretion, to disqualify any individual who tampers with the entry process and to cancel, terminate, modify or suspend the Contest or the Internet portion thereof. In the event the Internet portion must be terminated a notice will be posted on the website and all entries received prior to termination will be judged in accordance with these rules. In the event of a dispute regarding an on-line entry, the entry will be deemed submitted by the authorized holder of the e-mail account submitted at the time of entry. Authorized account holder is defined as the natural person who is assigned to an e-mail address by an Internet access provider, on-line service provider or other organization that is responsible for arranging e-mail address for the domain associated with the submitted e-mail address. Torstar Corp. and/or D.L. Blair Inc. assumes no responsibility for any computer injury or damage related to or resulting from accessing and/or downloading any sweepstakes material. Rules are subject to any requirements/limitations imposed by the FCC. **Purchase or acceptance of a product offer does not improve your chances of winning.**

For winner's name (available after May 1, 2002), send a self-addressed, stamped envelope to: Harlequin Mother's Day Contest Winners 2216, P.O. Box 4200 Blair, NE 68009-4200 or you may access the www.eHarlequin.com Web site through June 3, 2002.

Contest sponsored by Torstar Corp., P.O. Box 9042, Buffalo, NY 14269-9042.

If you enjoyed what you just read,
then we've got an offer you can't resist!

Take 2 bestselling
love stories FREE!

Plus get a FREE surprise gift!

Clip this page and mail it to Harlequin Reader Service®

IN U.S.A.
3010 Walden Ave.
P.O. Box 1867
Buffalo, N.Y. 14240-1867

IN CANADA
P.O. Box 609
Fort Erie, Ontario
L2A 5X3

YES! Please send me 2 free Harlequin Temptation® novels and my free surprise gift. After receiving them, if I don't wish to receive anymore, I can return the shipping statement marked cancel. If I don't cancel, I will receive 4 brand-new novels each month, before they're available in stores. In the U.S.A., bill me at the bargain price of $3.34 plus 25¢ shipping and handling per book and applicable sales tax, if any*. In Canada, bill me at the bargain price of $3.80 plus 25¢ shipping and handling per book and applicable taxes**. That's the complete price and a savings of 10% off the cover prices—what a great deal! I understand that accepting the 2 free books and gift places me under no obligation ever to buy any books. I can always return a shipment and cancel at any time. Even if I never buy another book from Harlequin, the 2 free books and gift are mine to keep forever.

142 HEN DFND
342 HEN DFNE

Name	(PLEASE PRINT)	
Address	Apt.#	
City	State/Prov.	Zip/Postal Code

* Terms and prices subject to change without notice. Sales tax applicable in N.Y.
** Canadian residents will be charged applicable provincial taxes and GST.
   All orders subject to approval. Offer limited to one per household and not valid to
   current Harlequin Temptation® subscribers.
® are registered trademarks of Harlequin Enterprises Limited.

TEMP01   ©1998 Harlequin Enterprises Limited

*Sit back, get comfortable and indulge yourself
with these passion-filled stories set in the*

Lap

of

Luxury

Three complete novels brimming with glamour,
wealth and breathtaking storytelling from
#1 Harlequin Temptation® author

KRISTINE ROLOFSON

Look for it in February 2002—wherever books are sold.

HARLEQUIN®
Makes any time special ®

Every day is

A Mother's Day

in this heartwarming anthology celebrating motherhood and romance!

Featuring the classic story "Nobody's Child" by Emilie Richards
He had come to a child's rescue, and now Officer Farrell Riley was
suddenly sharing parenthood with beautiful Gemma Hancock.
But would their ready-made family last forever?

Plus two brand-new romances:

"Baby on the Way" by Marie Ferrarella
Single and pregnant, Madeline Reed found the perfect husband in the
handsome cop who helped bring her infant son into the world. But did his
dutiful role in the surprise delivery make J. T. Walker a daddy?

"A Daddy for Her Daughters" by Elizabeth Bevarly
When confronted with spirited Naomi Carmichael and her brood of girls,
bachelor Sloan Sullivan realized he had a lot to learn about women!
Especially if he hoped to win this sexy single mom's heart....

Available this April from Silhouette Books!

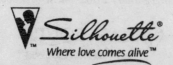

Where love comes alive™

Visit Silhouette at www.eHarlequin.com

PSAMD